MICKEY7

ALSO BY EDWARD ASHTON

Three Days in April

The End of Ordinary

Edward Ashton

ST. MARTIN'S PRESS

NEW YORK

First published in the United States by St. Martin's Press, an imprint of St. Martin's Publishing Group

MICKEY7. Copyright © 2022 by Edward Ashton. All rights reserved. Printed in the United States of America. For information, address St. Martin's Publishing Group, 120 Broadway, New York, NY 10271.

www.stmartins.com

Library of Congress Cataloging-in-Publication Data

Names: Ashton, Edward (Science fiction writer), author.
Title: Mickey7 / Edward Ashton.
Description: First edition. | New York : St. Martin's Press, 2022.
Identifiers: LCCN 2021042263 | ISBN 9781250275035 (hardcover) |
   ISBN 9781250275042 (ebook)
Subjects: LCGFT: Science fiction.
Classification: LCC PS3601.S567 M53 2022 | DDC 813/.6—dc23
LC record available at https://lccn.loc.gov/2021042263

Our books may be purchased in bulk for promotional, educational, or business use. Please contact your local bookseller or the Macmillan Corporate and Premium Sales Department at 1-800-221-7945, extension 5442, or by email at MacmillanSpecialMarkets@macmillan.com.

First Edition: 2022

10 9 8 7 6 5 4 3 2 1

For Jen. If you hadn't ended civilization, none of this would have happened.

MICKEY7

THIS IS GONNA be my stupidest death ever.

It's just past 26:00, and I'm sprawled on my back on a rough stone floor, in a darkness so black that I may as well be blind. My ocular wastes a long five seconds hunting for stray visible-spectrum photons before finally giving up and flipping over to infrared. There's still not much to see, but at least I can make out the roof of the chamber above me, glowing now in a pale, spectral gray, and the black ring of the ice-crusted opening that must have brought me here.

Question: What the hell happened?

The last few minutes of my memory are fragmentary—mostly unconnected images and snippets of sound. I remember Berto dropping me off at the head of the crevasse. I remember climbing down along a broken jumble of ice blocks. I remember walking. I remember looking up, seeing a boulder jutting out of the ice about thirty meters up the south wall. It looked a little like a monkey's head. I remember smiling, and then . . .

. . . and then there was nothing under my left foot, and I was falling.

Son of a bitch. I wasn't looking where I was going. I was staring up at that stupid monkey-head rock, thinking about how I'd describe it to Nasha when I got back to the dome, and I stepped into a hole.

Stupidest. Death. Ever.

A shiver runs the length of my body. The cold was bad enough up top, when I was moving. Down here, though, pressed against the bedrock, it's soaking into me, eating through the skin suit and the two layers of thermals, seeping down through hair and skin and muscle and all the way into my bones. I shiver again, and a sudden jolt of pain runs from my left wrist up to my shoulder. I look down. There's a bulge where there shouldn't be one, pressing against the fabric just at the point where my glove meets the sleeve of my outer thermal. I start to pull off the glove, thinking that maybe the cold will help keep the swelling down, but another jolt of pain stops that experiment almost before it's started. Even just trying to make a fist, the pain ramps up from bad to blinding as soon as my fingers start to curl.

Must have banged it on something during the fall. Broken? Maybe. Sprained? Definitely.

Pain means I'm still alive, right?

I sit up slowly, shake my head clear, and blink to a comm window. I'm too far out to pick up any of the colony repeaters, but Berto must still be close, because I'm getting just a hint of a signal. Not enough for voice or video, but I can probably manage text. My eye flickers to the keyboard icon, and it expands to fill a quarter of my field of view.

<Mickey7>:Berto. You getting this?

<RedHawk>:Affirmative. Still alive, huh?

<Mickey7>:So far. I'm stuck, though.

\<RedHawk\>:No kidding. I saw what happened. You walked right into a hole.

\<Mickey7\>:Yeah, I figured that out.

\<RedHawk\>:Not a little hole, Mickey. A big one. What the hell, buddy?

\<Mickey7\>:I was looking at a rock.

\<RedHawk\>:...

\<Mickey7\>:It looked like a monkey.

\<RedHawk\>:Stupidest death ever.

\<Mickey7\>:Yeah, well, only if I die, right? Speaking of which, any chance you're coming for me?

\<RedHawk\>:Uh...

\<RedHawk\>:No.

\<Mickey7\>:Seriously?

\<RedHawk\>:Seriously.

\<Mickey7\>:...

\<Mickey7\>:Why not?

\<RedHawk\>:Well, mostly because I'm hovering two hundred meters over the spot where you went down right now, and I'm still barely reading you. You're deep underground, my friend, and we are definitely in creeper territory. It would take a hell of an effort and a great deal of personal risk to get you back out—and I can't justify that kind of risk for an Expendable, you know?

\<Mickey7\>:Oh. Right.

\<Mickey7\>:Not for a friend either, huh?

\<RedHawk\>:Come on, Mickey. That's a cheap shot. It's not like you're really dying or anything. I'll file a loss report on you when I get back to the dome. This is line of duty. There's no way Marshall won't approve your regen. You'll be out of the tank and back in your bed tomorrow.

\<Mickey7\>:Oh, that's great. I mean, I'm sure that'll be convenient for you. But in the meantime, I have to die in a hole.

\<RedHawk\>:Yeah, that sucks.

\<Mickey7\>:That sucks? Really? That's all you've got?

\<RedHawk\>:I'm sorry, Mickey, but what do you want? I feel bad that you're about to die down there, but seriously, this is your job, right?

\<Mickey7\>:I'm not even current, you know. I haven't uploaded in over a month.

\<RedHawk\>:That . . . is not my fault. Don't worry, though. I'll fill you in on what you've been up to. Got any private stuff you've done since your last upload that you think you might need to know?

\<Mickey7\>:Um . . .

\<Mickey7\>:No, I guess not.

\<RedHawk\>:Perfect. Then we're all set.

\<Mickey7\>: . . .

\<RedHawk\>:All good, Mickey?

\<Mickey7\>:Yeah. All good. Thanks a lot, Berto.

I blink away from the window, lean back against the rock wall, and close my eyes. I can't believe that chickenshit bastard's not coming for me.

Oh, who am I kidding? I can totally believe it.

So, what next? Sit here and wait to die? I have no idea how far I tumbled down that bore hole or drop shaft or whatever it was before I hit ground in this . . . whatever this is. It might have been twenty meters. From the way Berto was talking, it might have been more like a hundred. The opening I dropped through is right there, no more than three meters up. Even if I could reach it, though, there's no way I'm climbing with this wrist.

In my line of work, you spend a lot of time pondering different ways to die—when you're not actually experiencing them, that is. I've never frozen to death before. I've definitely thought about it, though. It's been hard not to since we made landfall on this godforsaken ball of ice. It should be pretty easy, relatively speaking. You get chilly, fall asleep, and then don't wake up, right? I'm starting to drift, thinking that at least maybe this won't be such a bad way to go, when my ocular pings. I blink to answer.

<Black Hornet>:Hey babe.

<Mickey7>:Hey Nasha. What can I do for you?

<Black Hornet>:Just sit tight. I'm in the air, ETA two minutes.

<Mickey7>:Berto pinged you?

<Black Hornet>:Yeah. He doesn't think you're retrievable.

<Mickey7>:But?

<Black Hornet>:He's just not properly motivated.

You know, hope is a funny thing. Thirty seconds ago I was one hundred percent sure I was about to die, and I wasn't really afraid. Now, though, my heart is pounding in my ears and I find myself running down a checklist of everything that could go wrong if Nasha actually manages to get her lifter on the ground up there and makes a rescue attempt. Is the floor of the crevasse even wide enough for her to set down? If it is, will she be able to locate me? If she does, will she have enough cable to reach me?

If she does, what are the chances that all that activity brings the creepers down on her?

Shit.

Shit shit shit.

I can't let her do it.

<Mickey7>:Nasha?

<Black Hornet>:Yeah?

<Mickey7>:Berto's right. I'm not retrievable.

<Black Hornet>:...

<Mickey7>:Nasha?

<Black Hornet>:You sure about this, babe?

I close my eyes again, and breathe in, breathe out. It's just a trip to the tank, right?

<Mickey7>:Yeah, I'm sure. I'm buried deep here, and I'm pretty badly banged up. Honestly, even if you managed to get me back, they'd probably wind up scrapping me anyway.

<Black Hornet>:...

<Black Hornet>:Okay, Mickey. This is your call.

<Black Hornet>:You know I would have come for you, right?

<Mickey7>:Yeah, Nasha. I know.

She goes silent, and I sit there watching her signal strength rising and falling. She's orbiting the drop site. She's trying to triangulate my signal, trying to pin down my location.

I need to end this.

<Mickey7>:Go home, Nasha. I'm checking out now.

<Black Hornet>:Oh.

<Black Hornet>:Okay.

<Black Hornet>:How're you gonna do it?

<Mickey7>:Do what?

<Black Hornet>:Shut down, Mickey. I don't want you going out like Five did. You got a weapon?

<Mickey7>:Nope. Lost my burner on the way down. Honestly, I don't think I'd want to use one of those things on myself anyway. I guess it would be quick, but...

<Black Hornet>:Yeah, that's probably a good call. How about a knife? Or an ice ax?

<Mickey7>:No, and no. And what exactly are you expecting me to do with an ice ax?

<Black Hornet>:I don't know. They're sharp, right? Maybe you could chop yourself in the head or something.

\<Mickey7\>:Look, Nasha, I know you're trying to be helpful, but—

\<Black Hornet\>:You could just pop the seals on your rebreather. Not sure if the low O2 or the high CO would get you first, but either way it shouldn't take more than a few minutes.

\<Mickey7\>:Yeah. I know I haven't tried it, but somehow I don't think slow suffocation is my thing.

\<Black Hornet\>:So what're you gonna do?

\<Mickey7\>:Freeze to death, I guess.

\<Black Hornet\>:Yeah, that works. Peaceful, right?

\<Mickey7\>:I hope so.

Her signal dwindles almost to nothing, then hovers just above zero. She must be hanging just at the edge of transmission range.

\<Black Hornet\>:Hey. You're backed up, right?

\<Mickey7\>:Not for the last six weeks.

\<Black Hornet\>:Why haven't you been uploading?

I really don't want to get into that particular question right now.

\<Mickey7\>:Just lazy, I guess.

\<Black Hornet\>:...

\<Black Hornet\>: I'm sorry about this, babe. I really am.

\<Black Hornet\>:Want me to stay on the line with you?

\<Mickey7\>:No. This might take a while, and if you go down out there, you don't get to come back, remember? You should get back to the dome.

\<Black Hornet\>:You sure?

\<Mickey7\>:Yeah, I'm sure.

\<Black Hornet\>:Love you, babe. When I see you tomorrow, I'll let you know that you went down like a pro tonight.

<**Mickey7**>:Thanks, Nasha. Love you too.
<**Black Hornet**>:Goodbye, Mickey.

I blink the window closed, and watch as Nasha's comm signal dwindles the rest of the way down to zero. Berto's already long out of range. I look up. The opening is staring down at me like the devil's anus, and, backed up or not, I'm suddenly not cool with dying. I give my head another shake, and climb to my feet.

HERE'S A THOUGHT experiment for you: Imagine you found out that when you go to sleep at night, you don't just go to sleep. You die. You die, and someone else wakes up in your place the next morning. He's got all your memories. He's got all your hopes and dreams and fears and wishes. He thinks he's you, and all your friends and loved ones do too. He's not you, though, and you're not the guy who went to sleep the night before. You've only existed since this morning, and you will cease to exist when you close your eyes tonight. Ask yourself—would it make any practical difference in your life? Is there any way that you could even tell?

Replace "go to sleep" with "get crushed, or vaporized, or set on fire" and you've pretty much got my life. Trouble in the reactor core? I'm on it. Need to test a sketchy new vaccine? I'm your guy. Need to know if the bathtub absinthe you cooked up is poisonous? I'll get a glass, you bastards. If I die, you can always make another me.

The upside of all that dying is that I really am a shitty kind of immortal. I don't just remember what Mickey1 did. I remember being him. Well, all but the last few minutes of being him, anyway. He—I—died after a hull breach during transit. Mickey2 woke up a few hours later, sure as shit that he was thirty-one years old and had been born back on Midgard. And who knows?

Maybe he was. Maybe that was the original Mickey Barnes looking out through his eyes. How could you tell? And maybe if I lie down on the floor of this cavern, close my eyes, and pop my seals, I'll wake up tomorrow morning as Mickey8.

Somehow, though, I doubt it.

Nasha and Berto might not be able to tell the difference, but deep down on some level below reason, I'm pretty sure I'd know I was dead.

THERE'S PRETTY MUCH nothing in the way of visible-range photons down here, but my ocular is picking up just enough in the shortwave infrared to get a look around. As it turns out, there are a half dozen tunnels leading out of this chamber. All of them slope downward.

That shouldn't be.

None of this should be, actually.

The tunnels look like lava tubes, but according to the orbital survey, there isn't supposed to be any volcanism within a thousand kilometers of here. That's one of the reasons we picked this place for our first base camp, even though it's far enough off the equator that the crappy climate of this stupid planet is even crappier than it has to be. I walk slowly around the perimeter of the chamber. All the tunnels look the same, circular tubes about three meters in diameter, glowing faintly in a way that tells my conscious mind that there's a positive temperature gradient at work, and at the same time lets my subconscious know that they all probably lead directly to hell. I count six paces from each to the next.

That doesn't seem right either.

No time to worry about it, though. I pick a tunnel and start walking.

After a half hour or so, I start to wonder if maybe I should have tried to tell Nasha that I wasn't going to just sit there and freeze to death after all. It would be good if she knew not to let Berto file a loss report until and unless I actually die. The Union is pretty loose about a lot of stuff, morality-wise, but some really bad things happened in the early days of bio-printed bodies and personality downloads, and at this point on most colonies you're better off being a serial killer or a child stealer than a multiple.

I pop open a comm window, but of course I'm getting no signal here at all. Too much bedrock between me and the surface. Probably for the best. I'm pretty sure the only reason Nasha didn't force the issue on a rescue attempt is that I gave her the impression that I was broken anyway. If she knew I was up and walking around with nothing worse than a headache and a sprained wrist, she might swing back and try to come for me, whether I wanted it or not.

I can't have that. Nasha's the only clearly good thing I can point to from the past nine years of my life, and if she went down because of me, I couldn't live with myself.

I couldn't, but I'd have to, wouldn't I? I can't die—not and make it stick, anyway.

In any case, I'm not sure she could find me even if she wanted to at this point. It's like an ant farm down here, with cross-tunnels every dozen meters or so. I've tried to pick the ones that looked more up than down, but I don't think I'm having a lot of success, and I have no idea what direction I'm headed.

On the plus side, though, I'm not shivering anymore. I thought at first that I was going hypothermic, but the infrared glow from the walls has been brightening steadily, and I'm pretty sure now that it's getting warmer the deeper I go. I'm actually starting to sweat a little.

Which is okay for now, I guess—but it's gonna suck if I actually do manage to find my way back to the surface. It was negative ten

C when I broke through the crust covering the mouth of that drop shaft. Temperatures at night have been dipping to negative thirty or more, and the wind never stops. If I do find a way out, it might be a good idea to hang around inside until the sun comes back up.

I'M DAYDREAMING ABOUT Nasha the first time I hear the skittering. It's like a bunch of little rocks tumbling down a granite face, except that it starts and stops, starts and stops. I hurry on, and I don't look back. It's obvious to me by now that these tunnels are not a natural formation. I don't know what kind of burrowing animal digs three-meter-wide tunnels through solid rock, but whatever it is, I'm pretty sure I don't want to meet one.

As I press on, the noises come more often, and closer. I find myself walking faster and faster, until I'm almost running. I've just passed a cross-tunnel when I realize that I can't tell if the noises I'm hearing are coming from behind me or in front of me. I pull up short, and turn half around.

And there it is, almost close enough to touch.

It looks generally like a creeper, which I guess makes sense: segmented body, one pair of legs to a segment, hard, sharp claws for feet. The mandibles are different, though. Creepers have one pair on their front segments. This guy has two: a slightly longer pair held parallel to the ground, and a shorter pair held perpendicular to those. Just like a creeper, it has a short, dextrous pair of feeding legs inside the mandibles, and a round, toothy maw.

There are some other important differences. Creepers are pure white—evolved to blend in with the snow, maybe? It's hard to tell from the infrared I'm getting, but I'm guessing that in the visible spectrum this thing would be brown or black.

Also, of course, creepers are maybe a meter long and weigh a few dozen kilograms, while my new friend here is as wide as I am tall, and stretches back down the tunnel as far as I can see.

Fight or flight? Neither one seems like a good bet here. I raise my hands, show it my open palms, and take a slow step back. That gets a reaction. It rears up and spreads both sets of mandibles wide. The feeding legs beckon to me. Body language. To a thing like this, my arms up and spread probably look like a threat. I drop them to my side and take another step back. It slides toward me, its front segments weaving slowly back and forth like the head of a cobra, and I'm thinking I should have listened to Nasha, should have popped my seals and let the local atmosphere do its work, thinking that being eaten by a giant centipede is really not the way I wanted to check out, when it strikes.

The mandibles snap around me, faster than I can react—between my legs, over my right shoulder, and around my waist. The creeper lifts me off the ground, and the feeding legs pin me in place. The maw is opening and closing rhythmically, less than a meter away. There are rows and rows of cold black teeth in there, one behind the other, as far down the furnace-hot gullet as I can see.

It doesn't pull me in, though. It picks me up, and it moves.

The feeding legs are multi-jointed, and they end in nests of tentacles that could almost be fingers, tipped by two-centimeter-long claws. I struggle at first, but they hold my arms splayed and pressed back against the mandibles with a grip like a steel vise. I can kick my feet a little, but I can't reach anything worth kicking. I'm assuming at this point that I'm on my way back to the nest. A snack for the little ones, maybe? Or a special treat for the wife? Either way, if I could reach up to pop my seals now, I'd do it. Not an option, though, so I hang there, imagining what it's going to feel like being ground up in that churning maw.

The trip is a long one, and at one point I actually find myself dozing off. The clacking of the giant creeper's teeth wakes me, though, and I spend the rest of the ride watching them grind against one another as the maw irises open and closed. It's strangely fascinating. The teeth must either grow continuously or fall out and regenerate on a pretty regular basis, because they're really doing a number on each other.

After a while, I realize that the angles at which they strike one another are optimized to keep them sharpened.

We finally stop in a chamber similar to the one I first fell into. The creeper crosses the open space, then slides its head into a smaller side tunnel. I crane my neck around. The passage looks like it dead-ends after twenty meters or so. The family larder, maybe? It sets my feet on the ground, then opens its mandibles. The feeding legs give me a gentle shove, and the head withdraws.

I'm not sure what's happening now, but I'm pretty sure I want to be where that thing is not. I start up the tunnel. There's something strange about the wall at the end. It takes me a few seconds to realize that my ocular is registering visible-range photons for the first time in hours.

When I get to the end of the tunnel, the wall isn't rock. It's hard-packed snow. I put my hand against it and shove. A section a half meter across gives way. Daylight floods in.

At that moment, I suddenly remember being nine years old in my grandmother's country house back on Midgard. It was a sunny spring morning, and I'd caught a spider in my bedroom. I scooped him up in my cupped hands and trapped him, ran down the stairs and out the front door with his sharp little feet scrambling around and around my palms. I crouched down in the front garden, put my hands near the ground, and opened my fingers. As he scuttled away, I felt like a benevolent god.

Through the hole in the wall, I can see the snow-dusted bulge of our main dome, no more than a couple of kilometers away.

I'm the spider. I'm the spider, and that thing in the tunnel just set me down in the garden.

I TRY PINGING Berto, then Nasha, as soon as I'm clear of the tunnel. No response. Not too surprising, I guess. It's early yet, and they were both out on overnights. Would Berto have reported me as KIA as soon as he got back to the dome, or would he have waited until morning? And how long would it take them to actually re-instantiate me after that? I've never been around for that part, so I'm not exactly sure, but I'm guessing it's not very long. I think about leaving a message for Berto, but something tells me to hold off. If he went straight to his rack last night when he got in, I can tell him in person. If not . . . I honestly don't know what happens then, but I've got a weird feeling that I might want to keep my current not-dead status to myself for a while.

It's an hour-long slog through a knee-deep layer of fresh snow back to the perimeter. Despite that, it's actually a nice morning, for a change. The temperature is a hair over zero, for the first time in almost a week. The wind has died down, the sky is a soft, cloudless pink, and the sun is a fat red ball resting just above the southern horizon. We've got a security perimeter established about a hundred meters out from the dome—sensor towers, automated burner turrets, man traps, the works. I've never been sure what the point of this is supposed to be, since the creepers are the only big animals we've seen so far, and they seem to be able to move around under the snow where our sensors can't find them, but it's standard operating procedure, I guess.

Gabe Torricelli is manning the checkpoint leading to the main lock this morning. He's a Security goon, but as goons go he's an okay guy. He's wearing a full kit of powered combat armor, minus the helmet. He looks like an overgrown bodybuilder with a really tiny head.

"Mickey," he says. "You're out early."

I shrug. "You know. Just out for my constitutional. What's with the gear? Did we declare war on somebody while I was on crevasse duty?"

He grins behind his rebreather. "Not yet. Armor's voluntary for picket duty. I just like the way it looks." He gestures back toward the way I came. "Marshall's still got you scouting the foothills, huh?"

"Yup. No point in risking valuable equipment doing scut work when you've got me around, right?"

"Right you are. See anything good out there?"

Yeah, Gabe. I saw a creeper the size of a heavy lift shuttle. It carried me back to the dome and then let me go. Pretty sure it was sentient. Cool, right?

"Nope," I say. "Just a lot of rocks and snow."

"Yeah," he says. "Typical. Marshall's just wasting our time with this bullshit, am I right?"

Ugh. He's bored, and looking to chat. I need to short-circuit this.

"Look," I say. "I'd love to hang, but I've got a thing in the dome this morning. Okay if I head on in?"

"Yeah," he says. "Sure. I guess I don't need to ask for ID, huh?"

"No," I say. "Probably not."

He pulls out a tablet, punches something in, then passes me through and into the dome with a wave. That's good. It might mean nobody's registered Mickey8 with Security yet. Berto's laziness may have saved me an unknowable amount of trouble. On the other hand, it was basically Berto's laziness that got me into this situation in the first place. It would have been difficult, but I'm pretty sure he could have pulled some gear together and come back and extracted me last night.

I wouldn't let Nasha risk coming for me, but Berto? If he'd been willing, I think I would have rolled the dice.

Of course, the whole point of having Expendables is that you don't have to go back for them. Still, no matter how this winds up, I'm going to need to reassess my criteria for picking best friends.

First stop is my rack. I need to get changed, clean up a bit, and put a pressure wrap on my wrist. I don't think it's broken at this point, but it's swollen and purple and I'm guessing it's probably going to be unpleasant for the next few weeks at least. After that, I can get in touch with Berto and make sure he's not getting ready to do something stupid. I need to ping Nasha too, just to let her know I made it out.

Also to say thanks for being willing to try, I guess.

I follow the main corridor two-thirds of the way across the dome, then climb four floors of bare metal spiral staircase to the slums. The low-status racks are up here, dozens of three-by-two-meter rooms separated by extruded plastic dividers and thin foam doors, right up near the roof. My room is near the hub. I've got a double to myself, with enough vertical space to stand up and raise my hands over my head—one of the benefits of being an Expendable, I guess. It's kind of like the way the Aztecs were really nice to their ass-ball players, right up until they dragged them up to the altar and ripped their hearts out.

I first realize we may have an issue when I try to key my door. It's already unlocked. I push it open, heart pounding out a staccato rhythm in my chest. There's someone in my bed, with my blanket pulled up to his chin. His hair is plastered to his forehead, and his face is streaked with what looks like dried snot. I take two steps forward, and swing the door closed behind me. His eyes pop open at the sound of the latch closing.

"Hey," I say.

He sits half up and puts a hand to his face. "What the . . ." He looks at me, and his eyes go wide.

"Crap," he says. "I'm Mickey8, aren't I?"

AT THIS POINT, you may be wondering what I did to get myself designated as an Expendable. Must have been something awful, right? Murdered a puppy, maybe? Pushed an old lady down a staircase?

Nope, and nope. Believe it or not, I volunteered.

The way they sell you on becoming an Expendable is that they don't call it becoming an Expendable. They call it becoming an Immortal. That's got a much nicer ring to it, doesn't it?

I don't want to make it seem like I'm an idiot. I knew what I was getting into, more or less, when I put my thumb to the contract. I sat in the recruiter's office back on Midgard and listened to her entire spiel. Her name was Gwen Johansen. She was a tall, heavyset blonde, with an expressionless face and a voice that sounded like she'd spent most of the morning swallowing gravel. She sat behind her desk, staring down at a screen in her hands, and read off a list of things that I might be required to do that would likely result in the death of that particular instantiation of me.

External repairs during interstellar transit was on the list. So were exposure to local flora and fauna, necessary medical experiments, combat against any hostiles we might encounter, and on and on for so long that I finally tuned out. The plain fact was that it didn't matter what they were going to do to me. I didn't have a choice if I wanted a berth. I wasn't a pilot. I wasn't a medico. I wasn't a geneticist or botanist or xenobiologist. I wasn't even a spear-carrier. I had no practical skills of any sort—but I really, really needed to get the hell off of Midgard, and I needed to do it quickly. This was the first colony ship we'd chartered since our own landfall two hundred years prior, and signing on as an Expendable was the only way I was going to win passage.

I knew that once I submitted my tissue samples and let them run my upload, I'd be first in line for pretty much every dangerous-to-suicidal job that came down the pike. What I didn't really grasp even after hearing Gwen run through the entire litany, though, was how many dangerous-to-suicidal jobs there actually are on a beachhead colony, and how often I'd be called on to perform them. I mean, you'd think that we'd use remotes to handle most of the seriously stupid stuff—stuff like exploring possibly unstable crevasses filled with possibly carnivorous local fauna, just to pick a random example. That's what they did on Midgard, which is why I thought this posting might actually wind up being pretty soft.

Turns out, though, that there's a whole range of things, mostly involving lethal doses of radiation but extending to other abuses as well, that a human body can actually tolerate for a significantly longer period than a mech, and there's a whole other range of things, mostly involving medical experiments and the like, that a mech can't do at all. Moreover, an Expendable is actually a lot easier to replace on a beachhead than a mech is. We won't have any kind of serious mineral extraction, let alone heavy industry, for a long time to come. Any metal lost is lost for good until we can get that stuff up and running. The raw materials they need to make another one of me, on the other hand, just require us to get our agricultural base online.

Not that we've accomplished that either. Getting anything to grow outside the dome on Niflheim is going to be a serious challenge long-term, and something in the local microbiota seems to be screwing with the things we're trying to grow inside as well—but theoretically it's a much more short-term project.

When Gwen was done listing off all of the awful things that might happen to me—several of which actually *have* happened to me, of course—she leaned back in her chair, folded her arms across her chest, and stared at me for a long, awkward moment.

"So," she said finally. "Does this really sound like the sort of job you'd enjoy?"

I gave her what I hoped was a confident smile and said, "Yes, I think it does."

She kept staring, until I could feel little beads of flop sweat forming on my forehead. Have I mentioned that I really, really needed this gig? I was about to say something about how I'd always been comfortable with risk-taking, how I was confident in my ability to stay alive in the most challenging circumstances, when she leaned forward and said, "Are you a total, irretrievable moron?"

That set me back for a moment. "No," I said. "I don't think so, anyway."

"You heard what I said before, right? The whole list?"

I nodded.

"So when I said 'acute radiation poisoning,' for example, you got that. You understood that what I meant by that was that you might well be called upon to perform duties that would result in you deliberately being exposed to a lethal dose of ionizing radiation. You understood that subsequent to that, you would develop a fever, skin rashes, blistering, and eventually that your internal organs would more or less liquefy and leak out of your anus over a period of days, resulting in what I am led to believe is an exceedingly painful death. All of that was entirely clear to you?"

"Yeah," I said, "but that wouldn't really happen, right?"

"Yes," she said. "It very well might."

I shook my head. "Sure, I might get irradiated or whatever, but I wouldn't have some long, drawn-out, agonizing death. I'd just kill myself, right? Take a pill, close my eyes, and wake up as a new me? I mean, that's kind of the point of the whole backup thing, right?"

"Yes," Gwen said. "You'd think that, wouldn't you? The fact is, though, that most Expendables don't."

I waited for her to go on. When it was clear she wasn't going to, I said, "Don't what?"

She sighed. "Kill themselves. My understanding is that that very rarely happens, despite the fact that it would make eminent sense. Apparently three hours of training lectures aren't enough to overcome a billion years of ingrained instinct for self-preservation. Go figure. Also, in many cases the Expendable may be required to ride it out all the way to the bitter end, whether he wants to do so or not. Think about medical experiments, for example. Can't short-circuit one of those with a premature euthanasia. Same with exposure to local microbiota. Command needs to know exactly what biological effects are produced, and they won't let you check out until they've finished gathering data. Understand?"

I nodded. I couldn't think of a more elaborate response. Gwen looked up at the ceiling for a long while. When she finally looked back down at me, I got the feeling that she was disappointed to see me still sitting there.

"So tell me, Mr. Barnes. What, exactly, do you find appealing about the position on offer?"

She set her elbows on the desk then, and rested her chin on her hands.

"Well," I said, "I mean, even if I got killed once or twice, I'd basically be immortal, right? That's what you said."

She sighed again, louder this time. "Right. You're a moron. Ordinarily we try not to discriminate, but the problem in this case is that the Mission Expendable is actually an extremely important posting for a colony expedition. Even a mind as simple as yours obviously is takes up an almost inconceivable amount of storage space. Prepping you for backup is an enormous investment of resources. If you take this position, yours will be the only downloadable personality and the only biological pattern that your colony will carry. That means that if things go badly, you may find yourself the last living thing aboard the *Drakkar*, solely responsible for the welfare of thousands of stored human embryos, among other assets. Is that really a burden you're willing to accept?"

I gave her a nervous smile. She stared me down for what felt like a long time, then leaned back in her chair until the front legs lifted off the floor, folded her hands behind her head, and returned her attention to the ceiling.

"Do you know how many people we've had apply for this particular position?" she asked finally.

"Uh," I said. "No?"

"Guess," she said. "We've had over ten thousand applications for berths on this expedition, all told. Six hundred atmospheric pilots alone have made inquiries. Do you know how many berths we have for atmospheric pilots?"

I know the answer to that question now, because Berto has

mentioned it about a thousand times since we boosted out of orbit, but I didn't have a clue at the time.

"Two," she said. "We've had six hundred pilots apply for two goddamned slots—and these are not weekend-pilot randos. Every single one of those six hundred would be eminently qualified for the job. Miko Berrigan applied to head up our Physics Section. Can you believe that?"

I shook my head. I had no idea who Miko Berrigan was, but apparently he was hell on wheels, physics-wise.

I've since learned that that's true.

I've also since learned that Miko Berrigan is kind of an asshole, but that's not really relevant to the story.

"The point is," Gwen said, "we have had our pick of the litter for this expedition. As I'm sure you're aware, it is a tremendous honor to be selected for a beachhead colony mission, one that most people never even get the opportunity to try for. If we wanted to, we could fill every berth on the *Drakkar* with someone with one green eye and one blue one, and still have a fully qualified crew."

She brought her chair back down onto the floor with a bang then, and leaned across the desk toward me. I had to force myself not to flinch.

"Which brings me back to our Expendable," she said. "Do you know how many applications we've had for that slot?"

I shook my head.

"You," she said. "You are the only person who has stepped forward to fill this particular berth. We were seriously considering asking the Assembly for authority to *conscript* someone until you walked through my door. Now, I can see from your standardized test scores that you are not actually a completely stupid person. In fact, it says here that you're a . . . historian?"

I nodded.

"Is that a job?"

"Actually," I said, "it is—or at least it used to be. The study of history can—"

"Isn't every scrap of known history available to anyone at any time?"

I nodded.

"So what, exactly, makes you more of a historian than me, for example?"

"Well," I said, "I've actually bothered to access a lot of those scraps."

She rolled her eyes. "And someone pays you for this?"

I hesitated. "I suppose it's technically more of a hobby than a job."

She stared me down for five seconds or so, then shook her head and sighed.

"In any case, the post that you are applying for right now is not a hobby. It is most definitely a job, one which, if you take it on, you will never be able to relinquish—and what, exactly, does the fact that nobody else on this entire planet wants this job tell you, Mr. Barnes?"

She looked at me then as if she expected some kind of response, but I honestly had no idea what to say. Finally, she rolled her eyes again, and slid a bio-print reader across the desk to me. I pressed my thumb to the pad, and felt a tiny prick as it nipped off a DNA sample. She took the reader back and glanced down at the display.

"Can I ask a question?" I said.

She looked up at me. Her expression was unreadable. "Sure. Why not?"

"If nobody has applied for this job, if you were actually thinking about *drafting* someone for it, why are you trying so hard to discourage me from taking it?"

She looked back down at her tablet. "An excellent question, Mr. Barnes. I guess maybe you just strike me as a decent sort, and I'd rather this particular job went to an asshole."

She stood then, set the tablet down on her desk, and offered me her hand.

"Whatever," she said. "I guess it's going to you. Welcome aboard."

HERE'S THE QUESTION that Gwen should have asked me, but didn't: What's so rotten about Midgard that you're willing to take a chance on getting your insides liquefied to get away from it? I mean, Midgard's a nice enough place, as third-gen colony worlds go. It sits dead-center in the Goldilocks zone of a red giant that just finished eating its inner system. That means they had to do a bit of terraforming when the first boat showed up, which was probably a pain in the ass. On the plus side, though, unlike our current home, Midgard hasn't been habitable for long enough to have any sophisticated locals to deal with. I'm sure some bad things happened to their Expendable too, but at least he wasn't getting eaten right and left.

Midgard has almost no axial tilt, so there's not much in the way of seasons to worry about. It's warm at the equator and cold at the poles, with a couple of broad, shallow, low-salinity oceans, and one world-girdling continent that completely divides them. Crowding isn't a problem. There were more people in one mega-city on old Earth pre-Diaspora than there are on all of Midgard. The beaches are nice. The cities are clean. The government is elected, and mostly limits itself to managing the economy. I never even had a problem with that fat red sun filling half the sky, although I'll admit that the little yellow one we have here already feels more natural somehow.

So, what was the problem? You've probably got a few guesses, so let me run down the list. Love affair gone bad? Nope. I'd had a few girlfriends, some good and some bad, but none bad enough to drive me off-planet, and none at all in the year leading up to my first upload. Money problems? You wouldn't think so, would you? Almost nobody on Midgard had money problems. Virtually the entire industrial and agricultural base was automated, and the government distributed the spinoff on a per-citizen basis, just like nearly every other planet in the Union. In most ways you could measure, Midgard was almost a paradise.

As it turned out, the problem that I had with Midgard was exactly the problem that I had with getting off of Midgard. I wasn't a scientist. I wasn't an engineer. I had no talent for art, or entertainment, or rhetoric. I was—I am—the sort of person who in an earlier age would have been a low-level academic of some sort. I would have read obscure books that I found in obscure archives, and written obscure papers that nobody would ever have read. In an earlier age than that, I might have put in my time in a factory, or a mine, or maybe the infantry. On Midgard, though, there weren't any low-level academics. As Gwen so kindly pointed out, history was anyone's for the taking. With a blink of your ocular, or a few clicks on your tablet, you could know anything you ever needed to know about anything—not that anyone ever bothered to actually do that, of course.

There also weren't any factory jobs, or mining jobs, or even any infantry, for that matter. My standard stipend gave me enough to keep a roof over my head and food in my belly, but try as I might, I couldn't figure out what it was all for. I couldn't think of a single way the universe would be different if I stepped off of my balcony one morning.

And so, like bored young men throughout history, I spent an unfortunate amount of my time finding ways to get myself into trouble.

"So," I say. "It seems like we've got a problem."

I'm in my desk chair, turned to face the bed. Eight is sitting up now, leaning forward with his head in his hands. I know how he feels. Waking up straight out of the tank is like the world's worst hangover, with little bits of leprosy and the bends mixed in for flavor.

"You think? We're screwed, Seven. We're worse than screwed. How did you let this happen?"

I sigh, lean back, and rub my face with both hands. "Which part? The part where Berto assumed I was dead because he was too afraid of getting eaten to come back and rescue me? Or the part where I inconveniently didn't actually die?"

"I don't know. Either one. Could you hand me a towel?"

There's a hand towel hanging over the wardrobe door. I pull it down and toss it to him. He scrubs the worst of the gunk off of his face and neck, then tries to work it back through his hair.

"That's hopeless," I say.

He glares at me and keeps rubbing. "I know that, asshole. I remember when you woke up from the tank, right? I remember

27

when Six woke up, and Five and Three and . . . well, I guess that's all, actually. Anyway, I remember everything you remember."

"Not everything," I say. "I haven't uploaded in over a month."

"Great. Thanks for that."

I sigh. "Don't worry. You're not missing anything good."

He flings the goo-covered towel at me, climbs out of bed, and pulls open the wardrobe. "Haven't been keeping up with the laundry either, huh?"

"Not really. It's been a rough few weeks."

He pulls a grimy sweater and a pair of wind pants down from the top shelf. "Got any clean underwear at all?"

"Check under the bed."

He shoots me a look exactly halfway between hatred and disgust. "What's wrong with you? I don't remember us being a pig."

"I told you. It's been a rough few weeks."

He drops to one knee and pulls a pair of boxers out from under the bed, holds them up at arm's length, then brings them in close and gives them a tentative sniff.

"They're clean," I say. "They just got kicked under there."

He glares at me again, then turns around and dresses himself.

"Thanks," I say. "It's weirdly uncomfortable to look at yourself walking around naked."

"Yeah," he says. "I'm sure it is."

He sits down on the bed again, and runs his hands back through his hair. It's still stiff and shiny black, but at least it's starting to break up into individual strands. It won't look right until he's been through the scrubber a couple of times, though.

"So," he says. "What now?"

I stare at him. He quits playing with his hair and stares back.

"What?" he says.

"Well," I say. "I mean, you shouldn't have come out of the

tank, right? I'm not actually dead. If Command finds out we're a multiple . . ."

His eyes are hard now, and angry. "Say what you mean, Seven."

"Come on," I say. "You know this as well as I do. One of us has got to go."

THE CLOSEST ANALOGUE in the long human story to the Diaspora and the formation of the Union is probably the colonization of Micronesia. The islands of the Pacific back on Earth are small, they're separated by hundreds or sometimes thousands of miles of open ocean, and they were settled by people paddling twelve-meter-long outrigger canoes. When those folks landed on a new island, they had whatever was left in their boats after the journey to tide them over until they could make the new land yield them up something to eat.

That's basically the situation we're in, except that our boats are a little bigger, our journeys are a hell of a lot longer, and we can't even be sure that any of the crops we've brought with us will grow where we make landfall. As a consequence, there is one hard and fast rule that everyone who boards an ark knows and accepts: there are no fat guys in beachhead colonies.

Rations when we made landfall were set at fourteen hundred kilocalories per day, base, with bonuses based on current lean body mass and work schedule. They've been cut back twice since then because, for reasons unexplained, even the hydroponics tanks are having a hard time getting anything to grow here. We're not quite down to cannibalism yet, but most of us are definitely on the gaunt side these days.

The upshot of this is that even if having multiple copies of yourself hanging around at one time weren't the strongest taboo in the Union, there's not a lot of leftovers at dinnertime for a surplus Expendable.

"LOOK," EIGHT SAYS. "If you think I'm just itching to hop into the bio-cycler for you, you're about to be seriously disappointed. I get that this situation isn't one hundred percent your fault, but it's *zero* percent my fault."

I'm pacing back and forth now, which is not very satisfying in a four-by-three room. Eight is sitting on the edge of the bed, elbows on knees, trying to massage the tank-funk out of his temples.

"This isn't about fixing the blame," I say. "It's about fixing the problem."

"Okay, so let's fix both. *You* go jump in the cycler."

I shake my head. "No, that's not gonna happen."

He glares up at me, then grimaces and digs a chunk of hardened tank fluid out of one ear.

"How is this fair? I've been alive for, what, maybe twenty minutes? You've gotten a couple of months, at least. You should be the one to go."

I smile, but not in a friendly way. "Oh no," I say. "Don't try to pull that shit on me. You're thirty-nine years old, just like me. You've got every second of memory and experience that I have, less the six weeks since my last backup. You wouldn't even have known you just came out of the tank if you weren't covered in dried goo."

He stares at me.

I stare at him.

"There's no point in trying to argue this out, Seven. I mean, we can't really compromise on this, can we?" he says finally.

And he's right, of course. This isn't the kind of disagreement where one person or the other just gives up after a while. It's not like picking up the check in a restaurant. We can't take turns.

"Okay," I say. "So what do we do? Take it to Command?"

"No," Eight says, a little too quickly. "Bad idea. Marshall thinks we're an abomination already. If he finds out we're a multiple, he'll kill us both on the spot. We need to keep this between the two of us."

The truth is that if we went to him now, Marshall would probably just say that Eight never should have come out of the tank, and that therefore he should be converted back into slurry without delay. I think about mentioning that now, but . . .

I don't know. Maybe Eight has a point. It does seem unfair somehow to shove him back into the void before he's even had a chance to get the tank goo out of his ears.

What's the alternative, though? I don't want to go down the corpse hole any more than he does.

"Look," I say. "We can figure this out. Let me change my clothes and clean up a bit here. You go hit the chem shower on three, get the rest of the tank gunk off of you, and meet me at the cycler in thirty."

He gives me a wary look, then gets to his feet. "Fine," he says. "Thirty minutes. I'll see you there."

He takes two steps to the door, turns the latch, and pulls it open. He starts out into the corridor, then hesitates and looks back at me.

"Hey. You're not planning on being a dick about this, are you? I mean, you're not gonna call Command while I'm in the shower and try to make this judicial, are you?"

"No," I say. "I won't do that, even though I'm pretty sure I'd win if I did. We'll settle this ourselves."

He smiles. "Thanks, Seven. I'll see you in thirty."

The door swings closed behind him.

I FIGURE EIGHT probably actually needs at least an hour. Tank goo is a nightmare to get off of you, and the chem shower isn't the ideal way to do it. I'm just settling in for a quick nap when there's a soft knock-knock-knock at my door.

"Come," I say. The door swings open. Berto pokes his head in and looks around, then steps through and closes the door behind him.

"Hey, buddy," he says. "How're you feeling?"

Berto takes a seat at my desk, just like I did when I walked in on Eight. Unlike me, though, he doesn't really fit into the chair. Berto's almost two meters tall—a rarity on a beachhead, where compactness is important both for comfort and efficiency. I barely crack one-point-six myself, and I'm pretty average around here. Between the caloric restriction and the fact that he has to slouch and scrunch most of the time, Berto looks an awful lot like a pasty-pale, redheaded stick bug.

I sit up in bed and push my hair back with one hand. I keep my sprained wrist under the blanket. "I'm okay, I guess."

"You look pretty good for being fresh out of the tank," he says. "Been through the scrubber already?"

I nod. He stares at me for a moment, then looks away.

"So," I say. "What happened this time? What happened to Seven?"

Berto shakes his head. "Brother, you do not want to know."

"Huh. Isn't that exactly what you said about Six?"

He looks back at me. "Maybe. I don't know. Does it matter?"

"Yeah," I say. "It kind of does. You're a pilot, right? What's your last, most important duty if you go down?"

His eyes narrow. "Always let them know what killed you."

"Right. It's the same way with Expendables. That's why every time Marshall murders me, he makes me upload right before I check out. I'd like to know what happened to Seven, so I can make sure it doesn't happen to me. And while we're at it, you might as well fill me in on Six too. Whatever got him, I'm sure my constitution can handle it."

Berto stares me down, then shrugs and looks away again. I make a mental note to invite him to play poker for rations sometime. He's a terrible liar.

"Six and Seven both went down the same way," he says. "Swarmed by creepers."

"Okay. Where did this happen, and what was I doing at the time?"

He sighs. "You were out doing one of Marshall's stupid-ass walk-arounds. Over the past few months, he's had you spending most of your time mapping out the crevasses around the dome and scouting them for creepers. Personally I don't really get it, but he seems to have developed some kind of obsession with them." He hesitates, then continues. "Sometimes it seems like you have too, actually. When he first started in on this shit, you complained all the time. A week or so after Seven came out of the tank, though, that stopped. The last few weeks, you just saluted and went. Any idea what that was about?"

I shake my head. "My memories are six weeks out of date. Apparently Seven wasn't keeping up on his uploads."

"Yeah," Berto says. "He mentioned something about that last night when he realized he was going down."

I scratch my chin with my good hand. "Huh. Really? In the middle of getting torn apart by a swarm of creepers, the thing he had on his mind was that he hadn't been uploading?"

Berto's mouth opens and closes twice without making a sound, like a fish pulled out of water. I have to grit my teeth to keep from laughing. He really is a terrible, terrible liar.

"It was before that," he finally manages. "I guess he had a premonition?"

"A premonition."

"Yeah. I mean, I guess so."

I could push on this, but I've got my own secret to keep here, so I decide to let it go.

"Anyway," Berto says, "I dropped Seven off near a crevasse about eight klicks out from the perimeter yesterday afternoon. He had a burner with him. Per usual, he was supposed to be mapping the area and scouting for creepers, with the goal of bringing one back if possible. I was supposed to pick him up on my next circuit."

"But it didn't work out."

"No, it didn't work out. They came up out of the snow all at once, almost as soon as I dropped him, twenty or thirty of them. I was hovering right over him, but they tore him up before I could get the grapple deployed."

I get that he doesn't want to admit that he left me to die down there. That's the kind of thing that could definitely crimp a friendship. I'm wondering now, though, about what really happened to Six. Did Berto lie to me about that too?

"Anyway," he says, "I just wanted to come by and make sure you were all set. I thought we could file a quick report with Command, and maybe go grab some breakfast."

I definitely do *not* want to file a report with Command. Not until I settle things with Eight, anyway.

"You know," I say. "I'm actually still pretty whipped. You go ahead and get something to eat. I'm gonna take a quick nap. I'll register with Security when I wake up, and we can file with Command after that."

He gives me a searching look. He knows something's not right here. I usually head straight to the cafeteria after I come out of the tank. Nobody voluntarily skips meals around here, but beyond that, the bio-printer doesn't print any food into your digestive system. When you wake up, your stomach is pretty much where it would be after a seventy-two-hour fast.

"Okay," he says. "But don't take too long. You know synthesizing your ass takes a huge bite out of our protein budget. Command will want to know what happened, and why, and how we're planning on making up the deficit. This is your second regen in the last eight weeks, so we'll need to come up with something good this time."

"We could just tell them what actually happened."

He shakes his head. "We have to be a little creative with this. Command is really sensitive about losing calories and protein from the system right now, and Marshall is not about to accept responsibility for it, even though these stupid sorties are on his orders. He's probably going to be pissed at you for not defending yourself adequately, and he's definitely going to be pissed at me for not swooping in and recovering your body. Honestly, if this keeps up, he may just refuse to authorize your regen one of these times."

A shiver runs up my spine. Was that a premonition?

"Hey," he says. "Are you okay? You don't look so good, Mickey."

I rub my eyes with my right hand, and hope he doesn't notice that my left hasn't come out from under the blanket this entire time.

"Yeah," I say. "I'm good. Just need to sleep off the tank funk. I'll meet you at the caf in an hour."

He looks me up and down, then gets to his feet, reaches over, and pats me on the leg.

"Good man. I'll save you some cycler paste."

"Thanks, Berto. You're a pal."

"By the way," he says, just as the door is closing behind him.

"I couldn't help but notice that you've had your hand on your junk the entire time I've been here. Careful with that. Nasha gets jealous."

"Yeah, Berto. I know. Thanks for noticing, though."

"No problem. See you in an hour."

I can hear him snickering as the latch clicks closed.

I'VE DIED SIX times in the past eight years. You'd think I'd be used to it by now, wouldn't you?

To be fair, one of those was a surprise, one was an emergency situation, and one of my instantiations refused to upload before he died. I only remember what gets uploaded, so all I know about what happened to those iterations of me is what Nasha or Berto told me, or what I've seen on surveillance vids. The other three, though, were planned, and standard procedure is to have the Expendable upload as close to his termination as possible, basically for the reason I gave Berto—the next iteration needs to know what happened to the last one, so that hopefully he can keep it from happening again. So, I guess I'm more familiar with the hollow feeling that's settling into the pit of my stomach right now than most people ever get to be.

This isn't exactly like any of those times, of course. For one thing, those other Mickeys knew for shit sure they were going to die. Unless Eight is planning to shiv me or something, I've only got a fifty-fifty chance of going down this time.

I'm not really sure that's a good thing. There's a certain peace that comes from knowing without a doubt what's going to happen to you. The possibility that I might survive this morning is a source of anxiety as much as it is a source of hope.

The uncertainty isn't the big difference between this time and those others, though. The big difference is that up until now, every time I went down I could at least halfway believe the crap my handlers were feeding me about my own immortality. I knew that a few hours after Mickey3 died, Mickey4 would come out of the tank, and I could imagine that it would just be me both times, closing my eyes and then opening them.

If I die now, though, there won't be another me coming out of the tank. The other me is already here, and despite all appearances, Eight is most definitely not a continuation of me.

Honestly, he doesn't even seem to like me very much.

THE CYCLER IS on the lowest level, and halfway across the dome from my rack. It's not a long walk, realistically speaking, but it feels like one this morning. The corridors are nearly empty, and as I pace down them the only sounds are my footfalls and the pounding rush of blood in my ears. I know it's irrational, but deep in my belly I can feel that this isn't going to go my way. When I take the two shallow steps up to the entrance to the cycler chamber, it's like I'm mounting the stairs to the gallows.

The bio-cycler is the heart and soul of any beachhead colony. It takes our shit, our tomato stems, our potato peels and rabbit bones and half-chewed gristle, our hair clippings and fingernails, our dropped-off scabs and wadded-up tissues, and eventually our corpses. In return, it gives us protein paste and vitamin slurry and fertilizer. Nobody wants to live on cycler paste, but a desperate colony can do it for a very long time.

The cycler works by breaking down anything you drop down the corpse hole into its component atoms, then piecing them back together in whatever order you specify. This takes an obscene amount of energy, but our power plant is an antimatter-driven starship engine. Energy is the one thing we have more than enough of.

I've finished transmitting my access code to the control console when Eight walks in. I lift the safety cover and press the big red button, and the corpse hole irises open in the center of the floor.

The corpse hole is one of those things we try not to think too much about. I've only seen it open on the rare occasions that I've been seconded out to garbage duty, and I've never really looked inside. I'm not sure what you'd expect an antimatter-driven, all-devouring maw to look like—roaring flames and a stench of sulfur, maybe?—but it's actually quiet and odorless and kind of pretty. It's just a flat black disk at first, but then the disassembler field starts grabbing dust motes, and they disappear one by one in tiny firefly flashes.

It doesn't look so bad.

Better than being ripped apart by a swarm of creepers, anyway.

"So," Eight says. "You ready?"

I shrug. "Yeah, I guess so. Kinda regretting not going judicial at this point, to be honest, but let's do this."

He smiles, and claps me on the shoulder. "You're okay, Seven. I'm gonna feel really bad when I shove you down that hole."

My heart stutters. "What do you mean, shove me?"

His smile disappears. "Think about it. Do you really want to go into that thing conscious?"

Huh. That's a good point. Actual corpses get lowered into the hole pretty slowly. I don't know what the maximum feed rate is, but if it's less than infinite, unconscious or already deceased is probably a smarter way to go.

Eight turns to stand next to me, looking down into the hole.

"You know," he says, "you could still do the decent thing, and volunteer to be the one to go."

"Sure," I say. "So could you."

He puts his arm around my shoulder. "Not gonna happen, huh?"

"Probably not."

The disk has gone black again. Out of dust, I guess. Eight hawks up a glob of tank goo and spits. It flashes when it hits the threshold, sizzles for a second, and disappears.

"This may be less painless than I thought," he says.

"Truth," I say. "Tell you what—I could strangle you first, then push you through."

He grins. "Thanks, Seven. You're a real humanitarian."

We stand in silence for a while. His arm around my shoulder grows heavier and heavier. Finally, I step out from under it and turn to face him.

"Look," I say. "Are we doing this?"

"I guess so," he says.

He raises his left hand. I raise my right. We clench our fists and say the words together.

"One . . ."

"Two . . ."

"Three . . ."

"Shoot."

I'm planning to go with Rock, right up until we shoot. But then I remember that he's me. He's probably thinking the same thing. So it's Paper, right? But what if he's thinking that too? He could be figuring I'll go with Paper and shooting Scissors. So that brings me back to Rock, which is good because by the time I work my way through all of that it's too late and my fist is still clenched.

I look down.

His hand is held out flat.

"Sorry, brother," he says.

Yeah, sorry.

Thanks for that, asshole.

KNEELING THERE ON the decking, my face six inches from the disassembler field interface, looking at the prospect of being converted into slurry for the hungry colonists of Niflheim, I find myself once again contemplating the question of whether I made the right call when I pressed my thumb down onto that reader pad back in Gwen Johansen's office nine years ago.

Even now, though, I have to say—yeah, I did. No question about it, really.

I didn't go home after I left Gwen's office. I would've liked to, because I was hungry and tired and could've used a shower. I couldn't, though, for the same reason that I couldn't say no to Gwen's oh-so-tempting offer of half-assed immortality. I'd gotten onto Darius Blank's shit list, you see—and as far as I could tell, I didn't have any reasonable way to get back off of it.

The root of this particular problem, like the root of pretty much all of my problems, now that I think of it, was Berto.

Berto was the only person on the *Drakkar* that I'd known before I gave Gwen my DNA and signed my life away. We met in school, where he was tall, smart, athletic, and weirdly good-looking considering how he turned out, and I was . . . well, I was pretty much what I am now, only smaller. We bonded over our common love of the flight simulator, which he mastered in about an hour and which I was still crashing when we graduated, and our hatred of the school administrators, who hated me right back for obsessing about *history* when I could have been studying something useful, but despite all our best efforts loved Berto like the son they'd never had. In form ten, Berto's calculus instructor told him he should reconsider spending so much time with me if he wanted to reach his full potential.

I think Berto took that as just another challenge.

The thing you have to understand about Berto is that he was one of those obnoxious kids who was prodigy-level good at nearly everything he ever tried. When we were fifteen, his mom bought him a pog-ball racket. He didn't take lessons. He didn't join a recreational league. He spent a couple of months banging balls off of the wall of the admin building after classes to figure out how it worked, did one season on the school team, then turned around and entered a pro-am tournament. Nobody had any idea who he was when he showed up for his first match. He won that one going away, and by the end of the week he'd finished second in his age bracket. The next year, he won the amateur division. The summer after we graduated, he started playing for money. By the time he dropped the game to start serious flight training two years later, he was the tenth-ranked player on the planet.

All of which would have been apropos of nothing, except that nine years after that, I was living in an extremely unfashionable apartment in an extremely unfashionable part of Kiruna, and Berto had been selected for the crew of the *Drakkar*. We were sitting in a café called Shaky Joe's, sipping tea and killing time while we waited for a ball game to start on the viewscreen over the bar, when he mentioned that he was considering coming out of retirement for one last run at the spring pro-am before disappearing into the unknown forever.

"Think about it," he said. "If I take that trophy after all this time, I'll be a legend. They'll still be talking about me a hundred years from now."

I opened my mouth to tell him that he'd be a legend, all right, but it wouldn't be because he'd won a global tournament and then ridden off into the sunset. It would be because he thought he could do that after being out of the game for nine years, and then he'd lost his first match to some eighteen-year-old by a hundred points.

I didn't say that, though. I didn't because it suddenly occurred to me that while *I* knew that for the past nine years he'd been spending nearly every minute that he wasn't in the air or in orbit hanging around with me, most of the people in Kiruna did not. They still remembered twenty-year-old Berto Gomez beating seasoned pros and hardly seeming to break a sweat doing it. They remembered him doing things with a racket that people hadn't realized could be done up until then, and they remembered commentators calling him the most naturally talented player they'd ever seen. They didn't have any idea that he basically hadn't touched a racket in the past nine years.

"Yeah," I said. "Do it, man. You'll be a freaking *legend*."

So, he did. He registered for the tournament, and one of the news feeds picked up the story and did an interview with him that they paired with footage from his last tournament, which he'd won without dropping a single game.

Meanwhile, I scraped up every credit I had, and a bunch that I didn't, and I placed a bet on Berto to lose his first match.

I don't have a great defense for this decision, except to say that the market for amateur historians in Kiruna wasn't great, I had no real prospects for any kind of gainful employment, and the idea of living out the rest of my life on a basic subsidy was so depressing that I couldn't contemplate it.

Was it worse than the prospect of being dissolved headfirst? Maybe not, but I wasn't thinking along those lines yet.

You can probably see where this is going.

By the time Berto won the goddamned tournament, I was so far underwater from doubling down and doubling down again that even if I'd somehow found an actual paying job somewhere, it would have taken me half a lifetime to get back to the surface.

The person I was underwater to, specifically, was Darius Blank.

Vids are full of stories about guys who fall behind on their gambling debts and get murdered for it, but that's not actually how it usually works. After all, while it may be hard to collect a debt from a live guy, it's indisputably even harder to collect from a dead one—and in the end, collecting the debt is all somebody like Darius Blank really cares about. I wasn't worried about him killing me. I guess I had some vague idea that he'd garnish my subsidy, and maybe make me work as his valet or something. It would be unpleasant, but I'd survive.

Berto, to his credit, did his best to convince me that I was mistaken about all of this.

Also to his credit, Berto felt bad about what his win had cost me. He had a suggestion for how he could make it up to me. He wanted me to sign on to the *Drakkar*.

He had some vague idea that he could get me in as a Security goon. He was famous, after all, and he'd always gotten whatever he wanted up until that point in his life. Why wouldn't he be able to get this?

Gwen Johansen pretty much summed up the answer to that question for me during our interview. There were a lot of people who wanted Security berths, and there were only eighteen slots available. Most of them went to people with both some sort of qualification—experience in law enforcement, weapons training, etc.—and political connections. I didn't have any of those things, because having read extensively about the Battle of Midway does not count as military experience, and as it turned out Berto didn't have nearly as much pull as he thought he did.

I did put in a request to interview for a Security position. A rejection bounced back to me less than a second later.

The next afternoon I met Berto for coffee at Shaky Joe's. I showed him the rejection notice on my tablet.

"Ouch," he said. "That sucks."

"Yeah," I said. "It was kind of a dumb idea, anyway. I owe some money. You don't flee the planet over something like that."

Berto shook his head. "You owe a lot of money, Mickey, and guys like Darius Blank don't forgive and forget. What is it, a hundred thousand credits? How are you planning on paying that back?"

I shrugged. "Installment plan?"

"You didn't just buy a used flitter, buddy."

"Yeah," I said. "I know." I dropped my head into my hands. "I'm such an idiot. I can't believe I didn't just tell you to throw the freaking match."

He stared at me for a long moment, then laughed. "You could have asked," he said, "but I wouldn't have done it. This tournament was the last thing the yahoos on this planet will ever hear from me, Mickey. There's no way I wasn't going to win."

That's the thing about Berto. Friendship with him only ever went so far, and no farther.

On the way home from the coffee shop, I remember thinking that this really wasn't going to be so bad. Yeah, Blank would take a chunk of my subsidy, but he'd have to leave me enough to stay alive, right? If I starved to death, he'd never get his money back. And maybe being his valet wouldn't be so bad? It would give me a reason to get out of the apartment, anyway.

I got home. I took the lift tube up to my floor. I let myself into my apartment. The door was still swinging shut behind me when my legs stopped working and I fell flat on my face.

"Hello, Mickey," a voice said. I tried to answer, but my mouth wasn't working either, and all that came out was a low moan. "Just relax," the voice said. "This won't take long." Something pressed against the back of my neck.

I spent the next thirty seconds in hell.

I later learned that the thing that had been pressed against my neck was in fact a neural inducer. It was tuned to tap directly into my pain centers. It didn't do any physical damage, but if you're curious about what I experienced, try skinning yourself alive while a friend works you over with a blowtorch.

That might get you about ten percent of the way there.

When it was over, I was astonished to find that I was still alive. I was sobbing and paralyzed and I'd soiled myself, but I was still alive. A hand patted my shoulder.

"This was fun," the voice said. "We'll be working together, you and I, until you're all square with Mr. Blank. See you tomorrow, Mickey."

He didn't close the door behind himself on the way out.

It was about an hour before I could move again. I got to my feet, staggered into the bathroom, and cleaned myself up. That taken care of, I sat down and had a good cry.

That night, I logged on to the recruitment page for the *Drakkar*. It listed the various sections and positions, and who had been selected for each so far.

Every slot was full.

Every one but one.

I pinged Berto.

"Hey," I said. "What's an *Expendable*?"

"That," Berto said, "is the one berth on the *Drakkar* that you do *not* want."

"It's the only one that's still open. I want it."

He was silent for a while. When he spoke again, his voice had the tone you take when you're explaining to someone that you want them to come down off the ledge.

"Look," he said. "Don't get me wrong about this. I would really love to have you with me on this trip. This is a one-way, and it would be great to have a friend along. But Mickey—"

"Can you put in a word for me?"

"I mean—"

"Berto," I said. "I'm asking for your help here. You kind of did this to me, you know."

"I didn't," he said. "I didn't tell you to bet against me. If you'd asked, I would have told you to bet *on* me. I knew I was going to win."

"Will you help me?"

He sighed. "Honestly, Mickey? I don't think you're gonna need my help."

He cut the connection. I went back to the recruitment page and scheduled an interview for the next afternoon.

Twelve hours later, when Gwen ran down her list of all the horrible things that might happen to me during my tenure as an Expendable, all I could think was, *That doesn't sound so bad, actually.* They put some effort into training me not to fear the reaper once I'd boosted up to the *Drakkar* and couldn't change my mind about signing on, but honestly none of that made too much of an impression on me. I'd gotten all the training anyone ever needed on that front in that one afternoon.

I DON'T GET shoved into the cycler at this time. The disassembler field doesn't get me.

I'm explaining this now because you looked nervous.

I'm on my hands and knees, looking down at the hole. Swear to God, I'm gonna do it. I lower my face down, right next to the interface. I can feel the field pulling at me, a tingle along my cheeks and across the bridge of my nose as it strokes my skin, and I'm trying to figure out a way to do this that will be something less than agonizing, when I feel a hand on my shoulder.

"Give me a minute!" I bark, picturing Eight shoving me down the hole face-first.

"No," Eight says. He pulls me back onto my heels and offers me a hand up. "This isn't right. I can't just stand here and watch you do this."

I let him haul me to my feet. I'm shaking so badly that I can barely stand.

"Okay," I say. "I'm with you on that."

I take a deep breath, then another. For some reason, staring down into that black disk was much, much worse than staring down the gullet of that thing in the tunnel last night.

"So, ah . . . what do you suggest?"

"Let's go back upstairs," he says. "I can drown you in the toilet, then chop you up in the chem shower and feed you through the cycler a piece at a time."

I stare at him. He's grinning.

"Too soon," I say finally. "Much too soon. Seriously, Eight, what are we doing here? We've still only got one berth, and one ration card. More importantly, we've only got one registered identity. If *anybody* finds out we're a multiple . . ."

He shrugs. "These are unusual circumstances, right?"

"Yeah, maybe—but given the resource constraints we're under, I don't think Command is likely to be sympathetic. If we go to Marshall now, one of us is definitely going down that hole."

"Most likely," he says. "And if we try to be sneaky about it, there's a fair chance both of us wind up as slurry."

I squeeze my eyes closed and wait for my pulse to slow from jackhammer to frightened baby bird, then finally to something close to normal. When I open them, Eight is looking at me with concern that's clearly bordering on alarm.

"You okay, Seven?"

"Yeah," I say. I shake my head and breathe in, breathe out. "I'm good. They talk about staring death in the face, but . . ."

"A bit too literal, huh?"

"Right," I say. "If Marshall does wind up feeding me to the cycler, I really, really hope he has the decency to kill me first."

Eight puts one hand to my shoulder. "You and me both, brother. In the meantime, though, we need some kind of plan."

"Agreed. Do you have one?"

He runs both hands back through his hair. "I don't know . . . I don't know . . . they didn't cover this situation in training."

That's the truth, anyway. Training was one hundred percent about dying. I don't remember them dedicating much time at all to staying alive.

"Look," he says. "We've got a heavy ration card. Unless you've done something stupid since our last upload, we should still be getting two thousand kcal a day."

"Yeah," I say. "I think that's right."

"So if we split that down the middle, we've got enough to keep us alive for a while. Not happy, maybe, but alive."

I can feel my face twisting into a grimace. "A thousand kcal a day each? That's brutal, Eight. We have to be able to do better than that. What about Berto? This is mostly his fault. If we told him what's going on, think he might feel guilty enough to kick in a little cycler paste?"

Eight looks doubtful. "Maybe. I'd rather save that for desperation time, though. Berto's not the most altruistic guy on Niflheim, and I don't know how much of a fundamentalist he is about the multiple thing."

"Yeah," I say. "You make some good points. Also, he abandoned me to die in a cavern last night, so you can put that on the maybe-don't-trust-him side of the scales."

"Right," he says. "That. Okay. What about petitioning Marshall for a bump in our ration?"

I roll my eyes. "Sure. I'll get right on that."

"Look," Eight says. "When I stopped by the caf on my way down here, paste was selling at a twenty-five percent discount. If we stick to nothing but, that's twelve hundred and fifty kcal of actual nutrition each. It's not great, but . . ."

"Okay," I say. "Fine. I guess we won't starve to death right away, anyway. That still doesn't address our main problem, though. *There's two of us.* Marshall looks like he just stepped in something rotten every time he has to deal with the fact that there's one Mickey Barnes in his colony. If he gets a sniff of this, the cycler is a best-case scenario for us."

I should point out here that Commander Marshall found out about my run-in with Darius Blank about a week after we boosted out of orbit around Midgard, and interpreted that as evidence that a criminal element had infiltrated his colony. Add that to the fact that he comes from a religious tradition that considers the whole concept of pulling people out of the tank even one at a time to be an abomination, and you wound up with me about thirty seconds from being chucked out of an air lock before the captain of the *Drakkar,* a very nice woman named Mara Singh who is now head of our Engineering Section, reminded him that he wasn't actually in command of the mission until we made landfall on Niflheim.

Somehow, I don't think this situation is likely to improve his opinion of me.

"I know," Eight says. "I know . . . but unless you want to change your mind about going down the hole today, there's nothing we can do about that point, is there?"

"No," I say. "I guess not."

"Of course, if you did change your mind?"

"Don't worry, Eight. You'll be the first to know."

He's grinning. I'm definitely not.

"Thanks," he says. "Hey—what about Nasha? Do you think we can talk to her about this?"

I have to think about that one. Nasha and I have been together since I was Mickey3, and unlike Berto, she was ready to risk her one and only life to pull me out of that hole last night. If there was one person we could trust around here, she'd be it.

On the other hand, if we eventually do wind up in front of Marshall over this, I'd really, really rather she didn't have to go down with us.

"You know what?" I say. "Let's just keep this between us for now, huh?"

"Sure," Eight says. "I mean, the way things have gone since landfall, one of us will be dead pretty soon anyway, right? Problem solved."

Ugh. He's probably right about that.

ON THE TOPIC of being dead soon, here's a story for you: a few months after landfall, when I was still Mickey6, Berto took me out for a ride-along. We took up a fixed-wing, single-engine reconnaissance flitter that day instead of one of the heavy lifters that he usually flies. We were already up and circling over the dome when I asked him how they managed to fit a gravitic generator into such a tiny plane. He turned to look at me, a subtle smile on his face.

"Gravitics? You're kidding, right?"

"No," I said. "I'm not."

He shook his head, then throttled up and put us into a steep, banking climb.

"This is an aircraft, Mickey. The only thing keeping us up here is Bernoulli's principle."

I didn't have any idea who Bernoulli was or what principles he might have had, but I really didn't like the sound of that. I'd never been off the ground before without the sure knowledge that I was surrounded by a gravitic field that would not, under any circumstances, allow me to plunge into the ground at a hundred and fifty meters per second and burst open like an overripe melon.

"Berto?" I said. "Do you think you might want to level out or something? Or better yet, maybe head back in and switch this thing out for something a little more stable?"

He laughed. "Are you serious? Do you have any idea how

much wheedling I had to do to get them to let me sign out the flitter? The whole point of taking this thing out today is that it can do things that a heavy lifter can't."

I opened my mouth to say something about not really wanting to do things that a heavy lifter can't, but before I could get anything out we were in a barrel roll and I was screaming like a . . . well, like one of what I was, I guess, which was someone who was suddenly, shamelessly, gut-churningly terrified of dying.

I think that's when I first realized that despite all the training, despite the indoctrination, despite the incontrovertible fact that I'd died five times by then and I was clearly still alive—deep down, in my heart of hearts, I did not believe in immortality.

"So," Nasha says, "what's with the pauper's breakfast?"

I'm halfway through choking down a six-hundred-kcal bowl of unsweetened cycler paste. I should note here that in the economy of a beachhead colony, a kcal is not actually a kcal. Different items can come at anything from a steep discount to a premium, depending on how closely they resemble something that you'd actually want to put into your mouth. Like Eight said, paste and slurry are trading at a twenty-five percent discount at the moment, which means that if I stick to nothing but, I can probably hold most of my body weight for at least a week or two. Nasha's working on a mashed yam and Cajun-blackened cricket scramble. That's going at par this morning. They actually have a few rabbit haunches and some sickly-looking tomatoes on offer, but those are at a forty percent premium. I'm guessing I can forget about that kind of luxury as long as Eight is still around.

"Well," I say. "I've been thinking about doing some bodybuilding. Thought maybe if I max out my calories and bulk up a little, it'll take the creepers longer to eat me next time."

She giggles. Nasha's giggle is one of her best features. It's soft and delicate, and when she giggles she has a tendency to look to the side and cover her mouth with her hand. The effect is so at odds with her whole badass-combat-pilot thing that it's almost like she becomes a different person.

"I'm glad you've still got a sense of humor about this," she says. "You've been going down pretty often since we made landfall. Some folks might be getting bitter by now."

I refill my water glass. Cycler paste really isn't meant to be eaten by itself. It doesn't taste like anything in particular, but it's thick and gritty enough that it needs a lot of washing down.

"Well," I say, "I try to look at it this way. If Seven hadn't gotten himself whacked, I never would have come out of the tank, right?"

Her face clouds over. "I guess," she says.

I look up from my shitty breakfast. "What?"

She shakes her head. "This is hard for me, Mickey, and every time you go down it gets harder. I felt awful last night—worse than I did when Six died, maybe even worse than I did after what happened to Five. Even after you told me you were shutting down, I hung around just in comm range, hoping you'd change your mind. When I finally gave up and came back to the dome, I spent an hour in the bay sitting in my cockpit and crying like a baby. Now, though, here you are, and like you said, if I *had* saved you last night, *this* you wouldn't be here . . . and now I don't know what to feel."

"Yeah," I say. "Immortality is confusing, huh?"

"Right you are," says Berto. I look around to see him standing behind me, a tray of yams and crickets in his hands.

"Morning, Berto," Nasha says. "Have a seat. I guess."

He sets his tray down next to mine and folds himself onto the bench. "What's up with the gruel, Mickey? And what happened to your hand?"

I look down. I've got my wrist wrapped up tight, but you can still see bits of purple bruising sticking out around the edges.

"I fell getting out of bed," I say. "Tank funk, right?"

Berto gives me a long look, and I can see the wheels turning. "Right," he says. "When, exactly, did this happen?"

"After you stopped by my rack," I say. "Why do you care?"

Nasha looks up from her breakfast. "Am I missing something?"

"Maybe," Berto says. "How long after I stopped by?"

"I don't know. Right before I came down here. Maybe half an hour ago?"

"Your wrist was fine when I saw you in the shower room," Nasha says.

"Right," I say. "It was after that."

Berto's eyes narrow, and he shakes his head.

"Seriously," Nasha says. "What's going on?"

"I'm not sure," Berto says. "Mickey? What's going on?"

I spoon up the last of my cycler paste. I'm wondering if Berto might have run into Eight on his way down here. If so, I need to come clean now and hope he's willing to keep his mouth shut. If not, though . . .

"Nothing's going on," I say. "I'm just trying to finish my breakfast."

I take a quick look around. We're late for breakfast now, but early for lunch. There's nobody sitting close enough to us to overhear what we're saying. Berto's still staring at me.

"So?" I say. "What are you getting at, Berto?"

He takes a forkful of crickets and yam, chews slowly, and swallows. "I dunno, Mickey. I've seen you come out of the tank a lot lately. Something's just a little off about you this time."

I feel my face twist into a scowl. "Maybe if you focused less on how I act when I come out of the tank and more on not getting me killed and back in the tank in the first place, we wouldn't be having this discussion."

"Oh yeah," Nasha says. "There's the bitter."

"Anyway," Berto says, "I didn't sit down here so that I could get into it with Mickey over how he hurt his jerking hand. I was actually wondering if either of you had heard anything about what happened on the perimeter this morning."

Nasha grimaces into the remains of her breakfast and pokes halfheartedly at a scorched potato skin.

"I heard I'm on sweep again in an hour, even though I just came off shift four hours ago. I assumed there was a reason, but nobody's said shit to me about what it is."

Berto leans across the table toward her and drops his voice. "We lost someone."

"Lost?" Nasha says. "Lost how?"

Berto shrugs. "Nobody seems to know. It was the Security goon manning the east checkpoint. Dani said it was Gabe Torricelli. He pinged in at eight, but not at eight thirty. When they sent someone out to look for him, all they found was a bunch of churned-up snow."

I've already opened my mouth to say I saw Gabe this morning before I remember that neither of these two are supposed to know I was outside the dome today. Gabe was the one who waved me in when I got back from the labyrinth. That must have been around . . .

Eight fifteen?

Holy shit.

Did the creepers follow me back to the dome?

I flash back to that spider I set free in the garden all those years ago. What if that's not what happened at all last night? What if I was actually an ant they didn't stomp so that they could figure out where the nest is?

"What?" Nasha says.

I look from her to Berto, then back again. They're both staring at me.

"Seriously," Berto says. "You look like you just wet yourself, Mickey. What the hell? Were you tight with this guy?"

That's kind of a stupid question, considering that there are fewer than two hundred humans on this planet, and we've been cooped up with all of them for the past nine years. It says something about how little the three of us have interacted with our fellow colonists that, no, I was not tight with Gabe. In fact, I barely knew him beyond recognizing his face and having a vague sense that he wasn't one of the bad ones—and neither, obviously, did either of them.

"I know who he was," I say. "We weren't really friends. Does it matter, though? We just lost like point-six percent of our population, Berto."

"Yeah," Berto says. "I guess that's true. I wasn't actually a big fan of old Gabe, to be honest. During transit, he was one of those guys who was constantly busting people's asses about not putting in enough time in the carousel. You make a point, though. Until we start thawing out embryos, we really can't afford too many leaks in the bottom of the gene pool."

"I'm not worried about that," Nasha says. "I mean, if we need more generic white guys around here, we can always just crank out a few more Mickeys, right?"

They both laugh. I hesitate a bit too long before joining in.

"Seriously, though," Berto says. "Mickey does have a point."

I don't actually remember making any points, but okay.

"Truth," Nasha says. "Pretty sure Gabe didn't just wander off."

"Creepers got him," Berto says.

Nasha looks up from the last of her yams. "You know that?"

"Not for sure, but what else could it have been? We haven't seen anything else on this rock yet that's bigger than an amoeba."

Nasha shakes her head. "Creepers coming that close to the dome is bad news. Creepers taking down an armed goon is worse. Was he armored up?"

He was—but again, I'm not supposed to know that.

"Dunno," Berto says. "Probably not, though. No reason to be up until now, right? I mean, this is the first time the creepers have actually killed somebody."

"They killed me," I say. "Twice, actually."

Berto puts one arm around my shoulders and gives me a squeeze. "I know they did, buddy."

Nasha snickers. I shoot her a glare, but she's back in her breakfast and doesn't notice. I expect that kind of shit from Berto. Nasha's usually better than that.

"Armor or no," Berto says, "Gabe would have been carrying a heavy-duty burner, right? How do you get yourself killed by a bunch of bugs when you're armed with something that can flash-fry a buffalo?"

"Burners don't affect them," I say.

They both turn to look at me.

"What?" Nasha says.

"Yeah," Berto says. "What are you talking about, Mickey?"

I open my mouth to answer, then let it fall closed again when I see Berto's eyes widen. Again, I need to get him into a poker game.

"I feel like I'm missing something," Nasha says. "Friends don't keep secrets, Mickey."

"No," Berto says. "No, Mickey's right, actually. He had a burner when he got taken down last night. It didn't do him any good. I guess I forgot about that."

I give him my best dead-eye stare. "You forgot?"

"Yeah," he says. "I forgot."

"You forgot that you saw your best friend get torn to shreds less than twenty-four hours ago."

"Well," Berto says, "I don't know if I'd say *best* friend."

"Torn apart?" Nasha says. "I thought he wound up freezing to death at the bottom of a crevasse."

I give Berto my best confused-yet-angry look. "What's this about freezing to death, Berto?"

He shoots a quick, poisonous glare at Nasha, then shakes his head and says, "Not important. The point is, you went down, and there was nothing any of us could do about it."

"Not true," Nasha says, and goes back to poking at her breakfast. "I could have." She looks up at me, gives me a sad half smile. "He wouldn't let me. You were brave last night, Mickey. You wouldn't let me risk myself for you. Can't take that away from you, no matter how dumb you were to fall down that hole in the first place." Her smile fades then, replaced by a scowl. "Anyway, the actual point here is that, however he managed to do it, Gabe Torricelli got himself killed or kidnapped or eaten this morning, and because of that I now have to pull a double goddamned shift aloft." She looks over at Berto. "Speaking of which—why are you off duty this morning? You didn't spend any more time up last night than I did."

Berto shrugs. "I guess Marshall just likes me more."

That's still hanging in the air between us when a chat window pops up in my ocular.

<Command1>:You are required to report to Commander Marshall's office no later than 10:30. Failure to report will be considered insubordination and will result in a reduced ration allocation. Please acknowledge.

I've just bounced back a read receipt when a second window opens next to the first, partially covering Nasha's face with text.

<Mickey8>:You're seeing the summons from Command too, right?
<Mickey8>:Yeah, I see it.
<Mickey8>:Ugh. We're both Mickey8 now, huh?

<**Mickey8**>:Looks like it.

<**Mickey8**>:Great. This is gonna be confusing.

<**Mickey8**>:I'm sure we'll figure it out.

<**Mickey8**>:Think the network's gonna flag the fact that the same handle is pinging from two different locations?

<**Mickey8**>:Probably not unless somebody goes digging.

<**Mickey8**>:In which case, we're screwed anyway.

<**Mickey8**>:Right.

<**Mickey8**>:Anyway, I'm guessing this summons is Marshall looking to chew on us for getting killed again, and wasting seventy kilos of colony protein. You mind handling it? I've got a serious case of tank funk, and I could really use a nap.

<**Mickey8**>:Do I have a choice?

<**Mickey8**>:Zzzzzzz

I blink both windows closed. Berto and Nasha are staring at me.

"Rude," Nasha says.

"Yeah," Berto says. "Extremely." He pushes back from the table, stands, and picks up his tray. "That said, I've gotta run. Have a fun time out there, Nasha."

Nasha picks up a scrap of yam skin with her fork and flings it at his back as he walks away. I have to resist the urge to chase the scrap down and eat it.

"Anyway," Nasha says when he's gone, "I've got an hour to kill before I have to go up again. Want to finish what we started in the shower?"

It takes me a second or two to put that together with what she said earlier about seeing me in the shower room and realize what she must be talking about, then another two or three to get the image of her with Eight out of my head. I can't actually be jealous of myself, can I?

Yes, apparently I can.

Doesn't matter, though. For better or worse, I've got somewhere to be.

"Actually," I say, "I just got a ping from Command. I've got to go pay Marshall a visit."

"Oh," she says. "Right. Pissed about you flushing another hunk of protein down the toilet, huh?"

"Yeah," I say. "Probably something like that."

She half stands, leans across the table, grabs me by the back of the head, and pulls me into a kiss.

"Don't take any shit from him," she says. "Getting iced is your job, and you were out there on orders. He can't be mad at you for being a klutz." She kisses me again, this time on the forehead. "I'm gonna need some rack time after I get back in, but I'll ping you after that, huh?" She kisses me once more on the mouth. "Make sure you brush your teeth first, though. That cycler paste is nasty."

She pats me once on the cheek, picks up her tray, and goes.

I SHOULDN'T BE nervous about going to see Marshall. I mean, he's not likely to have me killed today. Especially lately, I can't always say that.

Anyway, he may be our supreme commander, but I've known Marshall longer than I've known anyone else on Niflheim other than Berto. He was the first person to greet me when my shuttle docked at the orbital assembly plant where they were putting the finishing touches on the *Drakkar,* two days after my interview with Gwen Johansen and three days after Darius Blank's minion made me spend the longest thirty seconds of my life staring into the face of Satan.

Well, *greet* might be a strong word for what Marshall did. He was definitely there, though.

In all fairness to him, I probably didn't make a very good first impression. I'd never experienced free fall before the shuttle's gravitics cut out for the approach to the station. I'd seen vids of people in orbit, of course. You couldn't spend five minutes on the entertainment nets without seeing advertisements for the orbital resorts with tourists in wing suits playing zero-g handball or some damn thing. I always assumed it would be kind of relaxing—like floating in the ocean, but without having to worry about getting eaten by a kraken.

The thing is, though, it's not called free float. It's called free *fall.*

The second the gravitic field shut down, my stomach climbed up into my throat, my heart started pounding so hard I could feel it in my fingertips, and my lizard brain let me know in no uncertain terms that, visual evidence aside, we were dropping like rain from a clear blue sky, and we were definitely, definitely about to die.

I didn't lose it like a few of my fellow passengers did. I didn't scream, I didn't start flailing around, and I didn't need to use the vacuum mask they provided in the seat back for folks who couldn't keep their lunches down. I was okay. I definitely wasn't *good,* though, and by the time we'd docked and I'd made my way through the air lock and into the arrivals lounge, I was drenched in sweat and trembling.

I probably looked like a morphine addict two days into withdrawal—and that's the first impression Commander Marshall got of me.

Marshall was in the lounge waiting for us, floating by the viewport opposite the air lock, staring down at the night side of Midgard as it spun past five hundred klicks below. He waited until the last of the dozen would-be colonists from the shuttle had drifted into the lounge and the air lock's inner door had clanged shut behind her to acknowledge us. I could see right away that we were in the presence of someone who thought of himself as In Charge of Things. From his jet-black tight-fade haircut to his perpetually clenched jaw to the fact that he somehow managed to look like he had a metal rod for a spine even in free fall, he was almost a parody of the sort of cold-eyed, combat-hardened military man that Midgard hadn't ever actually had or needed.

It took me three years and two reincarnations to realize that his whole aspect was ten percent genuine priggishness, ten percent insecurity, and eighty percent overcompensation for the fact that, as designated ground commander, he may as well have been cargo for the entirety of the transit.

"Well," Marshall said, and kicked off the floor toward us. He caught himself with one hand on a grab bar set into the ceiling, then drifted down to more or less stand in front of me. "Welcome to Himmel Station. This will be your home until the *Drakkar* is cleared for boarding. My name is Hieronymus Marshall, and I'll be in charge of this little expedition. Have any of you been off-planet before?" A half dozen hands went up. Marshall nodded. "Excellent. And how many of you others are trying desperately not to vomit right now?" Three hands went up, then a hesitant fourth. Marshall nodded again. "Yes, well. You'll get over that eventually. Or else you won't, I suppose. Either way, you're here for the duration, as they say."

"Sir?"

It was one of the vomiters. Marshall turned to look at him.

"Yes?"

"Dugan, sir. Biology. When—" He belched, then grimaced and swallowed. "Ugh . . . when will they be transferring up our personal effects? They wouldn't let us bring them onto the shuttle."

Marshall gave him a tight smile. "They will not be, unfortunately. Mass, as you can probably imagine, is a bit of an issue on a trip of this sort. As a result, we've made the decision to forbid the transfer of personal items." That got a round of groans from the group, but Marshall cut it off with a wave. "None of that, please. I promise you'll be given everything you need, and I think

you'll find there's little need for knickknacks on a beachhead colony." His eyes swept across us. "Any other questions?"

I raised my hand. This was the first of several mistakes I made
in my early days as a colonist.

"Yes," Marshall said. "You are?"

"Mickey Barnes," I said. "They told us we had a thirty-kilo
personal allowance."

His smile became slightly tighter, and significantly less of a
smile.

"As I said, Mr. Barnes, the decision was made to rescind that
allowance."

"Nobody told us that," I said. "I need some of the stuff that I
left in my bag."

Marshall was definitely not smiling anymore. "Mr. Barnes," he
said. "When we are fully loaded, there will be one hundred and
ninety-eight colonists and crew onboard the *Drakkar*. If each of
them brought aboard thirty kilos of figurines and hand lotion
and whatnot, that would increase the mass of the ship by nearly
six thousand kilograms."

"I know," I said. "I can do math. I just—"

"Do you know how much energy is required to accelerate six
thousand kilograms to point-nine *c*?"

"Um . . ." I said.

The smile came back. "Not so good at math after all, hmm?"

"It doesn't matter," I said. "Six thousand kilos can't be more
than a rounding error in the mass of the ship."

"It does matter," Marshall said. "The answer, in case you were
wondering, is just a bit more than four times ten to the twenty-
third joules, and a similar amount of energy is needed at journey's end to decelerate back to rest. Physics is cruel, Mr. Barnes,
and the antimatter that fuels starships is heinously expensive.
The mass of the *Drakkar* has been reduced to the absolute mini-

mum necessary to allow it to keep you alive for the nine years or so that it will take us to reach our destination, at astronomical expense to the government of Midgard. I assume you are aware that ninety percent of your fellow colonists are traveling in the form of frozen embryos, are you not?"

"Yes, but—"

"Why do you suppose that is, Mr. Barnes? Do you think it's because we all long to spend our waning years as nursemaids to a horde of children?" He paused and looked at me, as if he expected an answer. After it became clear that I wasn't going to give him one, he went on. "No, it is not. It's because embryos are light, and fully formed adult humans are heavy. Do you know what else is heavy? Food, Mr. Barnes. Once you see what your calorie ration is going to be for the remainder of your natural life, you may begin to wish that we had allocated those six thousand kilos to increasing our agricultural capacity. Personally, if we had that quantity of mass to spare, I would be much more inclined to allocate it to another seventy or eighty colonists. In any case, however, I'm sure we can all come up with hundreds of more productive ways to allocate any additional mass we might carry than to your *luggage.*"

I opened my mouth to point out that unlike another seventy colonists, my *luggage* wouldn't require increasing the ship's stores of food, water, oxygen, and living space by forty percent, and more importantly that if somebody had told me that my *luggage* would not be coming aboard with me I could have shoved my tablet and a couple of memory chips, which was all I really wanted, into a pocket or something before boarding the shuttle.

I'm not completely stupid, though. The look on Marshall's face made me decide that maybe silent protest was the way to go.

"By the way," Marshall said, "I didn't quite catch your function, Mr. Barnes."

"My what?"

"Your function, son. Mr. Dugan here is a biologist. What are you?"

This was where my initial mistake compounded itself. I grinned. "I'm your Expendable, sir."

Marshall did not return my smile. His face twisted into the kind of scowl I was used to seeing on people who'd just bitten into something rotten, or maybe stepped barefoot into a pile of dung.

"I suppose I should have guessed," he said. He kicked up to the grab bar again, pushed off with both hands toward an exit at the far side of the lounge, then executed a neat midair somersault that left him kicking off the floor and into a smooth swimmer's glide.

"There obviously aren't sufficient individual quarters available on the station to accommodate all of the mission's colonists and crew," he said over his shoulder as the exit door slid open. "There are, however, slings set up in many of the common spaces. Find one. That's your home until we can board the *Drakkar*."

He slipped through the door, and it slid shut behind him.

"Wow," Dugan said when he was gone. "What was that about?"

"Commander Marshall is a Natalist," a tall, dark-haired woman who'd been hanging back by the air lock said.

Dugan barked out a short, sharp laugh. "Seriously?" He turned to look at me. "You're screwed, friend."

I looked from Dugan to the woman and back. "I don't get it," I said. "What's a Natalist?"

"They're a cult," Dugan said.

"They're not a cult," the woman said. She kicked off the wall with almost as much dexterity as Marshall had shown, caught herself on the grab bar, and plopped down in front of me. "They're a serious religion, and Commander Marshall is a serious believer.

I checked his digital profile. I checked out everyone in Command before I signed on to this gig. Didn't you?"

I didn't feel like this was necessarily the best time to get into the fact that I'd been too busy fleeing from gangsters with torture machines to worry about being a social media detective, so I just shook my head.

She laughed. "You've got to be kidding. You realize these people are going to own us for the rest of our lives, right? You didn't even bother to look into who they are?"

"No," I said. "No, I did not."

Dugan laughed again. I had already decided that I didn't like his laugh.

"He wouldn't have," he said. "You were conscripted, right? What were you, a prisoner or something?"

"What? No, I wasn't a prisoner, and no, I wasn't conscripted. I was *selected* for the mission, just like you were."

"Right," Dugan said. "Selected, conscripted, whatever. The point is, you didn't have a choice."

I shook my head. "You're not listening. I had a choice. I walked into the recruitment office two days ago, all on my own. A lady named Gwen interviewed me. She said I was an excellent candidate, and they were very happy to have me."

They both stared at me like I'd grown a second head.

"You're kidding," Dugan said.

"No," I said. "I'm not."

"If you don't mind my asking," the woman said, "what the hell were you thinking?"

I considered just spilling it about Darius Blank then, but good sense stopped me at the last second. I didn't need the people I was going to be spending the rest of my life with thinking I was some kind of criminal.

"Doesn't matter," I said. "The point is, I volunteered, I've never been to prison, and no, I did not do a social media search on anyone before I signed on."

"I didn't either," Dugan said. "This is Midgard's first colony expedition, right? I assumed everyone involved would be the best and the brightest. I can't believe they put a Natalist in charge of the whole show."

"It's not a big deal," the woman said, then turned to look at me. "Well, not for anyone but this guy, anyway." She gave me a sad look, then held her hand out to Dugan. "I'm Bree, by the way. I'm with Agriculture. I'd guess we'll be working together."

The rest of the new arrivals had drifted away by then, presumably looking for a sling to call their own. As Bree and Dugan smiled and shook, I began to suspect that this whole escape-the-planet thing might not have been as solid a plan as I'd hoped.

"Look," I said. "I don't mean to be stupid, but could one of you please explain what Marshall's religion has to do with me?"

Bree pivoted back toward me. Her expression said that Dugan was much more interesting, probably because she'd concluded that there was something seriously wrong with me and that I was starting to get on her nerves.

"One of the prime doctrines of the Natalist Church," she said, "is the belief in the sanctity of the unitary soul."

"Uh . . ."

"They don't like backups," Dugan said. "They believe it's one soul to a body, and once your original body dies, your soul is dead as well."

"Right," Bree said. "Which means that a bio-printed body with a personality imprinted from backup is, in fact, a soulless monster."

"Yeah," Dugan said. "An abomination, you know?"

"Not fully human."

Dugan nodded. "Not human at all, really."

"Huh," I said. "That's . . ."

"I know," Bree said. "Unfortunate."

"But hey," Dugan said, "just because you're the Expendable doesn't mean you've been expended yet, right? I mean, you're still the original you right now, aren't you?"

"Well, yeah," I said. "I just signed on to the expedition two days ago. I'm not even sure how this whole backup thing is supposed to work. For now, at least, I'm still in the same body I was born in."

"Great," Dugan said, and clapped me on the shoulder. "All you have to do to stay on Marshall's good side is keep it that way."

That was some solid advice, brother.

Can't imagine why I didn't think to follow it.

I GENERALLY TRY not to be late for things, particularly when lateness might threaten my food supply. I'm not a big fan of early either, though, and that goes double when the thing I'm early for is a dressing-down from Hieronymus Marshall. I take my time walking the corridors, actually stop to chat with a couple of people along the way, then loiter in the hallway outside Marshall's office door until the chronometer at the edge of my field of view hits 10:29 before knocking.

"Come."

The door swings open. Marshall sits behind a squat metal-and-plastic desk. He's leaning forward in his chair, elbows on the armrests, hands folded across his belly. Berto is sitting across from him, turned half around to see me.

"Close the door," Marshall says. "Take a seat."

I pull a chair up next to Berto and sit. Marshall stares us both down wordlessly for a painfully long time.

"So—" Berto begins finally, but Marshall cuts him off with a glare.

"You," he says. "Barnes. What iteration are you?"

"Uh," I say. "Eight?"

He raises one eyebrow in question. "You don't sound sure of this."

"It's not stamped on the back of my neck, sir, and I don't remember most of the dying. I only know I'm Eight because you guys tell me so."

"You remember coming out of the tank, do you not?"

I glance over at Berto. He's staring straight ahead.

"Not really, sir. I don't generally regain consciousness for a few hours afterward. Mostly what I remember is waking up in my bed and feeling really hungover."

Marshall's face darkens, but his expression doesn't change.

"Considering that you have no access to alcohol here on Niflheim, Mr. Barnes, I think we can take it as a given that such experiences are more likely to indicate reboots than the results of three-day benders, wouldn't you say?"

I have a smart-ass answer to that, but I'm sensing that this probably isn't the time.

"Yes, sir," I say. "I believe that's a fair assumption."

"So how many times has that happened, Barnes?"

"Seven times, sir."

"So you are in fact the eighth iteration of Mickey Barnes?"

"Yes, sir," I say. "I am the eighth."

Marshall stares at me for a while longer, then turns his eyes to Berto. "Gomez. Why is this man the eighth iteration of Mr. Barnes?"

"Well, sir," he says. "Protocol states that we have to have a functioning Expendable at all times."

"And?"

"And as of last night, the seventh iteration was no longer functional. Therefore, per protocol, I submitted a request to initiate the production of Mickey8."

"Thank you," Marshall says. "That was very officious, Gomez. You actually managed to sound as if you gave a shit about protocol for a second there."

"Sir—" Berto begins, but Marshall shakes his head.

"Save it, son. Just explain to me, please, in normal words that don't sound as if you pulled them from a field manual, exactly how you managed to flush seventy-five kilos of protein and calcium down the toilet last night."

I'm actually only about seventy-one kilos, and most of that is water, which we have more than enough of piled up in drifts outside, but this doesn't seem like the right moment to raise the point.

"Right," Berto says. "Well, sir . . ."

Marshall leans forward, props his elbow on the desk, and rests his chin on one palm as his eyebrows creep up toward his hairline. Berto clears his throat. This may be the most nervous I've ever seen him.

"As I stated in my reboot request, Mickey was lost at approximately—"

"The seventh iteration of Mr. Barnes, you mean."

"Yes, sir. Mickey7. He was lost at approximately twenty-five-thirty last night, while exploring a crevasse roughly eight kilometers southwest of the main dome. This exploration was in compliance with your standing orders regarding reconnaissance of the colony's immediate surroundings and surveillance of the local fauna. After I had confirmed that his body was not recoverable—"

"Confirmed how?"

I glance over at Berto. He keeps his eyes straight ahead. This should be good.

"Sir?"

"I thought that was pretty clear," Marshall says. "How did you confirm that the body could not be recovered?"

"Well," Berto says, and then shoots me a quick glance.

"Don't look at me," I say. "I was the body, remember?"

"If this is making you uncomfortable, Barnes," Marshall says, "you can wait outside until I'm finished with this line of inquiry."

I shake my head. "Oh no. I'm as interested in hearing this as you are."

Marshall's eyes shift back to Berto. "So?"

"Well," Berto says, "he fell down a hole."

Marshall leans back in his chair and folds his arms across his chest.

"He what?"

"He fell down a hole," Berto says. "An extremely deep one. By the time he stopped moving, the signal from his transponder was practically nil."

"Practically? So you could have located him."

"I mean . . ."

"You could have located him," Marshall says, "which means that you could have retrieved him. Is this not correct?"

"Huh," I say. "That sounds pretty reasonable to me."

Marshall and Berto shoot me simultaneous glares. Berto clears his throat and tries again.

"In my judgment, sir, it would not have been safe to attempt a landing in the area where Mickey went down."

"I see," Marshall says. "And yet, you felt it was safe enough to drop him there in the first place. Is that correct?"

"Yeah," I say. "What was up with that?"

Marshall jabs a finger in my direction. "Quiet, Barnes. I'll deal with you when I'm finished with Gomez." He turns back to Berto. "Look, son, your orders are to explore the dome's immediate surroundings, and to make observations of the things you've taken to calling *creepers* where and when it is prudent to do so. However, I expect you to use some damned judgment in your execution of those orders. In particular, if in your estimation there is a reasonable probability that the Expendable may be killed in the course of carrying out his duties, I expect you to make provision for the recovery and recycling of his body. Do I make myself clear?"

Nine years ago I might have been offended at the clear inference that the problem was not the fact that Berto got me killed, but rather that he didn't put sufficient effort into dredging up my corpse afterward. At this point, though, I would have been surprised if Marshall hadn't put it that way.

Berto opens his mouth to reply, but Marshall's eyes narrow, and I guess Berto thinks better of it, because his jaw snaps closed again and he nods mutely.

Marshall turns to me. "Now, Barnes. What do you have to say about all of this?"

"Me, sir? I'm afraid I don't have any opinions on this matter at all. If you'll recall, I just came out of the tank, and Seven apparently hadn't uploaded for several weeks prior to his death last night. I have no idea what the two of you have been talking about."

"Hmm," Marshall says. "Yes, I suppose that's true. I forget sometimes that you're simply a construct."

Ordinarily I'd argue that point—but again, this really doesn't seem like the time for it.

"In any case," Marshall says, "I'm sure you're both aware that our Agricultural Section has been having great difficulty getting virtually anything to grow properly in this environment, and that as a result we are currently operating on a very thin margin, calorie-wise. Your activities of the past several weeks have permanently removed nearly three hundred thousand kilocalories from our energy budget. Unless and until we are able to bring our agricultural base up to full production, this loss will necessitate a further reduction in our calorie rations." He pauses then, and leans forward again with his elbows planted on his desk. "I'm sure you'd agree that it is only equitable that the two of you should bear the brunt of this reduction."

"Sir—" Berto begins, but Marshall shakes his head.

"No, Gomez. I don't want to hear it. Both of your ration cards are hereby permanently docked by twenty percent."

"But—"

"I said," Mashall grates, enunciating each word, "I do not want to hear it." He stares Berto down, then turns to me. "Do you have anything further, Barnes?"

"Well," I say, "to be honest, sir, it's not clear to me why I should be sanctioned for the failure to recover my own corpse."

Marshall stares me down for a long five seconds, then blinks and says, "Allow me to rephrase my question. Do you have anything further that is not simply an inane bit of smart-assery?"

I do, but it's pretty clear there's no real point, so I shake my head and say, "No, sir."

"Good," Marshall says. "Perhaps your growling bellies will remind you to take better care of colony assets in the future. Dismissed."

"So," BERTO SAYS when we're safely out of Marshall's earshot, "how does it feel to be a *colony asset*?"

"Good question," I say. "Here's one for you: How does it feel to be a lying sack of shit?"

He stops walking. I wheel around to face him. He actually manages to look hurt.

"Come on, Mickey. That's not fair."

"You told me I got eaten by creepers, Berto."

He looks away. "Yeah. That wasn't exactly true."

"Exactly? It wasn't true at all. You left me to die down there, didn't you?"

A woman from Bio scoots past us in the corridor, clearly doing her best to ignore whatever is going on between us. When you spend nine years crammed into an ark together like rabbits in a hutch, you learn to do whatever you can to grant one another at least a tiny modicum of privacy.

"Please," Berto says. "Keep your voice down, huh?"

"Fine."

I turn and start walking again. He hesitates, then hurries to catch up.

"Look," he says. "I'm sorry. Seriously. I should have told you the truth."

"Yeah," I say. "You definitely should have."

"Right," he says. "That's on me—but I did *not* leave you to die, Mickey. That fall you took must have been at least a hundred meters. By the time you hit bottom, you were already dead. I wasn't going to risk my ass for Marshall's seventy-five kilos of protein, but if there had been any chance of getting you out of there alive, I would have done it. You know that, right?"

Good God, I want to hit him right now. He was sitting right there when Nasha said she was in contact with me after the fall last night. It's like he thinks that spouting bullshit sincerely enough will make it true. If it weren't for the fact that he can't know that I know exactly what he actually did, and also that he's taller, faster, and stronger than I am and could probably break my neck like a chicken's, I might actually do it.

"Yeah," I say. "I know. You'd never leave your best friend to die, Berto. I mean, you might leave one *iteration* of a *colony asset* to die. What's the harm in that? If a *friend* was in trouble, though? You'd definitely be all over it."

He grabs my shoulder, pulls me up short, and spins me around. He lets me go, though, raises both hands in surrender, and takes a step back when he sees my face.

"Woah," he says. "I don't know what's going on here, Mickey, but you need to get a grip. It sucks that you went down last night, but come on, in your line of work, that's just part of the job, right? I mean, Marshall's killed you deliberately at least three times now. I don't remember you getting all pissy about any of those. What are you so worked up about now?"

I close my eyes, take a deep breath, and let it out slowly. "I am angry, Berto, because I live an extremely messed-up life. Every so often I wake up in my bed, hungover and covered in goo, and I realize that something horrible just happened to me, and I don't have any memory of what it was, or why it happened, or what I could possibly do to prevent it from happening again. And when that happens, I trust you and Nasha to fill me in, to tell me what happened. I have to trust you, because I have no way to remember this stuff for myself. And now I know for a certain fact that you have lied to me about what happened at least once, and that leads me to wonder how many other times you've lied to me. Can you understand that?"

Maybe that got to him, because now he can't meet my eyes.

"Yeah," he says softly. "I understand that. I'm sorry, Mickey. Honestly, I am. I never thought about it that way."

He actually seems sincere. Maybe he wouldn't be such a terrible poker player after all.

"Yeah, well," I say. "Maybe you should have."

"Maybe." He looks up, and breaks into a grin. "Tell you what— next time I'll see if I can get video of whatever takes you out. If I can, I'll show it to Nine as soon as he comes out of the tank."

I don't want to let this go just yet—but, lying sack of shit or not, he is more or less my best friend.

"That's really thoughtful, you asshole."

He reaches out then and pulls me into a bear hug with those goddamned gangly monkey arms.

"Seriously," he says. "I'm sorry I lied to you, Mickey. I won't let it happen again."

"Yeah," I mutter into his chest. "I'll just bet you won't."

IT OCCURS TO me at this point that I'm not painting Berto in a particularly positive light, and that you may be wondering why I was ever friends with this guy in the first place. The short answer is that I've always believed it's important to accept the people in your life for what they are. There's no such thing as a perfect friend, any more than there's any such thing as a perfect any-thing, and if you slag everyone in your life for their many and varied failings, you're going to miss appreciating the good stuff they bring to the table.

As an example, during my last couple of years in school, I had a friend named Ben Aslan. Ben was a good noodle. He was smart enough to get me through two semesters of astrophysics despite my complete lack of mathematical aptitude, funny enough to get me suspended for two days during twelfth form for cracking up during our late vice administrator's funeral, and loyal enough to stick around and take a beating with me when I got on the wrong side of a bunch of extremely drunk older guys at a Copper Fist concert the summer after we graduated.

Ben was also unbelievably, almost pathologically, cheap.

The Aslans owned a controlling interest in the company that held the intercity shipping franchise for the entire planet. His dad dipped in and out of the list of the twenty-five wealthiest people on Midgard. Ben himself owned a flitter, a ground car, a beach house, and a guy who cleaned up his dormitory room for him. Despite that, in all the time I knew him, I don't think Ben Aslan ever picked up a check. He didn't have implants, because he said he was afraid that if he did, somebody might cut his eye out to get access to his trust fund, and he never seemed to remember to bring a phone along when we went out because why would he? If he needed to talk to someone, he had people to do it for him. The upshot was that when the check came around, he'd smile and shrug and promise to pick up the next one.

This went on for years.

Why did I put up with it? Why did I, a kid who never had more than twenty credits in his account at any given time, buy gallons of beer and mountains of food for the richest person I'd ever met? Simple, really. I knew who Ben was, and I accepted it. I added up the benefits of having him in my life, deducted the annoyance of having to pay for everything anytime we went anywhere, and decided that on the balance, he was a net positive. Once I'd made that decision, I quit worrying about the checks. It wasn't worth it.

I guess it's kind of the same with Berto, except instead of cheaping out on restaurant tabs, he occasionally leaves me to freeze to death in a hole and then lies about it later. That's who he is. Everything's easier if you can just accept that and move on.

WHEN I GET back to my rack, I find Eight curled up in my bed, sound asleep. I think about letting him be—tank funk is rough—but I'm tired too, and we've got things to discuss. I latch the door, then grab the top sheet and yank it off of him. He's naked.

I make a mental note to change my sheets.

Eight lifts his head up and blinks at me, then grabs at the sheet and tries to pull it back over him. It's then that I notice that he's got a pressure wrap on his left wrist.

"Hey," I say. "What happened to your hand?"

He shoots me a withering look. "Nothing, idiot. We need to

look like the same person now, right? You can't take the wrap off of your wrist, so I needed to put one on mine."

"It's not purple."

He looks down at his hand, then up at me. "What?"

"Your hand," I say. "It's wrapped, but it's not purple. Anyone who looks at it closely will be able to see that you're not really hurt."

"If anybody's looking closely," he says, "we're probably already dead."

He flops back onto the pillow and pulls the sheet back up to his chin. I sigh, and yank it off again.

"Sorry," I say. "Time to wake up. We've got a few issues that we need to go over."

He sits up, rubs his knuckles into his eyes, and pulls the sheet up to his waist.

"Seriously? You know I just came out of the tank, right? Don't we usually get a day to recover?"

I sit down on the edge of the bed. "Yeah, we won't get a work detail today—which is a good thing, because exactly how we're going to handle our duty cycles is one of the things we're going to need to figure out. Only one of us can be out and about at a time if we don't want Marshall shoving us both down the corpse hole."

Eight yawns, rubs his eyes again, and looks at me. A smile slowly spreads across his face. "Hey, that's a good point. This could actually work out pretty well, couldn't it? Only having to pull half duty isn't so bad, right?"

"Yeah," I say. "As long as our shifts are getting seconded out to Agriculture or Engineering, we can share. What happens the next time Marshall decides he needs someone to scrub out the antimatter reaction chamber, though?"

His smile fades. "That is definitely gonna happen at some point, isn't it?"

"It is. We should probably figure out how we're going to handle it ahead of time, no?"

He shrugs. "Seems pretty obvious to me. I shouldn't have come out of the tank until you checked out. Ergo, if we want to set things right, you should be the one who takes on the next suicide mission."

That doesn't seem obvious to me. I'm about to explain to him exactly why his argument is utter bullshit, but . . .

I actually can't come up with a good reason why he isn't right.

"Fine," I say. "If and when Marshall comes up with an actual suicide mission for us—I mean something like what he did to Three—I'll fall on the sword. I'm not taking every hazardous job, though. If he sends us out on another recon mission, or posts us to the perimeter, or sends us up in the flitter with Berto again, we're throwing hands for it."

He squints at me, head tilted to one side, and for a second I think he's going to try to argue the point. Finally, though, he just shrugs and says, "Yeah, fair enough."

"Good," I say. "I guess we can play it by ear the next time a summons comes through."

"Anyway," he says, "until and unless one of us goes down, living on half rations is definitely going to suck."

"Yeah," I say. "About that."

"About what? Rations, or duty?"

"Rations," I say. "That meeting with Marshall didn't exactly go the way I was hoping."

His face falls. "Tell me."

"He cut our ration by twenty percent."

Eight groans.

"I know," I say. "This would be bad even if there were only one of us. As it is, the next however long is gonna be really, really rough."

He leans back against the wall, tilts his head back, and closes his eyes.

"You think? This is a disaster, Seven. I just came out of the tank. I am literally starving to death right now. If I don't get some calories in my belly, I'm liable to bite your arm off and eat it while you're sleeping."

I run my hands back through my hair. They come away with a light sheen of oil, which reminds me that I haven't showered in almost a week.

"Did you get anything to eat this morning?"

He opens his eyes, looks away, and scowls. "If you want to call it that. I grabbed a paste-and-slurry smoothie on my way past the caf."

"Nice. How many kcal did you burn?"

"Six hundred, I think."

"Yeah," I say. "Me too. That leaves us another four hundred total for the day."

"Good freaking lord," he moans. "Two hundred apiece?"

I breathe in deep, hold it, and then let it out. "You can have it."

His eyes widen. "Are you serious?"

"I'm giving you two hundred kcal of slurry," I say. "Don't make this a thing."

"What about tomorrow?"

"Don't push it. Tomorrow we're back to fifty-fifty."

He sighs. "Yeah, that's fair. In fact, it's more than fair. Thanks, Seven."

I clap one hand to his knee. "No problem. It's probably the least I can do after you decided not to kill me this morning."

"Yeah," he says. "That's true. That was pretty magnanimous of me, honestly. Sure you don't want to give me the whole card for tomorrow?"

I give his leg an almost-painful squeeze before letting go.

"Again," I say, "don't push it. I'm pretty sure the next time one of us gets a full day's rations, it'll be because the other one is dead."

He lies back and folds his hands behind his head. "There's something to look forward to."

"Yeah." I'm about to go on about how at some point scrubbing out the reaction chamber might not seem like such a bad idea when I remember my conversation in the caf. "Hey—while I'm thinking about it, did you happen to run into Berto on your way back up here?"

"No. Why?"

"I saw him in the caf this morning. He sort of implied that you did. I think he's got some suspicions about us."

He shrugs. "Well, if we have to tell him, we have to tell him. It'll probably gross him out, but it's not like he can go crying to Command. He's as much to blame for this as anyone."

"Truth." I start to say something more, but have to stifle a yawn. Eight's eyes are already closed.

I give him a nudge. "Scoot over, huh?"

He slides over to the edge of the bed. I pull off my boots and lie down beside him. It's a little weird sharing a bed with myself, but I guess we'll have to get used to it.

I'm just drifting off when my ocular flashes.

<Command1>:We need you at the main lock immediately, Barnes. We have a problem.

My heart gives a sudden lurch. Did Berto slink back to Marshall's office and turn us in?

No. If Command knew about us, they wouldn't have just pinged me. They would have sent Security up here with cable ties and burners. I turn my head to look at Eight. His eyes are still closed.

"I think they want you, friend," he says.

I sit up. "This is a summons, Eight."

"Yeah," he says. "If it's a terminal job, it's on you, right? If it's just some scut work, that should be on you today too, because I just came out of the tank."

"What if it's one of those in-betweens? Are we throwing hands?"

"Nah," he says. "I think you owe me this one."

He rolls onto his side and pulls the sheet up over his shoulder. I waste a few seconds glaring at the back of his head, then swing my legs over the edge of the bed, sit up, and pull my boots back on. He's already snoring when I latch the door behind me.

I DO A lot of things around the dome. I'm not attached to any particular section, so they generally rotate me every couple of days to wherever they need a bit of extra grunt labor. I've tended to the rabbit hutches for Agriculture. I've stood sentry for Security. Once I even filled in for Marshall's admin while he took a sick day that I found out later was actually the result of his having made an attempt at homemade booze that went really, really wrong. Those jobs, though, were just random assignments from the semiautonomous system that runs HR for the colony. When I get a direct summons from Command, it's not because they need somebody to help move boxes. It's because they need me to do my actual job.

What my actual job *is* was impressed on me pretty clearly right from the jump, beginning with my first day cycle on Himmel Station. I'd managed to find a bathroom by then, and after a couple of painful and messy errors had more or less figured out how peeing works in zero-g. I'd found the room where they were handing out food packets. I'd even found a sling to call my own, strung up with forty or so others in what appeared to be a conference room.

The smell wasn't great, but I was already starting to get used to it. All in all, I felt like I was settling into my new life pretty well.

I was napping, wrapped in my sling, finally almost able to imagine that I was floating rather than falling, when something hard and pointy dug itself into my ribs. I batted at it, which sent the sling spinning on its long axis. I opened my eyes to see floor, then wall, then ceiling, then the person who had poked me. She was tall, dark-skinned, and hairless, dressed in the shapeless gray jumpsuit that all the permanent station personnel wore. She reached out to grab me, braced her feet against the floor, and stopped my spin.

"You're Barnes, right?"

I blinked up at her. "Maybe. Who's asking?"

She grinned. "I'm Jemma. Get up. It's time to get to work."

FOR ALMOST ALL of my stay on Himmel Station, I liked Jemma. She was an excellent teacher. She was funny, and kind, and weirdly thoughtful. When we had morning sessions, she brought me bulbs of hot chai. When I had trouble picking something up, she slowed down, backed up, and repeated herself until she was sure I understood. If at any time during this process she got it into her head that I was a dimwit, she made a point not to ever let it show.

That first day, we started with the schematics for the *Drakkar*'s engine systems. I learned where the antimatter was stored, how it was contained, where they kept the reactants, how they brought the two together, and (this was the part Jemma emphasized) what would happen if any of these components broke down.

"We can skip a breakdown in the antimatter containment unit," she said. "That problem solves itself."

We were sitting across from one another at a card table in what looked to be a disused storage closet. Jemma gave me a half smile and waited. After five seconds or so, her face fell.

"Aren't you going to ask me how it does that?"

I rolled my eyes. "By killing us all?"

"Yes," she said. "But I was going to say it in a much funnier way."

I sighed. "Why do I need to know about any of this? We'll have engineers, right? If they're all dead, I don't think whatever you can cram into my head in the next two weeks is going to make much difference. I like history. I can tell you who Wernher von Braun was, but that's about my limit when it comes to propulsion tech. I barely passed high-energy physics in school, and that was a long time ago."

"I'm not trying to turn you into an engineer," she said. "The *Drakkar* will carry a fully redundant complement of propulsion specialists. They'll tell you exactly what needs to be done if the need arises—but time will likely be short if it comes to that, and things will go much faster if you already know the basics."

"And if something does go wrong, they'll need my help to fix it because . . ."

Her smile disappeared. "Because an hour after shutdown, the neutron flux in the combustion chamber is still high enough to provide a lethal dose even through full combat armor in less than sixty seconds—and if it comes to that, trust me, you will not be wearing full combat armor. That shit is expensive."

"Right," I said. "I didn't mean they'd crawl into the engines themselves. Who does that? I meant they'd use a drone."

She shook her head. "Drones are subject to damage from high-energy particles, just like you are. In fact, you'd be surprised how much longer a human will last in a stream of heavy particles than a mechanical. You may be dead for all practical purposes after sixty seconds in there, but it will take your body an hour or more to figure that out, and you can be doing useful work for that entire time. A drone in that environment will shut down in under a minute—and once you're away from Midgard's industrial base, a damaged drone will be a lot more difficult to replace than you will. Your official title is *Mission Expendable*, Mickey. Part of my job over the next twelve days or so is to make sure you really understand what that means."

I think that's probably the point where I started liking her slightly less.

WE DIDN'T ONLY talk about schematics and radiation poisoning, Jemma and I. When it was pretty clear that my head was full up with technical data for the moment, we switched over to philosophy, which was much more my speed.

Turns out that people have been poking around the periphery of what has become the central question of my life for a long time. That first day, after we were finished talking about the many different ways I could irradiate myself into oblivion, Jemma told me about the Ship of Theseus.

"Imagine," she said, "that one day Theseus sets out to sail around the world."

"Okay," I said. "I know I should know this, but who's Theseus?"

"An old Earth hero," she said. "Seriously old school—from maybe three thousand years before the Diaspora."

"Huh. And he's sailing around the world?"

"Right," she said. "He's sailing around the world in a wooden ship. As he goes, parts of the ship get damaged or wear out, and he has to replace them. Years later, when he finally comes home, every single board and timber of the original ship has been replaced. So. Is this, or is this not, the same ship that he departed in?"

"That's dumb," I said. "Of course it is."

"Okay," she said. "What if the ship is destroyed in a storm, and he has to rebuild it all at once before sailing on? Is it the same ship then?"

"No," I said. "That's totally different. If he has to rebuild the entire ship, that's Ship of Theseus II, the Sequel."

She leaned forward then, elbows on the table. "Really? Why? What difference does it make if he replaces every component one by one, or if he replaces them all at once?"

I opened my mouth to answer, but then realized that I had no idea what to say.

"This is the key to accepting this job, Mickey. *You* are the Ship of Theseus. We all are. There is not a single living cell in my body that was alive and a part of me ten years ago, and the same is true for you. We're constantly being rebuilt, one board at a time. If you actually take on this job, you'll probably be rebuilt all at once at some point, but at the end of the day, it's really no different, is it? When an Expendable takes a trip to the tank, he's just doing in one go what his body would naturally do over the course of time anyway. As long as memory is preserved, he hasn't really died. He's just undergone an unusually rapid remodeling."

I DON'T WANT to make it sound like my training was all engine schematics and Theseuses. Some of it was actually fun. Jemma taught me the basics of handling a linear accelerator, for example. I couldn't actually fire a real one on the station, but she ran me through a pretty realistic simulation where I got to fight space zombies, and when I finally did get a chance to use the real thing years later, it wasn't much different. She showed me how to get in and out of a vacuum suit. She showed me how to assemble a full set of combat armor. On Day Six she actually took me outside, and we clambered around the hull of the station for an hour and practiced using recoilless wrenches to tighten and loosen bolts. I will never forget standing with her on the underside of the station and looking up to see the night side of Midgard rolling by.

"I know," Jemma said. "It's something, right?"

"That bright patch," I said. "That's Kiruna, right?"

"Yeah," she said. "You from there?"

I nodded. She couldn't see that through my mirrored visor, but she seemed to understand.

"And now you're leaving forever," she said. We hung there in silence for a while and watched Midgard swing by until Kiruna disappeared over the horizon. "I admire you guys," she said then. "The colonists, I mean. I don't understand you, but I admire you. I get the romance of it. I get that spreading humanity as widely as we can, making us as disaster-proof as we can, is the whole point of the Diaspora—but I could never just go."

I shrugged. "Yeah, well. Some of us are just born explorers, I guess."

Jemma gave an incredulous snort. I turned to look at her, but I couldn't see her face any more than she could see mine.

"I've trained Expendables before," she said. "We need them here on the station from time to time. They're usually pretty difficult to deal with. You're a pain in the ass, but ordinarily when I take them outside like this I'm worried they'll cut my tether and shove me into the void. Any idea why that would be?"

I sighed. "I know most Expendables are convicts," I said. "It's different, though, signing on to be an Expendable on Himmel Station. That's just agreeing to get killed every once in a while for no good reason. I signed on for a colony mission. Like you said, it's a romance thing, right?"

Jemma laughed. "Oh please," she said. "I talked to your friend. Gomez? The pilot? I know why you signed on to this mission."

"Oh," I said. "Um . . ."

She laughed again. "Don't worry, I'm not about to tell anybody important. Your reasons for going are probably at least as valid as his, or Marshall's, or any of the others'. I hope you know, though, that this is a permanent solution to a temporary problem."

"Isn't that what they say about suicide?"

She put a hand on my shoulder. "Come on, Mickey. Let's get back inside. We need to have a talk about John Locke."

MY FIRST BACKUP came on the morning of my twelfth day on Himmel Station. The physical part was pretty straightforward. They took a blood sample, snipped some skin from my belly, tapped my cerebrospinal fluid, and then stuck me into a scanner that spent three hours mapping out the distribution and chemical makeup of every cell in my body. Jemma was waiting for me when I came out.

"Hope you're having a good hair day," she said. "The way you look right now is exactly how you're going to look every time you come out of the tank for the rest of your life."

"Huh," I said. "This is a onetime thing?"

"Afraid so," she said. "That scanner draws an unbelievable amount of power, and the recon software will be running for almost a week now sorting out the information it extracted. Also, you just absorbed what under normal circumstances would be a problematic amount of radiation."

"Oh."

She grabbed a handhold and pushed off down the hall. I followed.

"Wait," I said when we reached our next stop. "What did you mean, that 'would be' a problematic amount of radiation?"

She gave me a sad half smile. "You'll see."

THE PERSONALITY BACKUP, which I've been repeating on a regular basis ever since then, was both simpler and stranger than the physical one. I sat in a chair, and a technician placed a helmet on my head. The outside was smooth and metallic. The inside was covered in dull-pointed spikes that pressed into my scalp and forehead.

"This is a squid array," the technician said. "It's a little uncomfortable, but it won't hurt you."

I later learned that a squid, in addition to being a surprisingly intelligent marine invertebrate from old Earth, is also a superconducting quantum interference device. I hope that means more to you than it did to me.

The tech was right that the backup process isn't painful. It is, however, profoundly weird. Routine backups are just updates. They take about an hour to get through. That first one, though, took almost eighteen, and it felt much longer. The backup process is like a fever dream. Bits and pieces of your past flit by, pictures and sounds and smells and sensations, all out of your control and all too fast to process. The thing I remember most vividly from that first upload is a close shot of my mother's face. She died joyriding in a flitter when I was eight, and I barely remembered what she looked like . . . but in that image she was young and vivid and beautiful, and when they finally took the helmet off of me, I was sobbing.

When that was done, Jemma took me to the officers' mess, got us a table, and told me to order whatever I wanted. When I asked what was going on, she gave me that sad smile again and said, "We're celebrating, Mickey. Today's your graduation."

"Really?" I said. "When's the ceremony?"

She looked away. "As soon as we're done here. Take your time."

I still remember that as one of the strangest hours of my life. The food was pretty good, considering that most of it was vat-grown and it was prepared in zero-g. The conversation was

awkward, for reasons that I totally misunderstood. I knew the
Drakkar was almost ready to begin loading. Believe it or not, I
actually thought Jemma might be sad because she was going to
miss me when I was gone.

When dinner was over and Jemma had settled up, I thought
I'd head back to my sling to catch up on my sleep. I hadn't actually been awake for the entire time I'd been uploading, but I
hadn't really been resting either. I wasn't tired, exactly—more
like stretched out and worn thin, and not quite connected to re-
ality anymore. Jemma caught my arm when I started down the
corridor, though.

"No," she said. "Your graduation ceremony, remember?"

"Oh," I said. "I thought that was a joke."

She stared at me for a long few seconds, then shook her head
and pushed off back down the corridor toward our closet. I
shrugged, and followed.

"So," I SAID when she'd closed the door behind her. "Do I get a
cap and gown, or what?"

I drifted closer to her.

I thought we were about to have sex.

Yes, I am exactly that stupid.

Jemma's face was as blank as a wooden mask. She reached
into a pocket of her jumpsuit, and pulled out a shiny black . . .
something . . . a little bigger than her hand.

"What's that?" I asked.

She held it up. It had a pistol grip and a snub nose with a white
crystal tip. For the first time in almost two weeks, it felt like I was
falling again.

"It's a burner," she said. "Low power, so it's safe to use on-
station. It won't cut through metal, but it'll do a number on
pretty much any kind of organic matter."

She held it by the nose and offered it to me. After a moment, I took it.

"See the red switch on the side of the grip? That's the safety," she said. "Slide it forward."

I did. The tip took on a dull yellow glow.

"Okay," she said. "It's armed. Careful with the trigger. It's that nub next to your index finger."

I turned the weapon over in my hand. "I don't understand," I said.

But then she gave me that sad look again, and I did.

"This is your graduation, Mickey. Time to prove that you understand what it means to be an Expendable."

I looked at her. She looked back.

"You're not serious," I said.

"You want this to be quick," she said. "Turn your head as far to the side as you can, and press the tip against the soft spot just behind your ear. Try to angle the weapon slightly upward. It's set for a fan beam. If you do it right, you'll take out your entire medulla oblongata and a good chunk of your cerebellum with one shot. I promise, you won't feel a thing. If you miss, I might have to do cleanup for you. Neither one of us wants that."

"Jemma—"

"This isn't really your graduation ceremony," she said. "It's more like your final exam. If you don't do this, you'll be on a shuttle back down to Midgard in the morning, and I'll have to start over with a conscript tomorrow. Neither one of us wants that either. I'm sorry, Mickey, but this is what you signed on for. Immortality comes with a price."

I thought about it. I thought about going back to Midgard, back to my shitty apartment and starvation subsidy. I thought about telling my friends that I wasn't going with the *Drakkar* after all.

I thought about Darius Blank's torture machine. "It's just like going to sleep, right?" I said. "I do this, and I wake up in my sling, good as new?"

"Right," she said. "A little hungover, maybe, but yeah."

She smiled. I sighed, looked away, and put the burner to my head.

"Like this?"

"Sure," she said. "Close enough."

I closed my eyes, took a deep breath in, and let it out.

I pressed the trigger.

Nothing happened.

I stood there, frozen and shaking, until Jemma reached over and gently pried the burner from my hand.

"Congratulations," she said quietly. "As of today, you're officially Mickey1."

THERE'S QUITE A crowd waiting for me by the main lock. Marshall is there, along with Dugan from Biology and a gaggle of Security goons. Berto and Nasha are standing off to one side. Berto's hunched over, his face just inches from hers. He says something, short and sharp. She looks away and shakes her head.

"Hey," I say. "What's going on?"

Marshall waves me over. "Take a look," he says, and gestures to the monitor over the lock. I look up. The outer door is sealed. There's a blackened, mostly man-shaped blob slumped in one corner.

"Shit." I look closer. What I'd taken for blackened metal is actually a hole almost two meters across in the floor of the lock. "Where's the decking?"

"Gone," says Dugan. "Something punched through while Gallaher there was waiting for the lock to cycle and started peeling it away."

"Gallaher? You mean that lump in the corner?"

"Yes," says Marshall. "That's him. We had to use the murder hole."

I can feel my jaw sag. "You vented plasma into the main lock? While one of our people was *in it*?"

"We did," Marshall says. "Gallaher was seriously wounded, in the process of bleeding out. The thing that ripped out the first section of decking sheared off most of his left leg in the process. The AI controlling perimeter security made the call, and I'm not inclined to second-guess it. We couldn't risk penetration into the dome."

I'm not sure what to say to that.

"It was creepers," says Berto. "At least two or three of them."

I shake my head. "How . . ."

"Apparently those mandibles are sharper than they look," he says. "I mean, I've seen them go through stuff before—"

"Stuff?" I say. "You mean like my skull?"

That gets me five seconds of awkward silence.

"Anyway," Dugan says, "I was surprised to find that we don't have any hard data on these things. I was able to call up a couple of descriptions in picket reports from Gomez and Adjaya, but that's pretty much it. That's why we called you down."

I look to Berto, then back to Dugan.

"Gomez says you've got some personal experience with these things," he says. "Says you've developed a bit of an obsession with them, in fact, and Commander Marshall tells me he's had you out observing them for the past few weeks. We need more than that. We need to figure out exactly what we're dealing with. If they start knocking holes in the dome, we're finished."

I glance over at Berto again. He won't meet my eyes.

"Personal experience?"

"Right," Marshall says. "Because they've eaten you."

"True enough," says Berto. "Mickey's an expert at getting eaten by creepers."

Berto and Nasha are both looking at me now. I roll my eyes.

"We just went over this. I don't remember anything about what happened to Six or Seven. I wouldn't even know it'd happened if Berto hadn't told me about it."

"You sure, Mickey?" Berto says. "This is important. You don't remember anything from last night?"

Berto stares me down. Nasha looks away.

"I just came out of the tank this morning. You know this, Berto."

Marshall's eyes narrow. "Is there something going on here that I need to be made aware of?"

Berto gives me one more dubious look, then shakes his head.

"No, sir. We're good. Mickey's right. As we discussed this morning, he hadn't uploaded in some time when he went down last night."

Marshall's not an idiot, but I guess he decides he's got bigger fish to fry. After giving Berto another long, hard stare, he says, "Whatever. Get geared up, all of you. Gomez and Adjaya, you'll be providing air cover. I want a complete sweep with ground-penetrating radar from the dome out to two thousand meters beyond the perimeter. I want to know exactly how many of these things are out there, and where they're located. I also want you loaded for bear. Make sure your missile tubes are full before you lift. Once we've accomplished what we need to accomplish and extracted our people, I want the entire field cleared of those things out to a kilometer at least." He pauses to look around. "The rest of you, be ready to step out of the auxiliary lock on foot in fifteen minutes. Dugan—if you're going to develop an understanding of what these things are and what they can do, you need to have a specimen in your lab." He grins, but the expression is more ghoulish than happy. "You gentlemen are going on a snipe hunt."

"You know," I say, "I've done this before."

"Huh?"

Dugan looks up at me. He and I haven't interacted much since that first day on Himmel Station. I don't get seconded out to Biology often, and when I do it's mostly for things like cleaning the labs. He's strapping himself into combat armor at the moment, which under other circumstances would be kind of hilarious. For the right kind of guy, being half in and half out of a battle suit makes you look like a war god from one of the old stories. Dugan is not that kind of guy. He looks like a plucked chicken getting ready for a costume party.

"I said, I've done this before. You don't want that armor."

He looks around. The Security goons are already geared up. I've been trying to remember their names for the last ten minutes. The scowly bald guy is Robert something—whatever you do, don't call him Bob—and the shorter woman is Cat Chen. The third one I'm pretty sure is named Gillian, but I wouldn't swear to that one. They're clanking around the armory at the moment, making sure all their servos are working. This will be the first armored sortie we've attempted since landfall.

"Seems like that's a minority opinion," he says.

I shrug. "They're Security. They'd wear armor to bed at night if they could. Armor may make you feel like you're invincible, but those suits add almost a hundred kilos. That makes you too heavy for snowshoes, and you really want to be on top of the snow when we go out there. Slogging through a meter or more of loose powder is really, really unpleasant."

He looks me up and down. I'm bundled up pretty well, but strictly in cold-weather gear. He's got two burners in hip holsters. I'm carrying a linear accelerator. It's heavier than what he's bringing and a lot less versatile, and I'm pretty sure my sprained wrist is going to complain bitterly if I have to actually bring it to bear, but it's the only weapon I have any real training on—and anyway, ever since that last night on Himmel Station, I've had kind of an aversion to burners.

"I appreciate the advice," he says, "but I saw what those things in the lock did to Gallaher's leg. I'd like to have something a little more substantial than a snowsuit between them and me."

"You saw what they did to Gallaher. Did you see what they did to the decking?"

He's glaring now, looking back and forth between me and his right gauntlet, which he doesn't seem to be able to get to slip into the fitting on his sleeve.

"Let me see that," I say. He holds up his arm. I give the gauntlet a twist, and the connector latches.

"Thanks," he says. He flexes his hand, makes sure everything's hooked up, then reaches for his chest plate. "I get it," he says as he snaps that into place. "This is no big deal for you. But you've got to understand, Barnes—the rest of us don't get to just hit the reset button if we go down. Dead is dead for me. So, yeah, I'm wearing armor."

I smile. "Reset button, huh? That what you think a trip to the tank is?"

"Look," he says. "I'm not trying to start something here, but the fact is that you're an Expendable, and I'm not. Our incentives are different. I just want to go out there, collect our sample, and get back in here intact."

I lift the accelerator's strap over my head. I want it loose enough that I can bring the weapon to bear quickly, but tight enough that it's not banging against my back while I'm walking.

"I'm definitely not about to argue that point," I say. "The whole reset-button thing isn't as much fun as you apparently think it is."

My ocular pings.

<Command1>:Adjaya and Gomez are starting their sweep. Time
    to go.

I look around. The goons are clanking toward the lock. I seal up my rebreather. Dugan dogs his helmet, and we go.

THE LAST TIME anything native seriously opposed one of our landfalls was a bit under two hundred years ago, and maybe fifty lights spinward from here. The beachhead Command there probably gave the place a name, but if they did, they never let the rest of us know. These days, the planet is called Roanoke.

Roanoke is not what you'd call an ideal habitat. Its star is a red dwarf, and the planet itself is a tidally locked rock with almost no axial tilt, very little water, and a thirty-one-day orbital period. It's got a hot pole on one side, where the ambient temperature rarely drops below eighty C, a cold pole on the other side where it snows CO_2, and a more or less habitable strip of perpetual twilight circumscribing the planet in between that's maybe a thousand kilometers wide. Roanoke is an old world. Speculation is that it's harbored life for maybe seven billion years. And all that time, everything that's evolved there has been fighting for a toehold in that dry, wind-scoured, thousand-kilometer strip.

Apparently, bringing a few million liters of liquid water to a place like that is like bringing a giant sack of scrip to a shantytown, because the colony wasn't a week past landfall before things started coming after them. There were tiny biting things that came on the wind, burrowed into any exposed skin, and brought itching rashes, then pus-filled blisters, then sepsis, then death. There were things like sand-burrowing starfish with armor-piercing fangs. They injected a necrotizing venom that killed in minutes. There were insectile things half the size of a man that shot jets of concentrated sulfuric acid from glands in their heads. Most of the creatures on the planet seemed purpose-built to defeat the colony's defenses, and though it seems obvious to us now what was going on, as near as we can tell from the records their

Command transmitted before they went down, they never did figure it out.

Almost from day one, Command on Roanoke couldn't keep their people alive outside the main dome for more than an hour. They lost them in ones and twos, week after week, until finally, taboos be damned, they had to start making extra copies of their Expendable just to keep their berths filled.

They eventually did button the place up and try to hunker down and do some research into what was happening to them. By that time, though, something was reproducing inside the dome. Command tried a half dozen sterilization protocols, but whatever it was, it kept coming back. By the end, the entire colony was made up of copies. The central processor kept cranking them out until it ran out of amino acids.

One of the last of the Expendables to die got at least a glimmer of the truth, just before the end. Bio had released a phage tuned to take out one of the microorganisms that was tearing them up. A resistant strain showed up six hours later. The last words in his personal log, dictated as his innards were liquefying and pouring out of every orifice, were these: I am not paranoid. Someone here really is out to get me.

I'M THINKING ABOUT that guy, Jerrol-two-hundred-and-something, as we step out into the snow. The locals on Roanoke didn't ring any alarm bells with the colonists there because they weren't tool-users in the classic sense. They didn't produce any electromagnetic emissions, didn't have power plants or roads or cars or cities. Didn't even have agriculture, as far as we could tell. They were, as it turned out, crazy-good genetic engineers, though. Combine that with their extreme territoriality and xenophobia—pretty predictable, considering that they'd spent their entire evolutionary history fighting with each other and everything else on their crappy planet over a thin band of marginally habitable territory—and you got a bad outcome for the Roanoke beachhead.

I'm thinking about Jerrol, and I'm thinking about my gigantic tunnel-digging friend from last night. Everybody died on Roanoke because there were sentients there, and the colonists failed to notice them until it was too late. I'm wondering if somebody like me maybe had a run-in with one of the locals on Roanoke, identified it as a sentient, and then failed to report it in to Command.

A fair number of beachhead colonies fail for one reason or another. I'd really hate to have this one fail because of me.

THE LAST GLOW of sunset is fading on the horizon, and the first stars are already visible in the eastern sky. We're ten minutes out from the lock, maybe a half kilometer past the perimeter, and Dugan is conferring with Berto and Nasha over the comm about where best to find one creeper but not a hundred, when Cat clomps over to me. Back in the armory we were about the same height, but I'm standing on top of almost a meter of snow now, and she has to crane her neck to look up at me.

"Hey," she says. "What's with the LA? I thought we were all packing burners."

It takes me a second to realize that she's talking about my weapon. I don't really want to go into my Jemma-inspired aversion to burners at the moment. I don't know this person at all, and even after nine years, that story still feels a little raw.

"No reason," I say. "Just a feeling, really."

"A feeling, huh? That's a good way to pick an outfit for a first date, but it's a strange way to pick a weapon, isn't it?"

Okay. Apparently she's not going to let this go.

"My feeling, specifically, was that I don't think burners are likely to be effective against creepers."

"Oh. Speaking from personal experience?"

I shrug. I can't see her face through her mirrored visor, but there's definitely a hint of worry in her voice.

"Not really. But when we were in the armory, I asked myself what I'd usually pick out for something like this."

She cocks her head to one side. "Well?"

"A burner. Definitely a burner. The max rate of fire on this thing I'm carrying is one round per second, and it's heavy as shit. I mean, not nearly as heavy as all that stupid armor, but still."

"I don't get it."

I smile, though she can't see it behind my rebreather. "Doing what I usually do has gotten me taken down by these things twice now. So, this time I did the opposite."

She nods. "Got it. That's very Zen of you, Barnes."

"Well, I do keep getting reincarnated."

"True," she says. "Working your way toward Nirvana, right?"

This seems like a weird time for banter, but okay. I shake my head. "I don't think so. I keep expecting to come back as a tapeworm or something."

"But every time, you wake up as you. Maybe Mickey Barnes is as low as you can go, karmically speaking."

I look around. Nothing important seems to be happening.

"Yeah," I say. "I guess so."

Dugan is standing almost waist-deep in the snow twenty meters or so away, still jawing with Berto. I could tell him where he can find plenty of creepers—or at least one really big one—but I'm guessing that wouldn't go over well with anyone. I look up. It's a beautiful night, by Niflheim standards. The sky is clear and deep and black. There's enough light bleeding off from the dome to make it so that only a few stars are visible, but the ones that are there are hard, bright bits of silver.

"You know," Cat says, "I don't think we've ever really talked before, have we?"

I look back down at her. She's watching Dugan, one hand on her burner.

"No," I say. "Not that I remember, anyway."

"That's weird, isn't it? Have you been avoiding me?"

I'm about to tell her that, no, it's not weird that we've never spoken, because half the people on the *Drakkar* thought I was some kind of abomination, and half the rest just found me generally creepy, and so for the past nine years I've never really reached out to anybody who didn't reach out to me first—which she apparently never did. Before I can get into all that, though, the whine of gravitics rises and then dies away as Nasha sweeps by, maybe sixty meters overhead.

"Come on," Dugan says over the comm. "We're moving."

We trudge north, away from the dome and toward the place where I emerged from the tunnels this morning. What would Dugan do if my gigantic friend popped up out of the snow in front of him?

"Something funny?" Cat asks.

"Not really," I say. "I was just thinking of something."

"Tell me," she says. "I'm bored."

I can't tell her, of course. I also can't tell her that I can't tell her, because then I'd have to tell her *why* I can't tell her. I don't have to figure out where I'm going with that one, though, because just then Dugan starts yelling. Yelling, and dancing.

"Hey," Cat says. "What the . . ."

That's when Dugan lifts his right leg up out of the snow, and I see that it's wrapped in creeper. There are divots in the armor where the thing's pointy little feet are dug in, and its mandibles are working on the seam at the back of his knee.

Things happen quickly now. The other two goons, who have been flanking Dugan for the past ten minutes, turn their burners on his leg. He seems to be encouraging them at first, but then the armor starts glowing and the creeper is still chewing and its legs dig deeper and deeper into the softening armor and as a gout of live steam rises up from the snow to hide them, Dugan's yelling turns into screaming turns into a wordless shriek. I spin half around. Maybe thirty meters off, a hunk of gray granite juts out of the snow. I start running.

Running in snowshoes is not efficient, and it is not fun. I haven't gone three steps before I stumble and fall face-first into the snow. I'm flailing, expecting every second to feel a creeper's mandibles sinking into the back of my neck, when a powered gauntlet grabs me by the arm and hauls me to my feet.

"Come on," Cat says. "Move!"

She gives me a shove in the back, and I almost fall again before stumbling forward. I can hear Cat slogging after me, and farther away the cursing and then screaming of the other two goons. I risk a glance back. The steam is being carried away on a stiff north wind. Dugan is gone—dragged under the snow, I guess. The two from Security are still on their feet, but they're wearing a couple of creepers each, and I'm guessing that won't last long.

I scramble up onto the rock, reach over my shoulder for the accelerator, and bring it to bear, wincing as my left hand takes the weight of the barrel. A second later, Cat climbs up beside me. We're on a granite island maybe three meters across, sticking up a half meter or so above the snow. A creeper pokes its head up, almost close enough for me to touch. I aim and fire. The kick of the accelerator pushes me back into Cat, and in the same instant the creeper's first three segments explode into a hail of shrapnel.

"Shit," Cat says. "Zen for the win, huh?"

The other Security goons are down now, though I think I can still see some thrashing going on under the snow. I open my mouth to speak, but then a rising screech of gravitics announces Berto's arrival. Twin spotlights illuminate first us, then the place where Dugan and the others went down.

"Have you got a sample?" Berto asks over the comm.

"Part of one."

I hop down off the rock and grab what's left of the creeper. Berto's grapple is already descending. I climb back up and hand the creeper to Cat, then latch the grapple to her armor. She wraps one arm around my chest, and we ascend. When I look down a few seconds later, the top of the rock is swarming with creepers. We're barely into Berto's cargo bay when Nasha comes screaming in, low and fast, first two missiles already loosed. The bay door slams, and we ride the first wave of expanding plasma up and away.

GETTING SENT ON near-suicide missions like Marshall's snipe hunt is pretty much routine for me at this point. Getting rescued, on the other hand, is not. That part is a little disorienting. Even before she staged my mock execution, Jemma made sure I was one hundred percent clear on what to expect in situations like that, and it definitely wasn't Berto riding in like my guardian angel and spiriting me away.

I sometimes wonder if maybe Jemma didn't do *too* good a job of letting me know exactly what being an Expendable was about. After the *Drakkar* had slipped her moorings and boosted out of orbit around Midgard, I spent the first few weeks of the journey wandering around the corridors in a funk, waiting morosely for one of the things she had prepped me for to happen, waiting to be told to climb into the engines or step out an air lock or stick my head in a blender to see whether the blades were sharp enough.

For a long time, though, none of those things happened. That ship represented a huge fraction of Midgard's accumulated wealth, and the systems architects had put a fair amount of effort into making as certain as possible that she'd get where she was going without exploding—and despite my worst expectations, nobody seemed to be particularly interested in killing me just for fun.

The longer we went without any disasters, and the more I thought about what we were actually doing, the more I started to expect that I might actually reach Niflheim without ever having to go through the tank. I mean, the one thing everyone knows about interstellar travel is that it's boring, right? And, especially once you're finished with the boost phase, which is when the engines are working hard and the ship's frame is under stress and you'd think anything that's likely to break is going to do it, it really is. The cruise phase of a colony mission, as it turns out, is in fact dull as dirt.

Until it isn't, anyway.

The last thing I remember about life in the body I was born with is a technician slipping the upload helmet over my head as my arms and legs spasmed and blood seeped out of my mouth and nose and pooled under my blistering skin. We were a bit more than a year out from Midgard by then. We'd gotten through first boost, pushed through our sun's heliopause at sub-relativistic speed, cranked the engines back up for second boost, and finally settled in at a hair under point-nine c for the long glide to Niflheim.

Life on the *Drakkar* was easy, for the most part. As far as the actual ship's crew were concerned, the bulk of the colonists were basically baggage during transit. Because I wasn't attached to any particular branch, I was even more so. I was supposed to be doing two hours of training per day, rotating among branches so that I could serve as a stopgap for any of them as the need arose, but a lot of the folks who should have been training me thought I was spooky, and some of the others, like the engineers, were actually busy doing their jobs and didn't have time to spare for training someone with zero technical expertise, so it mostly worked out to more like two hours a week. Outside of that I fed myself, took naps, and hung around the common areas with Berto playing puzzle games on our tablets. Throw in some gravity, and it wouldn't have been that different from my life on Midgard.

As I was about to be reminded, though, we weren't on Midgard. We were moving through interstellar space at two hundred and seventy million meters per second—and at those sorts of speeds, high-energy physics takes over from Mr. Newton, and things get wacky.

Space, as Jemma carefully explained to me, is not as empty as you might think. Any given cubic meter of what we think of as hard vacuum actually contains on the order of a hundred thousand hydrogen atoms, for instance. Hydrogen atoms are benign at rest, but at point-nine c they're dangerous projectiles. The *Drakkar* had a field generator in her nose that shunted them aside, and turned them into a continuous stream of cosmic rays just above the surface of the hull as we plowed through the interstellar medium—so, not a problem as long as you stayed inside, which everyone on the ship other than possibly me was definitely going to do for the duration.

Interstellar space also contains the occasional dust grain—only about one in every million cubic meters, but every square meter of the ship's surface area was passing through two hundred and seventy million cubic meters of space every second, so we bumped into those on a pretty regular basis as well. The vast majority of those grains carried enough net charge to get funneled along the surface and away by our field generator. Some of them didn't, which produced a continuous patter of tiny explosions against the nose cone. The ship was designed to withstand that, though. The armor on the nose was ablative, and thick enough to survive twenty years or more of normal wear and tear.

The armor was not, however, designed to withstand the impact of anything much bigger than a dust grain.

In fairness to the folks who put the *Drakkar* together, things bigger than that are pretty rare once you're past the heliopause, and there's no such thing as armor thick enough to protect you from an actual macro object. A rock the size of my head carries a hundred times the energy of a fusion bomb at *Drakkar*'s cruising speed.

Luckily, the thing that hit us wasn't quite that big.

We don't know what, exactly, the object was, obviously. It got reduced to its component quarks and gluons on impact. We know it massed between fifteen and twenty grams, though. One of the engineers calculated that based on the volume of armor that it vaporized, and the amount of kinetic energy the ship gave up on impact.

The jolt wasn't trivial, by the way. We were in free fall, so most things were reasonably well secured, but anything that wasn't—including a fair number of the crew—went flying into the forward bulkheads. There were a couple of broken arms, and one significant concussion. I clipped the edge of a table as I fell, and wound up spraining an ankle.

Nobody cared about any of that. There was a hole in the nose cone and one of the field generation modules was gone. Twenty percent of the interior volume of the ship was suddenly flooded with hard radiation.

It was my time to shine.

The summons came from Maggie Ling, who was the head of Systems Engineering during transit. She met me in the machine shop, which was the nearest safe compartment to the nose cone access hatch. Two of her people stuffed me into a vacuum suit while she explained exactly what she needed me to do.

"We think the power coupling is shot," she said. "We're not

sure, though, and we don't have time to screw around, so you're replacing the entire unit." Another of the engineers had just finished unpacking a half-meter-square silver cube from a storage crate. It had two floating connector cables on one side, and two maneuvering handles on the other. "When you're done with that, get the old unit back here if you can."

"If I can?"

"Yeah," she said. "Before you die, right? That compartment is open to space at the moment. Until you can get this unit running, you'll be absorbing a lethal full-body radiation dose every three-point-five seconds."

I must have given her a look then, because she rolled her eyes.

"Don't worry. That doesn't mean you're going to die the minute you go through the hatch. The human body takes a surprisingly long time to actually shut down, even after it's picked up many times a fatal dose. As long as you don't take a direct hit from a grain, you should have plenty of time to upload before you go, and we've already got your next instantiation cooking in the tank."

There were a bunch of things in that short statement that I wanted to argue with. Start with the fact that I was a lot more concerned about the dying part than about the specific timing of it, or whether I'd be able to upload before that happened, and follow that up with her assumption that I was going to do this despite the fact that nobody had actually asked me.

The fact was, though . . . she was right. I was doing this. Jemma had gone over the importance of the field generator with me in painful detail, and I was perfectly clear on how boned we were until that unit was replaced.

Once they'd finished securing my helmet, I very, very carefully hefted the generator and guided it over toward the portable air lock they'd rigged over the access hatch.

"Did I mention we're in a bit of a hurry?" Maggie asked over the comm. I grunted a reply, but I didn't move any faster. Heavy things don't have weight in free fall, but they still have mass, and it's really easy to smash things up if you get them moving too quickly. Once I was inside the lock, they sealed the outer door behind me, and my suit went taut as they evacuated the chamber. When the whistle of escaping air had completely died away, the hatch slid open.

The field generator was an array of six cubes, each exactly like the one I was carrying. I could see immediately which one was the problem. The unit nearest me as I entered the chamber had a black-rimmed hole maybe two or three centimeters wide punched straight through the top. I looked up. There was a slightly larger hole in the roof of the chamber. A beam of bluish light passed through it, and illuminated the top of the wrecked unit like a spotlight.

It was just about then that my skin started burning.

It wasn't too bad at first. As Maggie and Jemma had said, the human body is surprisingly slow to react to acute radiation poisoning. I pulled the cables from the old unit, opened the docking latches, and got it up and out without any real trouble. When I was trying to get the new unit positioned, though, my head must have passed through that beam of light.

About ten seconds later, I was blind.

The skin on my hands was bubbling up by then, and I didn't have much sense of touch left. The unit was latched down, and I'd managed to get the first docking cable engaged—but when I moved to the second one, I couldn't figure out where the port was. I groped around for a few seconds, cable in hand, increasingly panicked, before Maggie spoke in my ear.

"Barnes? You okay?"

I tried to say *no*, but my tongue was too swollen to make the sounds, and all that came out was a moan.

"Stop," she said. "Don't yank on the cable."

I stopped, or tried to. My body was shaking too badly to really hold still.

"Your helmet camera is still functioning for the moment. Try to position it so that I can see what you're doing."

I felt for the edge of the unit, then bowed my head toward where I thought the connector should go.

"Okay," Maggie said. "Hold the camera there. Now move the connector to your left. Approximately ten centimeters."

I slid the connector across the floor.

"Good," Maggie said. "Now forward about three.

"Right one.

"Back one.

"Press."

I felt a click as the connector snapped into place.

"Perfect," Maggie said. "Field is reestablished. Good job, Barnes. Try to relax now. We'll get somebody in there to retrieve you."

It's surprisingly difficult to relax when your body is burning from the inside out. If I could have just popped the seals on my helmet and decompressed then, I would have done it, but my hands were worse than useless, my fingers too swollen to bend. So I floated there, shaking and moaning and grinding my teeth, and waited for someone to pull me back into the world.

I understand why they forced me to upload before they let me die. Jemma covered that too. Knowledge and experience gained during a critical situation is valuable, and that can't be permitted to die with one particular instantiation of me.

Some things, though, just really need to be forgotten.

The situation was slightly less critical by the time I came out of the tank as Mickey2. The field generator was functioning, and conditions inside the *Drakkar* were basically back to normal—at least if you set aside the thirty-four people who were now suffering from various degrees of radiation poisoning because they'd been in the wrong parts of the ship when the field went down. We still had a hole in our armor, though, and all it would have taken was a stray grain in the right spot to put us right back where we'd been. So, as soon as I was conscious and functioning, Maggie and her people crammed me into another vacuum suit and sent me out onto the hull with a tank full of high-density emergency patch nanites, and five minutes' worth of direction on how to use them.

The highest intensity in the stream of protons being channeled along the hull was about two meters off the surface. Maggie told me that if I stayed close to the hull and was lucky enough to avoid getting clipped by a grain, I might even keep my exposure low enough to survive. So, I tried. Rather than just giving me force locks for my boots, like Jemma and I wore when we hiked out over Midgard, Maggie had them strap smaller attractors to my palms and knees. I went out through the forward air lock, and crawled the hundred meters or so to the impact point.

At first I thought I might be okay. As I approached the nose, though, the proton stream closed in. I started seeing flashes of light with maybe twenty meters to go, and by the time I reached the hole, my vision was blurring and my mouth tasted of iron. I pulled the nanite tank from my back, unlimbered the applicator, and pressed the trigger.

The nanites came out in a thick, sticky stream. They clung to the ragged walls of the hole, and even as I was still dispensing them they started to knit themselves together into the same hyper-dense material as the surrounding armor.

It took almost twenty minutes to empty the tank. When it was done, there was a mound of goo where the hole had been. Over the next few minutes, it flattened and smoothed itself until it would have taken an electron microscope to tell the difference between the patch and the original armor.

I only know any of this because when I came out of the tank as Mickey3 the next morning, the first thing they made me do was watch the video feed from my suit camera and listen to the running narrative I'd kept up right until the point when, halfway back to the air lock, I stopped moving, popped the seals at my collar, and showed my naked face to the universe.

"WELL," BERTO SAYS from the cockpit, "that could have gone better."

Cat shoots him a murderous glance. Berto's never been much for sensitivity.

"Three people just died," I say.

"Yeah," Berto says. "I saw. What the hell happened down there? It looked like Security turned their burners on Dugan?"

"They were trying to save him," Cat says.

"Hell of a way to do it," Berto says as we bank over the main dome and slow to a hover over the landing pad. "Even combat armor won't stand up to a burner set to full power for long. What were they thinking?"

I glance over at Cat. Her hands are clenched into fists.

"They were thinking Dugan had two creepers wrapped around his leg," she says. "And not for nothing, but those were my friends down there, asshole. Also not for nothing, maybe if you'd warned us that we were standing on top of a nest of those fucking things, the whole sortie would have gone a little better, huh?"

Berto glances back from the cockpit as we settle down onto

the pad. I'm slightly surprised to see that he actually looks embarrassed.

"Sorry," he says. "No disrespect intended."

"Yeah, well," Cat says. "Disrespect taken."

Berto powers the lifter down, then starts working through his shutdown checklist. I can feel my weight settle a little more firmly into the padding of my jump seat as the gravitic field dissipates.

"I really am sorry about what happened out there," Berto says. "I would have warned you if I could have. I don't know where those things came from, but they weren't just moving under the snow. There was nothing on my radar the last time I passed over you, and that was no more than a minute before the attack."

"Whatever," Cat says. I can't see her face through her visor, but I can hear the scowl in her voice.

"Anyway," Berto says, "mission accomplished, right?" As Cat and I unbuckle, he climbs out of his seat and comes back to stand over us. What's left of the creeper lies on the floor of the cabin. Berto nudges it with the toe of one boot. Two of its legs spasm, and he almost trips himself yanking his foot back. "Shit!" He regains his balance, grimaces, then steps forward again and crouches down between us. The carcass is vibrating. He touches the carapace with one finger, but this time it doesn't react. "Huh," he says. "I hope this turns out to've been worth it."

"YOU'RE GOING TO need to help me out here," Marshall says. "Because I'm having a lot of trouble understanding how we lost three people in the last two hours—four, if you count Gallaher, and five if you count Torricelli—and you weren't one of them."

Cat shifts uncomfortably in her seat next to me. Marshall leans forward, elbows on his desk. He doesn't look like he's trying to decide whether to kill me or not. He looks like he's trying to settle on the method.

"You're right, sir," I say. "I apologize for surviving. I'll try to do better next time."

That brings him to his feet. "Don't give me that shit, Barnes! You're an Expendable! You're not supposed to be worried about surviving!"

He sits back down slowly, while I wipe his spittle from my forehead.

"Now," he says, "I want you to explain to me, clearly and concisely, why you chose to save your own ass out there rather than rendering aid to Mr. Dugan. Give this some thought, Barnes, because if I don't find your answer convincing, I'm going to personally shove you down the corpse hole balls-first."

"Sir—" Cat says.

"Shut up, Chen. I'll deal with you when I'm done with him."

They're both looking at me now, Cat with a mixture of pity and concern, Marshall with the same basic expression a hawk might give to a field mouse.

"Well," I begin, then hesitate. I was going to say something about how it's all well and good to say I shouldn't be worried about surviving when he's sitting safe and sound in the same body he was born with, while I'm getting irradiated or eaten or dissolved every six weeks, but looking at his face, I suddenly realize that he might be serious about the whole corpse hole thing. I begin again.

"Well, sir, we were sent out there for a reason. You ordered us to retrieve a creeper. Given what happened to Torricelli and Gallaher, we were all very much aware that this was a hazardous sortie, but you decided that we should attempt it anyway. Therefore, I concluded that doing what we were sent out there to do was our first priority. By the time we realized what was happening to Mr. Dugan, it was my judgment that there was nothing we could have done to help him. Therefore, I decided to put my efforts to accomplishing the mission—which, I will note, I succeeded in doing."

Marshall stares at me for what feels like a very long time. "So what you're saying," he says, "is that what I saw on Gomez's video feed was not in fact you running for your life in abject terror, but rather you calmly doing what was necessary to further the mission and protect the colony. Is that correct?"

I look at Cat. She shrugs.

"Uh . . . yes?"

The silence stretches on for a long five seconds. Cat opens her mouth to speak, but Marshall silences her with a glance.

"Did you know, prior to leaving the dome, that our burners would be ineffective against those things?"

"No," I say. "Not for sure."

"Then why did you choose to carry an accelerator?"

"Primarily because I'm better trained in the use of an accelerator than in the use of a burner, sir. Also, I'm aware that I was carrying a burner on two other occasions when I encountered creepers, and that I did not survive either of those missions. So, I thought this time it might be wise to change tactics."

Marshall's eyebrows come together at the bridge of his nose, and his mouth shrinks down into a thin, hard line. I risk a glance over at Cat. She's staring straight ahead. Marshall turns his attention to her.

"What about you, Chen? Can you explain your actions? You were out there to protect Mr. Dugan, were you not?"

"Yes, sir," she says. "I was."

"And you abandoned him because . . ."

"I abandoned him because I could see what was happening, sir. The other two Security officers were my friends. If I had believed that I could do anything to help them, I would have done it. But the fact is, our weapons were not useful, and I couldn't see any point in feeding myself to those things along with Mr. Dugan."

"Barnes's weapon was useful. You could have commandeered it."

"I could have," she says, "but I couldn't have done anything useful with it. A linear accelerator isn't a precision weapon, sir. I could have blown Mr. Dugan's leg off, but I couldn't have saved him."

Marshall leans back from his desk and runs his hands back through his brush-cut salt-and-pepper hair.

"Look," he says. "We began this expedition with one hundred and ninety-eight people. We made landfall with one hundred and eighty, and we are now down to one hundred and seventy-five. From a population standpoint, we are fast approaching the limit of viability for a beachhead colony. Because of this, I unfortunately can't actually shove either one of you down the corpse hole at this time, or even punish you in any meaningful way, much though I might like to do so.

"Barnes, I have a strong suspicion that you know more about those things out there than you're telling us. If this is true, I can only ask you to think very carefully about what you're doing, because if this colony goes down, you will wind up spending your last days like that poor sick bastard on Roanoke, in the company of a whole shitload of Mickey Barneses—which, I can tell you from my experience with just one of you, would be absolutely unbearable.

"Chen, I really don't know what to make of you at this point. I'm beginning to suspect that you may have had some preexisting relationship with Barnes, which you should have disclosed prior to the sortie. In the future, please remember that you need to let Command know if the possibility exists that personal issues may interfere with the performance of your mission."

Cat opens her mouth to speak, but Marshall cuts her off again with a slash of one hand.

"I don't want to hear it," he says. "I just want you to think very carefully about who you choose to associate with in the future."

He looks at me, then Cat, then back at me. "That's all," he says. "Go. We'll let you know when you're needed again."

"So," CAT SAYS. "That was fun."

We're in the cafeteria, catching a late-shift dinner. There are at least thirty people here, gathered in groups of three or four, leaning over their tables, heads close together, talking in low voices. Five deaths in one day is a scary thing on a beachhead colony, and we're mostly engaged in the ancient human custom of telling one another what idiots the recently deceased were, in order to convince ourselves that what happened to them can't possibly happen to us.

"Yeah," I say. "He didn't actually murder us. I call that a win."

That gets a smile. Cat's much prettier in a jumpsuit than she was in battle gear. Her face is soft and heart-shaped, and her hair is thick and black and pulled back into a shoulder-length ponytail. She's picking at a plate of roasted tomatoes and a stringy-looking rabbit haunch. I'm working my way through a hundred-kcal half-full mug of cycler paste. I know I promised Eight the rest of our ration for the day, but I just nearly died while he was napping. That has to count for something, right?

"So," I say. "Marshall thinks we're sexing, huh?"

Cat's face hardens into a scowl. "Marshall can fuck himself."

"Wow," I say. "That's pretty harsh. Don't want anyone thinking that you're associating with the Expendable, huh?"

She shakes her head. "Nah. I'm not a Natalist or anything. As far as I'm concerned, you're no different from any of the other

weirdos who signed up for this trip. What I don't like is the insinu-
ation that I didn't do my job because my *hormones* got in the way.
I mean, I didn't hear him giving you any shit about that, right?"

"I didn't . . ." I trail off, because I was about to say *I didn't
think he meant it that way,* and it's just occurred to me that yeah,
he probably did.

"You didn't what?"

"Nothing," I say. "You're one hundred percent right. Fuck
that guy."

"Amen," she says, and raises her water cup to me. "Fuck that
guy."

I tap my mug to her cup, and we drink.

While she's distracted with that, I snatch a tomato from her
tray and cram it into my mouth before she can react.

"Hey," she growls, then reaches across the table and punches
my shoulder hard enough to leave a bruise. "No screwing around,
Barnes. You touch my food again and I'll break your arm."

"Sorry," I say, and push my mug of paste toward her. "You can
have some of mine if you want."

She scowls again and pushes it back. "Thanks, I'm good. If
you want a tomato, why don't you just go get one? Did you seriously eat through your entire day's rations before the sortie?"

"Yeah," I say. "Pretty much. I've had a rough few days."

"Oh," she says. "Right. I forgot you went down last night.
You're fresh out of the tank, huh?" She takes a bite, chews, and
swallows. "What's that like?"

"What, coming out of the tank?"

She nods, picks up the rabbit bone, and gnaws at a bit of meat
left around the joint. "Yeah. I've always wondered what it's like
to wake up and know that you just died, that the body you're in
was a bunch of protein paste in the bio-cycler a few hours before.
How does that feel?"

"Well," I say, "you're not conscious in the tank. You wake up in your bed. You're a little disoriented and a lot hungover, and you can't remember how you got there. You think maybe you were out drinking the night before, except that you can't remember that either. The last thing you remember is plugging in to upload."

She leans back and nods. "Right. That's when you realize."

"Yeah, that's it. I've done it seven times now, and it's a kick in the crotch every time."

She gives me a sympathetic smile, but then her eyes focus over my left shoulder and the smile fades. I turn my head to see Nasha standing behind me, arms folded across her chest.

"Hey," she says. "How'd it go with Command?"

I slide over to make room for her. She steps over the bench and sits.

"Good," I say. "Well, more like adequate, I guess. Marshall threatened to cram me down the corpse hole, but he didn't actually do it."

Nasha grimaces. "Is that even a threat for you? After the shit that bastard did to you when we first made landfall, why would he think that would scare you?"

Cat looks at Nasha, then back at me. "Well," she says. "He did threaten to put him through balls-first."

Nasha shakes her head, and moves her hand to the small of my back. "Sister, you have no idea what this man has been through."

"You're talking about the medical stuff?"

"Yeah," Nasha says. "I'm talking about the medical stuff."

Cat looks away then, and goes back to picking at her rabbit bone. I nudge Nasha. Cat's had a rough go. She doesn't need to catch shade right now. Nasha sighs.

"Anyway," she says, "I'm sorry about what happened to Gillian and Rob out there. I know you guys were tight."

"Thanks," Cat says. "I already asked Gomez this, but . . . did you guys pick up anything before those things hit us? I mean, they couldn't have just materialized out of nothing, right?"

Nasha shakes her head. "Nope. Nothing. I was running visible, infrared, and ground-penetrating radar, and I swear you guys were one hundred percent clear the last time I passed over."

"Yeah," Cat says. "That's the same thing Gomez said. Between the two of you, we couldn't have been exposed for more than thirty seconds at a time. It doesn't make sense, does it?"

"I don't know," Nasha says. "They came at the main lock from underneath, right? GPR can't see through granite. Maybe they're miners. Hell, maybe they've got tunnels running straight up under us right now."

Cat glances down at her feet. "Thanks, Nasha. I hate that."

Nasha grins. "Lucky thing we've all got top-level racks, right?"

"Yeah," Cat says. "Lucky." She pokes halfheartedly at the last scraps of tomato skin on her tray, then looks over at me. "So you two have been together forever, right? Since Midgard?"

I look at Nasha. She shrugs.

"Almost. When he's not getting eaten or set on fire or crushed by falling storage bins, anyway. Why? You want a crack at him?"

"Doubtful," Cat says. "Why? Would it be worth the trouble?"

Nasha glances over at me. "Maybe. Depends on what you're into, I guess."

I can feel my face redden as they both burst out laughing.

"Just kidding," Nasha says, and wraps one arm around my shoulder. "This one's mine. You touch him, and I'll gut you like a fish."

Cat raises both hands in surrender. "Oh, no worries," she says. "His tomato-stealing ass is all yours. I was just leaving, actually."

She pushes back from the table and gathers her things. When she's gone, Nasha leans her forehead against mine and cups my cheek in one hand.

"Just so you know," she says, "she's not the only one I'd be gutting."

She kisses me quickly, gets to her feet, and goes.

I GET BACK to my rack to find Eight sitting in my chair, at my desk, reading something on my tablet. He shuts it down when he hears me enter. He's taken the pressure wrap off of his unsprained wrist.

"Hey," he says without looking up. "How'd it go?"

"Great," I say. "We're five corpses closer to getting you a berth of your own."

"Huh." He puts the tablet into the desk drawer, stands, and stretches. "Were we always a sociopath, or is this another one of your post-upload innovations?"

"Really? Were we always a sociopath?"

He grins. "Sorry. Pronouns weren't really designed for this situation, were they?"

"No," I say. "I guess not. And in answer to your question, no, we are not a sociopath. What we are is really, really hungry."

Eight barks out a humorless laugh. "Oh no," he says. "I don't want to hear anything from you about hungry. I just came out of the tank, remember? Try doing that on nothing but cycler paste."

"About that," I say, "I just used a hundred kcal. You've only got two hundred left now. Sorry."

His face hardens. "So much for being a good guy, huh?"

I shake my head. "Don't, Eight. I just almost got killed while you were napping. That's got to count for something."

"I may not have mentioned this," he says, "but I am literally starving to death, Seven."

He's right, of course. Six and I both bitched incessantly about the rations when we came out, and we were eating like kings compared to what Eight is getting. I peel out of my shirt and drop it on the floor, sit down on the bed and start unlacing my boots. Eight sits down next to me.

"Anyway," he says, "what's going on out there? The feed just says four accidental deaths and one gone missing, all outside the dome. How does that happen?"

I finish with the boots, pull them off, and lie back on the bed. "Well," I say. "First, they weren't all outside, strictly speaking. One was in the main lock, which by the way is no longer in service, since they just used the murder hole."

That hangs in the air for a long, awkward moment.

"The murder hole," Eight says finally. "They used it on what?"

I fold my hands behind my head and close my eyes. "Creepers."

Eight laughs, with a little more warmth this time. "Okay. Got it. You're shitting me. Really, what happened?"

"Really, they vented plasma into the lock to kill creepers that had breached the decking, and roasted a mostly dead Security goon named Gallaher in the process."

"Creepers are animals, Seven. You don't use live plasma to kill an animal."

"I don't think you're hearing me," I say. "*They breached the deck.*"

"By 'breached' you mean . . ."

"I mean they cut directly through the decking and started peeling it away."

"Peeling it away? You mean they . . . took it?"

I shrug. "Seems like it. This planet is metal-poor, you know. Maybe they need it for something."

"Huh." He scratches the top of his head. "Scoot over."

I slide over to make room for him, and he lies down next to me. This still feels weird, but there's been so much weirdness in my life in the past twenty-four hours that it barely registers.

"It's not like anybody thought they were harmless," Eight

says, "but it's a little hard to swallow an animal being able to rip through the ship's decking, isn't it?"

"You're not wrong." I'm about to go on, but I have to stop to yawn. I haven't slept except in two-hour stretches since the night before last. "I didn't see the bit with the decking, to be honest, but I saw the hole in the floor of the main lock. I also saw a bunch of creepers take down two fully armored goons and one very frightened biologist. It was not pretty."

"You're saying you saw creepers bite through ten-mil fiber armor?"

"Well," I say, "not that specifically. I saw them crawling around on ten-mil fiber armor, and I saw the guys wearing the armor go down. The actual biting-through-armor part was pretty strongly implied, though."

Eight rises up on one elbow and leans over me. "That doesn't make sense. Species don't evolve abilities that don't have uses in their environment. Why would an ice worm evolve the ability to bite through armor designed to stop a ten-gram LA slug?"

"That's an excellent question," I say, and yawn again. "I will definitely give you a good answer for it when I wake up."

Eight keeps talking, but his words slur into a dull background hum. The last conscious thing I remember is the bed shifting slightly as he stands.

ALMOST EVERY NIGHT for the past few weeks, I've had the same recurring . . . dream? No, more like a vision, I guess. It always comes just when I'm drifting off, or just when I'm waking. This is one reason why I haven't been uploading. I'm a little concerned that I might have suffered some kind of glitch during the regen process. If I did, I don't want to inject any of it into my personality record.

More importantly, I don't want anyone in psych to notice, and suggest that maybe they ought to scrap me and try again.

In the dream I'm back on Midgard, out in the woods that run along the crest of the Ullr Mountains. There's a trail there, eight hundred kilometers of untouched wilderness filled with waterfalls, hundred-kilometer vistas, and trees that have been growing since the original terraformers seeded the place three hundred years ago. I've walked it end-to-end four times. There's a lot of empty space on Midgard, but those mountains are the emptiest place on a mostly empty planet. In all the time I spent out there, I don't think I saw more than two or three other human beings.

I'm camped for the night, sitting on a log in front of a little fire, staring into the flames. So far, so good, right? Maybe I'm just homesick. But then I hear a noise, like someone clearing his throat. I look up, and there's this giant caterpillar sitting across the fire from me.

I know I should be freaking out right now, but I'm not. That's the part of the whole experience that's most like an actual dream.

The caterpillar and I talk—or try to, anyway. His mouth moves, and sounds come out that sound like words, but I can't make any sense of them. I tell him to stop, to slow down, that if he would just speak a little more clearly I could understand what he's saying. He doesn't, though. He just keeps going, until the listening makes my head start to ache. I look into the fire. It's running backward, unburning the pile of sticks it's feeding on and sucking smoke back out of the air. When I look up again, the caterpillar is fading, becoming less and less substantial, until only the smile remains.

Eventually even the smile disappears, and as it does I slide from this half world into a real dream, one I've had on and off for years. I'm Mickey2, out on the hull of the *Drakkar* again, crawling back toward the forward lock as my skin sloughs away and my blood begins seeping from ruptured vessels, covering me like fever sweat and draining into my mouth, my throat, my lungs.

I stop, and reach for the clasps at my neck. My fingers are like sausages now, swelling and splitting, but somehow I manage to fumble one clasp open, then the other. My helmet flies away, and hard vacuum sucks everything out of me.

Air.

Blood.

Shit.

Everything.

I should be dead now, but I'm not, and I can't understand why.

I open my cracked mouth and pull in a lungful of nothing. Before I can use it to scream, though, I snap awake, wide-eyed and sweating in the coal-black dark.

MICKEY2 WAS MY shortest-lived instantiation.

Mickey3 was my longest.

It took me a while to get over what happened to One. You never forget your first kiss, right? Well, you never forget your first death either, and the death that my original body experienced was a pretty traumatic one. Two's ending shouldn't have been as scarring, mostly because I didn't actually remember anything about being him—but just knowing that what he went through was bad enough that explosive decompression seemed like a good idea weighed on me. I spent most of my time those first few weeks as Three moping around, jumping at every loud noise and waiting for something bad to happen.

Time went by, though. Weeks turned to months, months turned to the better part of a year full of nothing, and nothing bad happened. Funny thing. As it turns out, even waiting expectantly for a sudden, violent death gets boring after a while.

It was about that time that my general interest in history morphed into a morbid interest in the histories of failed colonies. You wouldn't think they'd have that sort of material available in the ship's library—bad for morale and all—but they did. My teachers didn't talk about the failures in school. I wouldn't necessarily call what they fed us *propaganda,* but in every subject, from biology to history to physics, they made sure to weave in something about the importance and nobility of the Diaspora, and the idea that it's been an uninterrupted parade of successes as humanity has spread across the spiral arm was pretty strongly implied if never actually stated—so I was surprised to learn that there have been almost as many failed efforts as successes over the past thousand years.

When colonists set out in a ship like the *Drakkar,* they really have no idea what they're likely to find at the end of the journey. The physics of antimatter drives dictate that they only work at scale, and antimatter production is insanely difficult and expensive, so a world looking to launch a colony ship can't just send out probes to a bunch of likely stars to scout things out before they go. So, they make do with what they can observe from their home system. When we left Midgard, for example, we knew we were headed to a G-type main-sequence star. We knew it had at least three smallish, rocky planets, and that one of them was at the outer edge of the star's Goldilocks zone. We knew that planet—our target—had water vapor and at least some free oxygen in its atmosphere, from which we inferred that it almost certainly supported some form of life.

That was about it, honestly—and because Midgard and Niflheim aren't actually that far apart as these things go, and also because our powers of observation have improved substantially as time has gone on, we knew more than a lot of colony ships have. One of the shortest records I found was for an expedition launched from Asher's World a bit more than a hundred years ago. Asher's World is about as far out toward the rim as we've ventured, and the stars are spread thin there. Their target was over twenty lights distant, which is at the outer range of what a colony ship can do, and maybe a little beyond. The adult colonists were old, and tired, and really hungry by the time they finished their deceleration burn, and their ship was practically falling apart.

Unfortunately, the world they'd been targeting wasn't in the orbit they'd been expecting. It was just slightly too close to its star. They'd been fooled by the fact that they'd seen O_2 absorption spectra in its atmosphere. There was some oxygen there, but there was no liquid water, because the surface temperature was too high to permit it. Theory said that shouldn't have been possible, but the universe is a funny place, and it was what it was. Their best guess was that the planet may have been habitable—may in fact have been inhabited by something or other that was able to split carbon from CO_2 and produce free oxygen—but that a runaway greenhouse effect, something like the one that was pushing the limits of habitability of some parts of old Earth in the years before the Diaspora, had fairly recently sterilized the place. If they were right, the residual oxygen they'd detected just hadn't had time to bind itself out of the atmosphere yet.

With a hundred years to terraform, they might have been able to make it work. They didn't have a hundred years, though. With the condition of their ship, they probably didn't have ten. So, they beamed their findings back home, then put their ship into a stable orbit, doped everyone who wanted to be doped, and popped their air locks. As Two could tell you, explosive decompression isn't a fun time, but at least it's quick.

Reading that got me thinking about Two. That sent me into a spiral that lasted the better part of a month.

The thing that pulled me back out of that spiral was Nasha.

I'd seen Nasha around, obviously, going all the way back to Himmel Station. When you're living in a giant canister with fewer than two hundred other people, you see everybody around at some point. I'd never spoken to her, though—mostly for the same reason I'd never spoken to most of the other people on the

Drakkar. Lots of them didn't want anything to do with me, and I compensated by not wanting anything to do with them.

We met for real about a year after the collision that wound up killing One and Two. We were well into the coast phase of the journey by then, humming along through the vacuum at just a hair under point-nine *c,* weightless and on short rations and bored out of our minds. Command had ordered all personnel to spend at least two hours of every duty cycle in the carousel—nominally so that we'd still have bones and whatnot when we finally made landfall, but actually I think so that we'd be less likely to start murdering one another just to break up the monotony.

The carousel was exactly what it sounds like: a spinning ring around the waist of the ship a hundred and twenty meters across, with a flat, rubberized inner surface about six meters wide. They had it going at three revs per minute, which was fast enough to get us about half a standard g, but also slow enough that you could stand upright without having the Coriolis effect bring up your lunch.

We were supposed to spend our time in the carousel working out, but as long as we were in there for the designated time, nobody who mattered really seemed to care what we did. There were a few prigs who'd shoot you a look as they ran past if you weren't doing squat thrusts or yoga or practicing Krav Maga, but as far as I know none of them ever actually went to the trouble of filing a delinquency report on anyone.

I'd been pretty good about jogging around the ring at least a few times every day, right up until One and Two went down. After that, though, my motivation dropped off pretty radically. Not much point in worrying about bone mineral density and muscle tone when your bones and muscles have the shelf life of an open package of yogurt, right? I started bringing a tablet to the carousel, finding a place as far away from the squat thrusters as I could to plant myself against a wall, and reading through the records of other beachhead colonies. That's when I learned all about Asher's World, and Roanoke, and a bunch of other recent disasters.

Needless to say, reading that kind of stuff didn't increase my motivation to exercise.

So one day I was there in the carousel, squatting against the wall and reading through a first-person account of a near-failure that had occurred almost a thousand years prior, on what's now one of the most heavily populated worlds in the Union. The issue there was persistent agricultural failure, which they eventually traced to a virus that was endemic in the soil. They didn't have bio-cyclers then, and the narrator made it sound like things got pretty hungry before they cracked the problem.

I was just getting to the part where the head of the colony's Biology Section, who also happens to be the narrator, hero-ically saves the day with a tailored phage that clears the way for human-friendly plants to grow—while coincidentally wiping out the microorganism that had made it possible for local plants to grow, and thereby completely destroying the native ecosystem—when a boot nudged my shoulder, hard enough to knock me half over. I looked up to see a woman in black Security togs standing over me, arms folded across her chest.

"Hey," she said. "Shouldn't you be doing push-ups right now?"

I glared up at her. She broke into a grin and squatted down beside me.

"I'm just messing with you. You're the Expendable, right?"

"I'm Mickey Barnes," I said. "Who are you?"

"Mickey Barnes, huh? Don't you mean Mickey3 now?"

Ouch.

"Yeah," I said. "That."

She settled back against the wall. I sighed, straightened up, and tucked my tablet into my chest pocket.

"I'm Nasha Adjaya," she said. "Combat pilot."

I glanced over at her. Her braids had fallen across her face, but I could still see the grin.

"Combat pilot, huh? You must be pals with Berto."

"Gomez? Yeah, he's okay. Better pog-ball player than a pilot, but we get along."

I smiled. "You're not wrong. I wonder which we'll need more of when we get where we're going."

She leaned toward me. "You're not questioning the importance of combat pilots to the mission, are you?"

"Yeah," I said. "Kind of. Do they need a lot of those on beach-head colonies? I mean, do we expect to make landfall on a planet that's already got an air force?"

Her grin widened. "Guess you never know, right? Just 'cause it's never happened before doesn't mean it never will."

"There's only two of you," I said. "Better hope it's a *small* air force, right?"

She laughed. "Doesn't matter, friend. I'm a hell of a pilot."

"Yeah," I said. "I'm sure that's true."

We sat in silence then. I was starting to wonder whether I should pull my tablet back out, or maybe just get up and leave, when she turned to look at me. I looked back. The grin was gone and her eyes had narrowed. Her irises were so dark they were almost black.

"So," she said. "What's dying like?"

I shrugged. "Like being born, only backward."

"Ha! I like that." She smiled. "You know, you're pretty cute for a zombie."

"Thanks," I said. "I use a lot of moisturizer."

She touched my hand, then ran one finger up along my fore-arm. "I bet you do," she said.

Her smile morphed into a leer.

"I just bet . . . you . . . do."

IT WAS LATER, and we were back in my rack, halfway to naked and tangled around one another in the darkness, when she said, "I'm not a ghost chaser, you know."

That was the first time I'd heard that term. It definitely wasn't the last.

"Ghost chaser?" I said.

"Yeah," she said. "You know."

I waited for a while for her to go on. Instead, she ran her hand up my back and nipped at my ear hard enough to make me wince.

"No," I said. "I do not."

"Oh," she said. "Well, you know there's a bunch of Natalists on this boat, right?"

I scowled. "Yeah, I'm aware. That's one of the reasons I keep to myself so much."

"Well," she said. "Not all of them want you to keep to yourself."

I twisted around until our foreheads were touching. "What?"

She kissed me. "How many women have you been with on this trip?"

"I don't know," I said. "A few?"

She kissed me again. "All of them since the collision, right? All of them since you went through the tank?"

I didn't answer. It was pretty obvious that she knew.

"Ghost chasers," she said. "To a Natalist, you're some serious forbidden fruit. I've heard them talking."

"But that's not you."

"No," she whispered. "That's not me."

IT'S KIND OF tough to date on a colony ship. There just aren't a lot of options, activity-wise. You can eat together, but sucking food out of a plastic bulb while attached to a tether in the mess so that you don't float into somebody else who is also sucking food out of a plastic bulb is even less romantic than it sounds. You can take walks together, but the only place where walking is possible is around the carousel, and you spend most of your time there slightly nauseous while you put more time and attention to avoiding the squat thrusters than you do to your date. You can star-watch at the forward viewing ports, but I couldn't do that without thinking about the stream of high-energy protons flowing past, and what they would do to me—again—if something happened to one of the field generation units. PTSD-related panic attacks are also not romantic.

So mostly, we banged.

When we weren't doing that, we spent a lot of time talking. Nasha had stories. Her parents were immigrants, which, given the colossal expense and time required to get anywhere in the Union, is something that almost nobody other than beachhead colonists can say. They'd come to Midgard thirty years earlier on the *Lost Hope,* a refugee ship from New Hope, the world that had been, up until its inhabitants decided to kill one another, Midgard's nearest neighbor.

You wouldn't think a place like Midgard would be hard on immigrants. It's not like we didn't have the room or resources to take in a few hundred lost souls. You'd be wrong, though. Humans are tribal, and the refugees' accents were enough to mark them as outsiders, even setting aside the fact that the majority of them had skin a few shades darker than most of Midgard's original population. They hadn't been on Midgard for a month before anonymous articles started popping up on the feeds arguing that they were carriers for whatever lunacy had engulfed New Hope, and that if they were allowed to insinuate themselves into our social and political life, they'd drag Midgard down that same path.

The government set them up with basic stipends and places to live, but right from the jump it was almost impossible for them to find real jobs. Two years after they landed, a few dozen of them staged a sit-in that turned into a protest that turned into a minor riot. After that, they had a hard time even getting their kids admitted into the general schools.

It was right about then that Nasha was born.

Nasha never told me much about her childhood, but she dropped enough pieces here and there for me to figure out that it was rough. She was pretty up-front about why she learned to fly, though. She'd known since she was a kid that this mission was coming, and she wanted to be on it. She couldn't get into the kind of academic track that would have ended with a doctorate in exobiology, and she didn't have the connections that would have landed her a slot in Security or Command—but she could learn how to pilot a combat skimmer. Killing stuff was the one thing the people from New Hope were good at, right?

"Midgard was never my home," she said to me one night as we curled around one another in her sleeping mesh. "It was never going to be. This place where we're going, though . . ."

"It'll be good," I said. "Warm breezes and white sand beaches, and nothing that wants to eat us."

Famous last words, right?

I WAS WITH Nasha and maybe twenty or thirty other people in the forward common room when we finally shut down the main torch and switched over to ion thrusters for orbital insertion around Niflheim. We hadn't been able to make any kind of observations of our new home yet through the glare of our own exhaust, and everyone was pretty excited to finally see where we were going. A free-fall warning popped up in our oculars, and then thirty seconds later our weight eased away, and we drifted free of the deck.

A minute or so after that, an image of the planet we'd crossed almost eight lights to colonize popped up on the main wallscreen.

Someone up front tried to start a cheer. That died away almost before it began.

I don't know what we were expecting. Green continents and blue oceans? City lights?

What we saw was white. We were still several million klicks out, but from here the planet looked like a pog-ball—smooth, white, and featureless.

"Is that . . ." someone said. "Is that . . . clouds?"

We watched in silence as our maneuvering and the planet's rotation slowly shifted our viewpoint. Nothing changed. After what felt like hours but was probably actually more like ten minutes, Nasha said, "That's not cloud cover. It's ice. This planet's a snowball."

We were holding hands then, mostly just to keep from drifting apart. I squeezed her fingers. She squeezed mine back. I was thinking about all those stories I'd read about colonies that had failed to take root for one reason or another. This didn't look like the sort of place that would welcome us with open arms, but maybe . . .

I pulled her close, and brought my mouth next to her ear.

"This is doable," I said. "Old Earth was like this once, just before life took off. There's plenty of water here, and an oxygen-nitrogen atmosphere. That's all we really need."

She sighed, and turned her head to kiss my cheek.

"I hope so. I'd hate to come all this way just to die."

Those words were still hanging in the air between us when my ocular pinged.

<Command1>: Report to Biology immediately. Come prepared to
   deploy.

IT'S HARD TO get back to sleep under the best of circumstances after that creepy-ass *out on the hull* dream. With Eight crammed into the bed next to me, wriggling around and mumbling in his sleep, it's impossible. After a half hour or so of trying, I give up and slip out of bed, grab my tablet from my desk, and head down to the caf to do some reading. The corridors are deserted this early except for the occasional Security goon, and I've got the place to myself when I get there. I pick a table in the corner opposite the entrance. On the off chance that someone else wanders in while I'm down here, I'd rather they just left me alone.

My stomach starts rumbling as soon as I sit down. Apparently it knows this is where we go to eat. I'd love to oblige it, but my ration card is zeroed out, and it won't reset until 08:00, which is still a couple of hours away. Downside? I may digest my own liver by then. Upside? I've got plenty of time now to learn a bunch of stuff I don't actually want to know about some colony that crashed and burned in an interesting way somewhere, without being interrupted.

I'm not in the middle of anything right now, so I spend a few minutes browsing through the archives. Nothing's really grabbing me, though, and eventually, out of curiosity, I pull up a file on New Hope. I haven't dug into that particular story since I started my doom-and-gloom tour of the history of the Diaspora—mostly because, like everyone who's lived on Midgard for the past thirty years, I already have a general idea of what happened there.

New Hope failed about twenty-five years after their initial beachhead was established, mostly because of a short, brutal civil war fought between the remaining original colonists and the first wave of the New Hope–born that wrecked most of the infrastructure they still needed in order to survive on a semi-hostile planet. A group of refugees, all from the younger cohort, managed to boost up to the original colony ship that brought them there, which was, like ours here on Niflheim, mostly still in orbit around the planet. They stripped it down to the bare minimum needed to sustain them for a five-year hop—no embryos, no terraforming gear, no Agricultural Section—nothing but life support, a cycler, and a bare minimum of feedstock, basically. They even cut away most of the remaining living space.

When they were done, the ship massed less than ten percent of what the *Drakkar* did when it boosted out. Between the residual fuel that had been left in the ship's tanks, and the antimatter they managed to scavenge from the colony's wrecked power plant, they had just enough juice to limp across the gap to Midgard, where they were welcomed with slightly less than open arms.

As I start reading, it slowly dawns on me that the details the article is filling in give the story a significantly different valance than the one I'd picked up in school. They'd glossed over the reasons for the war, and I'd always assumed it was over the kind of stuff that civil wars are usually over—race, religion, resources, political philosophy, blah blah blah. According to this piece, though, the stated *casus belli* was the question of whether a native corvidlike avian species was sentient, and therefore deserving of protection and respect, or delicious, and therefore deserving of a spicy dry rub and an hour on the grill.

I guess I can see why that wouldn't get a lot of mention. If a colony can go down over something like that, we're all only one step from the corpse hole. I'm not sure what lesson to take from the story, though . . . except maybe that once things start to spiral, it can be really hard to pull them back.

I'm counting down the last ten minutes until I can show the scanner my ocular and draw a mug of cycler paste with equal parts anticipation and disgust when I get a ping from HR. It's my duty cycle for the day. They're seconding me out to Security. I need to be at Lock Two by 08:30, suited up and armed for perimeter patrol.

This sounds like a job for Eight.

I'm just about to tell him this when he pings me instead.

<Mickey8>:Hey Seven. You on your way to the lock?

<Mickey8>:Actually, I kind of thought you might take duty today. You know, considering I almost got eaten while you were napping yesterday.

<Mickey8>:I mean, I would, but . . .

<Mickey8>:Come on, Eight. You owe me.

<Mickey8>:Disagree, friend. If you'll recall, I'm the one who magnanimously did not shove you face-first down the corpse hole after I won our death match of rock-paper-scissors fair and square. Seems to me that you're the one with a debt to repay. Also, I haven't had time to get breakfast yet. You get this one. I'll pick up whatever they assign us to tomorrow.

I'm composing my response, which is definitely going to begin with, *Look, asshole,* when a second window pops open.

<CChen0197>:Hi Mickey. Saw you were on our roster this morning. They've got me on perimeter too. Want to partner? I feel like we made a pretty good team yesterday, right?

I'm trying to decide how to answer that when Eight comes back again.

<Mickey8>:Well, that decides it, huh? I have no idea what shenanigans you and Chen got up to yesterday. Five minutes of talking to me and we'd be outed, right? Right. So, I'm going back to sleep now, okay? Let me know how it goes.

He closes the window. I think about reopening it, and also about storming up there and dragging him out of bed and down to the lock by his ankles, but . . .

But the truth is, he's right.

<CChen0197>:You there?

<Mickey8>:Hi Cat. Yeah, I'm here. Just getting some breakfast before heading over. I'll see you in twenty.

"So," CAT SAYS. "No to the armor, yes to the accelerator, right?"

I look up from strapping on my snowshoes, shake my head, and go back to my laces.

"I'm not telling you what to do, Cat. Dugan was right yesterday. You guys have a different incentive structure than I do."

"Incentive structure?" Cat says. "You mean like the incentive to not get pulled to shreds by those things out there?"

"Yeah," I say. "That one."

I stand, shuffle away from the bench I'd been sitting on, and stomp my feet to make sure the shoes are secure. Cat's geared up the same way I am, with three layers of white camo thermals, snowshoes, and a rebreather pushed up to her forehead. Our weapons are still racked, but she's right about those too. Particularly after yesterday, I'm definitely carrying an accelerator.

"I don't think I buy that," she says. "I saw you yesterday. You didn't want to get pulled down any more than the rest of us did. I know you're supposed to be immortal, but you don't act like you believe it."

I give her a long look, then shrug and shuffle over to the weapons rack. "Have you ever shoved your hand into a shredder?"

She laughs. "What? No."

I pull an accelerator down from the wall, verify that it's powered, and check the load. "Why not? It wouldn't kill you, and the prosthetic they'd give you would be stronger than your real hand. A few hours in Medical and you'd be better than new."

"Oh," she says. "I see where you're going with this."

"You got it," I say. "Even if I don't believe it's permanent, I'm really not interested in dying any more often than I have to. Dying hurts." I shoulder the accelerator and pull on my gloves. "That said, I've got a theory about the creepers. I don't think they're going after us. I think they're after our metal, just like the natives on Roanoke were after their water. If I'm right, wearing combat armor out there is like walking into a wolf's den wrapped in bacon."

"Metal?" Cat says. "They're animals, Mickey. What would they want with metal?"

I shrug. "Who knows? Maybe they're not animals."

Cat pulls down a weapon for herself. "I don't like that. Let's get back to immortality. Do you?"

I look over at her. "Do I what?"

She rolls her eyes. "Believe that you're immortal, Mickey."

I sigh. "Ever heard of the Ship of Theseus?"

She pauses to think. "Maybe? Was that the one that they used to settle Eden?"

"No," I say. "It was not. The Ship of Theseus was a wooden sailing vessel from old Earth days. It got wrecked and had to be rebuilt . . . or else it didn't, I guess, but it still needed to get fixed—"

"Wait," Cat says. "A sailing vessel? Like on the water?"

"Yeah. Theseus sailed around the world in this boat, and it either got wrecked or it didn't, but either way he had to fix it."

"I'm confused. Is this a Schrödinger's cat kind of thing?"

"A what?"

"Schrödinger's cat," she says. "You know, with the box and the poison gas? Quantum superposition and all that?"

"What? No. I told you, it's a boat, not a cat."

"I heard you," she says. "I didn't think your boat was a cat. I'm just saying, it's the same kind of thing, right?"

I have to stop and think about that. For a second it seems like she's actually making sense.

Only for a second, though.

"No," I say. "Not at all. Why would you think that?"

Cat opens her mouth to answer, but before she can, the inner door to the air lock cycles open, and the bored-looking goon sitting beside it waves us over.

"Chen. Barnes. You're up."

"We'll finish this later," Cat says.

We pull down our rebreathers. Cat checks my seals, and I check hers.

"This thing cycles in ten seconds whether you're in it or not," the goon says.

Cat shoulders her weapon, and we go.

"This is bullshit," Cat says.

I look back at her. She's not using the comm, and the combination of the rebreather and Niflheim's atmosphere makes her voice higher than it should be, harsh and tinny. We're walking the perimeter now, shuffling along in our snowshoes, moving from pylon to pylon looking for signs of incursion. There are two other teams out here, spaced equidistant around the kilometer-wide ring that defines the human presence on this planet. We're supposed to keep moving at a steady pace, each team circling the perimeter twice in a six-hour shift. Every time we pass a pylon, it notes our presence and updates our oculars on the positions of the other teams.

"Which part?" I say. "The part where we spend our entire day freezing our asses off walking circles around the dome? Or the part where we maybe get shredded by creepers for no particular good reason?"

"Neither," Cat says. "Walking is good for you, and I guess getting shredded is part of the job when you sign on as Security. What's bullshit is this." She swings her arm in a gesture that takes in everything around us—from the dome, to the snow, to the mountains off in the distance. "This place was supposed to be habitable, remember? Goldilocks zone, oxygen-nitrogen atmosphere, yada yada." She kicks a clump of snow into the air, then watches as it breaks apart into a powdery cloud, glittering in the low yellow sun as it falls back to the ground. "This is not freaking habitable, Mickey. This is, in fact, bullshit."

I open my mouth to start in about the place Asher's World sent her people to. At least this planet didn't kill us dead right away. She turns away and starts walking, though, and I think better of it. I'm not the most sensitive person, but I've been alive long enough to figure out that telling a miserable person about how much worse things could be is usually a bad idea.

The pylons are spaced out at hundred-meter intervals around the perimeter. When we shuffle up to the next one, my ocular pings to let me know that we're moving more quickly than the other two teams, and that we need to slow down by ten percent.

"Ugh," Cat says. "How much slower can we go?"

"They're probably in full armor," I say. "No snowshoes. Remember how much fun that was yesterday?"

"Right. Still, though."

My ocular pings again. Command wants us to wait here for twelve minutes before proceeding. Cat sighs, leans back against the pylon, and sights down along the length of her accelerator, aiming toward a knob of bare rock jutting up out of the snow fifty or so meters away.

"I haven't fired one of these things since basic, back on Midgard," she says. "Hope I still remember how it works."

"Point and click," I say. "The targeting software does most of the work, and the size of the exit wound does the rest."

Her weapon whirs and slams back against her shoulder, and an instant later the top of the rock explodes into a cloud of powdered granite.

"Yeah," she says. "I guess it works."

I'm about to say something about maybe saving her rounds for when we need them when the debris around the rock settles out.

There's a creeper crouched there, head poking up just where Cat's round struck, rear segments trailing back into the snow. Its mandibles are spread wide, and its feeding arms are beckoning.

"Cat?" I say.

"Hush," she says. "I see it."

She aims carefully, and again the accelerator whirs and kicks. The creeper's front segments vanish in a hail of shrapnel, and the body drops back into the snow.

"Yeah," she says. "It definitely works."

The snow around the rock begins to churn.

The disturbance spreads like a wave, snow heaving up and settling back, then heaving again.

It sweeps toward us.

"Mickey?" Cat says.

A creeper breaks through the snow maybe thirty meters off. Cat aims and fires, but it's a panicky shot that raises a gout of steam and snow, but leaves the creeper untouched. The burner on the pylon we're standing under comes to life. Its beam plays across the snow around the rock, and an instant later those from the pylons to our left and right join in. Steam rises in boiling clouds, obscuring my view of the oncoming wave. I've brought my weapon to bear by now, but before I can fire, my field of view splits. My right eye is sighting down the length of my accelerator at where I'm guessing the leading creepers are swarming forward. My left eye, though, is looking back at the dome from a distance. I see the rock Cat destroyed, and the billows of steam where the burners are vaporizing the snow. The images are distorted, colors washed out and features flattened.

Through a break in the steam clouds, I catch a glimpse of two stick-figure humans staring back at me.

I squeeze my eyes shut, but now all I can see is the stylized view coming through my ocular. I must be catching a feed from one of the pylons, maybe? I shake my head and take a half step back. My left snowshoe catches, and I feel myself start to fall. In the view from my ocular, one of the stick figures drops its cartoon rifle and staggers backward as the other turns its balloon head to stare back at me. I'm flailing now and toppling, but my point of view doesn't shift as the disarmed stick figure disappears into the pixelated snow. The other raises its weapon and fires again and again, each shot producing an explosion in the mid-distance between it and me.

I can hear voices, but I can't separate the shouting over the comm from Cat's bellowing rage from something else, something calmer and quieter but not quite understandable. The remaining stick figure raises its aim point, and its line-drawing rifle shrinks down to a dot . . .

"HE'S COMING AROUND."

The voice is unfamiliar. It takes me a long moment to realize that it's referring to me.

"Can he hear us?"

That's Cat. I open my eyes to find myself flat on my back in an exam cube somewhere in Medical. Cat is leaning over me. She looks worried.

"Hey," she says. "You in there?"

It takes me a few seconds to scare up enough saliva to speak.

"Yeah," I say finally. "I'm in here. What happened?"

Cat straightens, and I try to sit up. Hands grasp my shoulders from behind, though, and gently press me back down.

"Easy, Barnes. Let's make sure you're functioning before we try moving too much."

I look back, and find myself gazing up into the white-haired nostrils of a middle-aged, balding medico named Burke.

I don't find his presence all that reassuring. He's killed me several times.

"Sorry," I say. "Is there something wrong with me?"

"Don't know," Burke says. "I can't find any sign of physical trauma, and your EEG looks normal at the moment. From what Chen tells me, though, you dropped like a sack of flour for no obvious reason out there. That's generally not a great sign from a medical standpoint."

"Why aren't we dead? The creepers were coming for us, weren't they?"

"They were," Cat says. "I don't know why they stopped."

"The pylons," I say. "They were firing, right?"

"Yeah," Cat says. "The burners on the pylons are a lot more powerful than the man-portable ones. There weren't any dead creepers lying around when the steam cleared, but maybe they forced them to ground?"

"Maybe," I say. For some reason, though, I don't think so.

"Or," Cat says, "maybe I got the boss creeper."

I shrug out from under Burke's hands and sit up. "What?"

"After the pylons kicked in, I couldn't see what was happening in front of us. Too much steam, you know? So I looked up, and a bit up the hillside there was this gigantic creeper reared up out of the snow."

That gets my attention. "How gigantic?"

She shrugs. "Hard to say. It was at least a hundred meters off. Maybe twice the size of the other ones? Maybe more? Anyway, it was the only target I could actually get a bead on, so I popped it. A few seconds later, the pylons shut down, and the creepers were gone."

I swing my legs over the side of the table. "How many mandibles did it have?"

Cat's eyebrows come together at the bridge of her nose. "None, after I popped it. Before that? I didn't stop to count."

I get to my feet. The world swims briefly, then comes back into focus.

"You should stick around for a while," Burke says. "Neurological events like this are no joke, Barnes. I'd like to get some imaging done. You might have a tumor."

I shoot him a look, then shake my head and pick up my shirt from the swivel chair where someone apparently tossed it when they brought me in.

"I don't have a tumor," I mutter.

"You don't know that," Burke says.

"We've had this conversation before," I say. "Don't you remember? Tumors take a long time to grow, and I've only been alive for a day and a half."

He winces. I guess he does remember.

"Fine," he says. "It's not a tumor. Let me check one more thing, though."

He turns to rummage in a drawer, and pulls out a slim wand with what looks like a suction cup on one end and a readout on the other. He comes over to me as I'm pulling my shirt on over my head and puts one hand on my shoulder.

"Hold still," he says, "and look up at the ceiling."

I let my breath out in a put-upon sigh and roll my eyes up as far as they'll go. Burke cups the back of my head with one hand, and presses the tip of the wand against my left eye.

"Ouch."

"Oh, don't be a baby. This will only take a second."

The wand beeps, and he pulls it away. "Huh," he says.

Cat steps forward and peers over his shoulder at the readout. "What does that mean?"

He turns to look at her. "Looks like there's been a power surge in his ocular sometime in the past hour. You should get that checked, Barnes. Those things have a direct connection to your brain, you know. A fritzing ocular is dangerous."

"Okay," I say. "Can you check it?"

He shakes his head. "I only handle wetware. You need someone from Bioelectronics."

Of course.

"Thanks," I say. "I'll be sure to get right on that."

"So," CAT SAYS. "What actually happened to you out there, Mickey?"

We're in the first-level main corridor now, near the cycler. I understand why that and Medical are co-located, but it still gives me the creeps as we walk past the entrance.

"No idea," I say. "I just blacked out."

Did I, though? The memory of seeing cartoon-me and cartoon-Cat is starting to feel more and more like the sort of thing an electroshocked brain would come up with just before shutting down, but . . .

"I would say you should see a doctor," Cat says, "but I guess you just did, huh? Are you going to try to get in to see somebody about your ocular, like Burke said?"

"Maybe," I say. "I've got some stuff I need to take care of this afternoon, but I'll see if I can get an appointment with somebody tomorrow if I have a chance."

"Sounds like something you might want to get looked at sooner than later, but I guess it's your call."

"Thanks," I say. "I'll give it some thought."

This is a lie. I've already done all the thinking I need to do on this topic. Like Burke said, ocular implants are interwoven with our optic nerves, and they interface with our brains in a half dozen other places. You can't just snap one out and snap another one in. Anybody else with a glitching ocular would be in for a long, tricky microsurgery to install a replacement unit.

Somehow, I don't think they'd spare that kind of effort for me. Easier to just give me a trip to the tank.

We've reached the central stairs. I take one step up, then turn to look back. Cat isn't following.

"I've still got three hours on shift," she says. "Amundsen said I could make sure you were okay, but I've got to get back now."

"Oh," I say. "Do they need me?"

Cat gives me a half smile. "After what just happened? No. Not now, and probably not anytime soon. Security isn't too keen on people who faint under fire."

Ouch.

"I didn't faint," I say. "I glitched. I was picking something up . . ."

She raises one eyebrow. "Picking something up?"

"Yeah," I say. "I was . . ."

It suddenly occurs to me that I might not want to tell Cat what I was seeing when I went down out there. I don't want her to think I'm breaking down.

I don't want to think about what it means if I'm *not* breaking down.

"I don't know," I say. "Something weird happened, for sure, but I definitely didn't just faint."

Cat looks uncomfortable now. "It's okay, Mickey. You wouldn't be the first person to panic under fire."

"Is that what you think happened?"

She looks away. "Doesn't matter what I think, does it? I'll see you later, Mickey."

AFTER I LEAVE Cat, I stop by the caf for another shot of cycler paste, then head back up to my rack. What else can I do? When I get there, I find Eight sitting up in bed, our tablet propped on his knees.

"Hey," he says. "You're back early."

I drop into our chair and start unlacing my boots. "Got attacked again. Almost died again. Wound up in Medical this time. They said I should go home and tell you to start doing your share of this bullshit from now on."

Eight sets the tablet aside, stretches, and gets to his feet. "Uh-huh. Well, since you're back, I'm gonna go get myself something to eat. How much of our ration did you leave me?"

"Not sure," I say. "Maybe nine hundred kcal?"

"Great," he says. "I'm taking it all."

I start to protest, but he's already on his way out the door.

"Don't even," he says without looking back. "I just came out of the tank."

"Hey," I say to his retreating back. "Put the wrap back on your wrist, huh?"

He pulls up his sleeve to show me. It's there, but it's not even on straight. I open my mouth to say something, but he cuts me off with an eye roll.

"Don't worry," he says. "If anyone asks, I'll tell them I'm a quick healer."

When he's gone, I crawl into bed and pick up the tablet. He'd been reading about Asher's World. I spend five seconds wondering at the fact that he's perseverating over the exact same stuff that I am before I remember that the surprising thing would be if he weren't, considering that he's basically me, to within a rounding error.

Well, me minus the past six weeks or so, anyway. For some reason, that seems to have made an increasingly big difference.

I've been giving this some thought, and here's the thing about the Asher's World expedition: Their situation wasn't actually all that different from ours. Their target planet was too hot to support life. This one isn't quite too cold, but it's close. A better reading on the O_2 levels in the atmosphere might have clued the mission planners back on Midgard in to the fact that the biosphere on Niflheim is barely hanging on, but I guess at seven-plus lights distance you get what you get.

I can't help wondering what we'd have done if this place had been just a little bit worse—a few degrees colder, a bit less oxygen, something really toxic in the atmosphere, maybe? We brought terraforming gear, but that's an insanely slow process. I've read about dozens of colonies that faced similar predicaments. Some tried to regroup, refuel, and reach for another target. Some tried to hunker down in orbit, drop their terraformers, and make it work.

Some, like the folks from Asher's World, just gave up and called it a day.

Of the ones that kept trying, I could count on one hand the number that actually succeeded. Seeding a colony is hard on a hospitable planet. On an inhospitable one, it's damn near impossible.

And what about one like Niflheim? Time will tell, I guess.

I'm pondering that question, and thinking about what it'll mean for me if things go south here, when my ocular pings.

> **\<RedHawk>:**Hey Mick. I heard you had a rough day today. I'm off shift at 16:00. Want to meet for dinner? My treat.

The answer is, *Hell, yes,* but that's competing in my head with, *How the shit can you afford to spring for dinner?* and before I can sort that out and formulate an answer, another message pops up.

> **\<Mickey8>:**Absolutely. See you then, pal.

Oh *hell* no. I open up a private window.

> **\<Mickey8>:**No you don't, Eight. This one's mine.
> **\<Mickey8>:**Tank funk, Seven. I need real food. There's still three hundred kcal on our card for the day. You can have it back.
> **\<Mickey8>:**Look, friend. I've almost died twice in the past twenty-four hours, and you were napping both times. If you want to push this, we can meet back at the cycler in twenty and go for real this time.
> **\<Mickey8>:**Wow. That escalated quickly.
> **\<Mickey8>:**No joke, Eight. If you're not back here by 15:45, it's go time.
> **\<Mickey8>:**...
> **\<Mickey8>:**So?
> **\<Mickey8>:**Fine. Fine. Have your fancy dinner, you big baby. Man, I cannot wait until you get eaten.

"Go nuts," Berto says. "Anything you want, buddy."

My eyes drift to the rabbit.

"Within reason," he adds. "I'm not made of kcal, you know."

I glance around the caf. We're on the early side for dinner, so it's not too crowded yet. There's a bunch of Security types at one table near the door, though. One of them meets my eyes. He says something to his friends, and the table bursts out laughing.

Great. Now I'm the Expendable who's afraid to die. I'm pretty sure that's as low as you can sink in terms of social standing around here.

"Hey," Berto says. "You still with me?"

I turn back to the service counter. "Give me a limit," I say. "I could literally eat everything they have back there."

Berto looks down at the counter and scratches the back of his head. "Tell you what. Keep it under a thousand kcal, okay?"

I stare up at him. "A thousand? Seriously?"

"Yeah," he says. "I meant what I said before, buddy. You're my best friend. I shouldn't have lied to you. I guess this is my way of apologizing."

He's still lying to me, but at this moment I don't remotely care. I order potatoes, fried crickets, and a tiny bowl of chopped lettuce and tomatoes. That only comes to seven hundred kcal, so I top it off with a mug of paste. Waste not, want not, right? As my tray slides out of the dispenser, I see that Berto's ordering as well.

He gets the rabbit.

"Berto?" I say. "What the hell, friend?"

He grins. "You didn't think I was starving myself for you, did you? Come on, Mickey. I feel bad, but not that bad. This isn't me flagellating myself. It's more of a share-the-wealth kind of thing."

Our total is twenty-four hundred kcal. Berto shows his ocular to the scanner. It flashes green.

"Seriously," I say. "What. The. Hell."

Berto's grin widens. "You remember when I took you out in the flitter?"

Oh God, do I remember.

"Yeah," I say. "I think so."

His tray pops out. We gather our food and head toward a table in the back. I can feel the Security guys' eyes on the back of my neck as we go.

"Remember when we swung out over that ridge line, about twenty klicks south of the dome?"

That whole trip is actually a blur, and I have no idea what he's talking about, but in the interest of moving the story along, I nod. We sit, and he immediately tears into his rabbit haunch.

"There was a rock formation at the top of the ridge," he says around a mouthful of meat. "We flew right over it. Do you remember?"

At this point, I think we've reached the limits of bullshit. "No," I say. "I honestly don't."

He shrugs. "Doesn't matter. Picture a spike of granite, maybe thirty meters tall, with another slab just a little shorter leaning against it. The space between is maybe ten meters at the base, tapering down to nothing at the top."

"Okay," I say. "I guess I can picture that." Actually, now that he's described it, I think I do remember seeing the place he's talking about. I thought at the time that it might be a good spot for bouldering.

That was before the creepers, obviously.

"Right," Berto says. "So for the last few weeks I've been telling anybody who would listen that I thought I could get the flitter through the gap. Crazy, right? I mean, even rolled ninety degrees, the clearance on either side would be like half a meter at the top end, and you'd have to initiate the roll with a margin of maybe a tenth of a second."

"Yeah," I say. "That does sound crazy. So?"

"So," Berto says, "everybody else thought it was crazy too. I've been collecting bets."

He stops there to take a bite, but I don't need him to finish that thought.

"You did it?"

"Yeah," he says, with a grin that I don't think I've seen since he won that goddamned pog-ball tournament. "I did. I collected three thousand kcal, all told. Sweet, right?"

"You . . ." I begin, then have to stop to collect myself. "You could have died, Berto."

"Could have," he says. "Didn't."

I set my fork down beside my tray, and my hands clench into fists. "You risked your life. You risked your fucking life for two days' rations."

His smug grin fades. "Hey," he says. "Easy, there, buddy. It wasn't that big a deal."

"Not a big deal? You risked your life for goddamned *kcal,* Berto. You wouldn't risk jack fucking shit for me."

Berto's face goes slack. He stares at me. I stare back.

This is the point where I realize that I've just told him something that I'm not supposed to know . . . or, wait, did I? Good lord, I can't keep track of my own lies at this point, let alone Berto's.

"Mickey?" Berto says. "What do you mean by that, exactly?"

I open my mouth to reply, then let it fall closed again.

"You just came out of the tank," he says. "Isn't that right, Mickey?"

I look away. One of the Security guys is staring at us.

"Yeah, Berto. You know I did."

"I thought I did," Berto says. "Gotta admit, though. You're making me wonder."

I stab a potato, bring it to my mouth, and chew. This meal is the first solid food I've eaten in over two days. It's a sin that I'm not enjoying this as much as I should be. Over the course of five seconds I decide to come clean with him and then change my mind again a half dozen times. When I look back at Berto, he's chewing slowly and watching me through narrowed eyes. *I didn't die*, I picture myself saying. *You left me in that fucking crevasse, but I didn't die.* As he takes another bite of rabbit, I imagine adding, *Maybe I should have offered you a couple days' rations to come back for me, huh?* I'm working my way up to actually opening my mouth and saying it when the goon who's been watching us gets up from his table and starts over toward ours.

I know this guy, vaguely at least. His name is Darren. He's big for a colonist, almost as tall as Berto and probably ten kilos heavier, with close-cut dark hair and a weird curly tuft of beard growing from the bottom of his chin. He's not stupid—nobody who was selected for this expedition is stupid—but he's always struck me as having the kind of attitude that dumb guys get when you give them just a little bit of power. He stops a pace or two behind Berto, folds his arms across his chest, and tilts his head to one side.

"Hey," he says. "You gentlemen enjoying our rations tonight?"

Berto turns to look, then brings the rabbit haunch to his mouth and takes a slow, deliberate bite.

"Yeah," he says with his mouth still full. "Very much, actually."

Darren's face twists into a scowl. "You're an ass, Gomez. You could have wasted yourself and our only functional flitter out there this morning."

Berto shrugs, turns back to me, and takes another bite.

"Flitter's no use without me anyway. Nasha won't fly anything without a gravitic grid." He chews, swallows, and wipes his mouth with his sleeve. "Anyway, if you felt so strongly about protecting colony assets, why'd you put kcal into the pool? I wouldn't have done it if there weren't any stakes." The grin comes back now, and he looks up at me and winks. "Oh, who am I kidding? Sure I would have. This place is boring, and that was a hell of a ride."

A hell of a ride. I just fucking bet it was. My jaw is knotted so tight that it feels like my teeth might crack. Darren's eyes shift to me.

"What's your problem, Barnes?"

I don't trust my voice to answer. Darren's eyebrows come together at the bridge of his nose, and he takes a half step forward.

"Seriously," he says. "If you've got something to say, say it. If you don't, wipe that look off your face."

"Back off," Berto says. "Mickey's had a rough couple of days."

"Yeah," Darren says. "I heard. He got two of our guys killed yesterday, and then today he dipped out of a fight and left Chen to rescue his ass for the second time in twenty-four hours. I feel for you, man."

Berto sets the rabbit bone he'd been gnawing carefully onto

his tray, then puts both hands flat on the table. He's not smirking anymore.

"Step away, Darren."

"Suck it, Gomez. I just ate goddamned cycler paste for dinner, and I'm not in the mood for—"

He stops there, because he's made the extremely poor choice to shove the back of Berto's head. As I said, Darren's a big guy, and he's Security. He's probably used to people letting him get away with that kind of stuff.

Berto, to my knowledge, has never let anyone get away with that kind of stuff.

Berto pushes up from the table and pivots on his back leg, already swinging as the bench he'd been sitting on slams into Darren's shins.

There's a reason Berto is hell at pog-ball. For someone as tall and lanky as he is, he's inhumanly fast. Darren hasn't even managed to get his hands up when Berto's fist smacks into the left side of his face and drops him.

At this point, what had been standard middle-school bullshit turns into a riot.

I'm up and coming around the table as Darren tries to get back to his feet. He makes it as far as one knee before Berto puts a foot to his shoulder and shoves him back down. Berto still has one foot in the air when the first of the goons from Darren's table slams into him and drives him facedown onto our table hard enough that I have to jump back to keep from being knocked down as it slides a half meter across the floor under the impact. Berto tries to wriggle free, but two more are on him now, kicking his legs out from under him and pinning his arms behind his back. I manage to get my good hand on one of their shoulders before someone grabs me by the collar, yanks me off my feet, slams me facedown onto the floor, and plants a knee in the middle of my back. The last thing I feel is the tines of a Taser pressed against the back of my neck.

"EXPLAIN YOURSELVES."

I glance over at Berto. He's staring at a spot on the wall behind Marshall's head. After an awkward five seconds of silence, I say, "This was a bit of a misunderstanding, sir."

Marshall closes his eyes and visibly unclenches his jaw. When he opens them again, they're narrowed to slits.

"A misunderstanding," he says. "Is that how you would characterize the events of this afternoon, Mr. Gomez?"

"No, sir," Berto says. "I believe everyone involved understood what was happening quite clearly."

"I see," Marshall says. "And what, exactly, was this thing that everyone so clearly understood?"

Berto can't keep a hint of a smile from creeping onto his face.

"Primarily that the Security officers involved were upset about the consequences of their own poor judgment, and one of them decided to work out his frustrations by assaulting an innocent bystander."

"Huh," Marshall says. "Mr. Drake assaulted you? How is it, then, that he's in Medical with a cracked zygomatic arch, while you appear to be completely uninjured?"

Berto shrugs. "I said he assaulted me. I didn't say he did a good job of it."

Marshall's scowl deepens, and he turns to me. "Do you agree with the way Gomez is characterizing this incident, Mr. Barnes?"

"Basically, yes," I say. "Darren came over to talk to us on his own. We weren't even looking at him. He was clearly pretty upset about having to eat cycler paste for dinner, and it seemed like he was hoping to start something with me over it. Once things got going he did seem to be a bit surprised, but I'm not sure why he should have been. I mean, he did lay hands on Berto first."

Marshall's face twists into a *just ate dog shit* grimace.

"Yes, well. I'd like to come down on you over this, especially since this is the second time I've had the two of you in my office in the past twenty-four hours. Unfortunately, however, surveillance video appears to back up your claim for the most part. Drake clearly approached you unsolicited, and he does appear to have at least touched Gomez prior to being coldcocked. Honestly, I expect better from our Security team." He doesn't clarify whether he means better judgment, or better skills at fistfighting. Instead, he leans back in his chair and folds his arms across his chest. "I am curious, though. Why was Drake eating cycler paste while the two of you were enjoying a comparative feast? If I recall correctly, I docked both of your rations yesterday, while he's currently allocated two thousand kcal per day." He strokes his chin thoughtfully. "And regardless of his reasons, why in the world would he have held you responsible?"

Berto shoots me a quick look, but I've got nothing.

"It's hard to say, sir," he says. "Maybe he had a big breakfast?"

"I see," Marshall says. "So it wouldn't have had anything to do with this?"

He taps a tablet lying on his desk, and a video clip pops up in my ocular. I blink to stream. It's a grainy, long-distance view of Berto's flitter diving toward a jumble of rocks piled at the crest of a snowy ridgeline. The formation looks pretty much the way I remember it, with two slabs rising up from a boulder field to form a narrow triangle. From this angle, there doesn't appear to be any possible way that the flitter can fit through the gap, and even though I know what happens, I can feel my stomach clenching. Berto pulls up level about a hundred meters out, adjusts his altitude slightly, and then rolls the plane at the last instant so that it passes through the rocks without so much as scratching the paint.

"Oh," Berto says. "You caught that, huh?"

"Yes," Marshall says. "We caught that. We are in a state of heightened alert at the moment, Gomez. We have been losing people, and we have precious few to spare. As a result, we are keeping an eye on things. There is very little you can do that we won't catch. Now, given that you are aware of our precarious position in terms of both personnel and material resources, would you care to explain why you found it necessary to risk both your own life and, more importantly, two thousand kilos of irreplaceable metal and electronics for what appears to be a juvenile stunt?"

Berto sits silent, eyes fixed on the wall. Marshall stares him down for what feels like a very long time.

"Fine," Marshall says finally. "I'm aware of your wager, obviously. I don't suppose there's any point in explaining to you all the regulations you've violated in the past two days, because you clearly don't care." He leans forward, plants his elbows on his desk, and sighs. "At this point, I'm not sure what to do with you, Gomez. I can't afford to ground you, which honestly is the very least that you deserve, and sadly flogging is not an approved disciplinary technique under standard Union guidelines." He pauses then, and turns to me. "Barnes—do you have any suggestions?"

I glance quickly at Berto, then back to Marshall. "Me, sir? No, sir."

Marshall sighs again, and leans back in his chair. "Given my limited options, I suppose the best I can do is increase your workload and cut your rations. You'll cover Adjaya's shifts aloft as well as your own for the next five days, Gomez. That should keep you out of trouble, at the least. In addition, I'm reducing your rations a further ten percent. That shouldn't bother you, as you won't have time to eat in any case. I'm also blocking your ability to accept transfers from any other personnel, just in case you have any more ideas for scamming your fellow colonists."

"Sir—" Berto begins, but Marshall cuts him off before he can even finish that first syllable.

"Don't waste your breath, Gomez. As I said, this is the absolute *least* that you deserve. If you press me on this, you may force me to examine more radical solutions to the problem you present."

Berto looks like he has more to say, but with a visible struggle he swallows, fixes his eyes back on that spot behind Marshall's head, and says, "Yes, sir. Thank you, sir."

"Excellent," Marshall says. "Go." As we rise and turn to leave, he says, "Oh, Barnes? I don't know what your involvement in this incident was, but on the presumption that you probably had something to do with it, I'll be reducing your rations by five percent as well."

I turn back to him. "What? No!"

"Ten percent," Marshall says. When I open my mouth again, he says, "Care to make it fifteen?"

My jaw snaps shut with an audible click.

"No, sir," I say. "Thank you, sir."

"Another ten percent? Come on, Seven! You can't do that to me!"

"First," I say, "I'm not doing it to *you*. I'm doing it to *us*. And second, *I'm* not doing it. If you want to bitch at somebody, bitch at Berto. He's the one who decided to screw half the Security Section out of their rations and then clock one of them in the caf."

Eight slumps down onto the bed and drops his face into his hands. "I can't do this, Seven. I never got a chance to recover from the tank. You know this body still hasn't eaten a single damned bite of solid food, right? Eating is all I think about from the time I wake up until the time I go to sleep. Now we're down to, what, seven-twenty each? I can't do it. I cannot fucking do it."

"I'm sorry," I say. "Seriously, I know you must be going through hell right now, but look—there's nothing to be done. Unless we want to go back to the corpse hole, we're just going to have to deal with this."

He looks up. "I'm not gonna lie, Seven. The corpse hole is sounding better and better right now."

I drop into the desk chair, pull my boots off, and prop my feet up on the bed beside him. "It might come to that, friend-o, but we're not there yet. Tell you what—you can have whatever's left on our account for today, and I guess . . . nine hundred tomorrow? Does that help?"

He groans.

"Look," I say, "that's only leaving me five-forty for the next thirty-six hours, and I didn't even get to finish my dinner before Berto started his little riot. I know you're dying right now, but this isn't exactly a picnic for me either."

He sighs, and flops over onto his back.

"I know," he says to the ceiling, "I know you're hurting too, and I do appreciate the offer. You're a good guy, Seven. I'm gonna feel terrible when I finally wind up strangling you in your sleep and eating your corpse."

I don't have time to come up with a response to that before my ocular pings.

<Black Hornet>:Hey there. You off-shift?

I start to compose an answer, but Eight beats me to the punch.

<Mickey8>:Yeah. Thought you were flying tonight?
<Black Hornet>:I was, but now I'm not. Looks like they swapped Berto into my slots for the next few days for some reason, so I'm free until further notice. Want to hang?
<Mickey8>:Hells yes!
<Black Hornet>:Sweet. See you in ten.

"Sorry," Eight says. "You gotta go."

"Hey," I begin, but he cuts me off.

"No, Seven. Don't even. I need this. I *need* this. I was mostly joking about strangling you in your sleep, but if you try to fight me on this, I swear that I will end you."

The rage that boils up in me now is completely out of proportion to anything that he said. I recognize that.

I recognize it, but I don't care.

"Look," I say. "I get that you're having a rough go, you big fucking baby, but you're really starting to push it, you know that? I've taken two days of hazard duty while you've been napping up here, and I just offered to give you three-quarters of our rations for the next two days out of the goodness of my dumbass heart. You just came out of the tank, fine, you're hungry—but I'm hungry too, and I almost got killed today, and anyway there's nothing I remember about tank funk that makes us extra-horny. So if you want to keep walking this road, we can head down to Marshall's office together right now and settle this for good."

He stares at me for a long five seconds, his jaw hanging slightly open.

"Wait," he says finally. "What? You think this is a sex thing?"

That sets me back. "Uh . . . yes?"

He groans, sits up, and rubs his face with both hands. "Good God, Seven. Did I not just tell you that I'm starving to death? You think I've got the energy for sex right now? When Nasha gets here, I'm not gonna try to get her out of her jumpsuit, you idiot. I'm gonna try to talk her into feeding me. You got yours from Berto, even if you didn't get all of it down your neck, for some reason. You've got to give me this."

And just like that, the anger drains away.

"Oh," I say. "Right."

"Right. So?"

I stare at him. He stares back. After a few seconds of this, he rolls his eyes and points to the door.

"Right," I say again.

I pull on my boots, and I go.

SO HERE'S A fun story about starvation. Everybody knows Eden was the first colony, right? The first place old Earth successfully infected with her children. Not everybody knows, though, that the mission that dropped the beachhead on Eden was actually our second attempt.

The first, on a ship called the *Ching Shih,* went off almost forty years prior, twenty years or so after the end of the Bubble War. That mission was our species' first desperate attempt at flinging ourselves past our own heliopause—and like most of our first attempts at most things, it didn't go particularly well. The ship didn't have a cycler, and their engines weren't anywhere near as efficient as ours, and Earth to Eden is a long jump even by modern standards. They were expecting to be twenty-one years in transit, and they were expecting to sustain themselves for that entire time with shipboard agriculture.

Given what they were up against, and the primitive state of their technology base, and their woeful ignorance about what the interstellar environment can do to you at relativistic speeds, it's actually pretty impressive that they got as far as they did. They were almost twelve years out when their crops began failing. As far as anyone could tell from their transmissions, they never did fully understand what was happening. The best guess in the account I read was that the plants were suffering from cumulative radiation damage, compounded over multiple generations until there were just too many mutations for the organisms to be viable anymore. The *Ching Shih*'s field generators weren't as efficient as ours, and their Agriculture Section was located in the front third of the ship, apparently on the theory that the humans were the ones who really needed the shielding, so those poor plants were taking a serious beating.

The thing about disasters in interstellar space is that some of them are fast, and some of them are slow—but either kind can leave you really, really dead. The *Ching Shih* died slowly. To their credit, they documented the entire process, even when it was clear that their situation was completely hopeless, in the interest of making sure the next mission wouldn't make the same mistakes. They got through most of a year by progressively cutting rations. When it was obvious that wasn't going to be enough, the mission commander put out a standing request for volunteers to be converted from calorie sinks to calorie sources.

Starvation hurts. She got a surprising number of takers.

It took another three years before she finally faced up to the fact that even if she cut the crew down to the minimum needed to keep the ship running, and maybe still be able to unpack their stored embryos at the journey's end, they weren't going to make it. Their Agriculture Section was producing next to nothing by then, and the mission plan had relied on the crops to do a fair bit of their carbon cycling as well as providing food for the crew, so things were falling apart on multiple levels. They were still four years out from Eden when the last twelve crew members powered the ship down, stripped to their underwear, and stepped out of the main air lock.

The *Ching Shih* is still out there somewhere, humming through the void at point-six *c* or so—and so, I suppose, are the bodies of those last twelve would-be colonists. I find myself wondering sometimes if someone somewhere might see them zip by someday and wonder where they're going in such a hurry . . . and why the hell they're not wearing suits.

THE PROBLEM WITH getting kicked out of your room when you live in a rat-warren dome on a planet with a poisonous atmosphere and hostile natives is that there aren't a lot of places to

go. We don't have theaters. We don't have coffee shops. We don't
have parks, or plazas, or hangouts. What we have, mostly, is
workspaces, the majority of which range from unpleasant (sew-
age reclamation) to hostile (Security's ready room). The Agriculture Section is actually not a bad place to be, if you can avoid
getting depressed about the feeble state of most of the growing
things, but I'm not welcome there except on days when I've been
seconded out to them, so that's a no-go.

For lack of better options, I head down to the caf.

It's on the late side for dinner now, so I don't anticipate finding
a big crowd there, but when I walk through the door, it's even
more sparse than I expected. There's a group of four at a table
near the back, picking over two trays of potatoes between them,
and a guy I know vaguely from the Biology Section sitting alone in
the opposite corner, nursing what looks like a paste smoothie and
staring down at his tablet. His name is Highsmith. He's a history
buff of sorts. I once had a fun conversation with him about the
parallels between the Diaspora and the original spread of the human species out of Africa on old Earth. Most of his opinions were
wrong, but I had a good time telling him exactly why that was so.

I briefly—very briefly—consider asking if he wants company,
before realizing first that my ration is zeroed out for the day, and
then how weird it would be for me to sit down across from him
in the cafeteria with no food of my own and then try to strike up
a conversation. Instead, I take a bench at a table near the door,
as far from both him and the others as I can get, pull out my own
tablet, and start browsing for a distraction.

After ten minutes or so without inspiration, I finally decide to
go old school, with an article about the failure of the old Earth
Vikings' Greenland colony. Their situation, as it turns out, wasn't
all that different from ours in a lot of ways. They tried to build a
sustainable society in a cold, inhospitable place where their tradi-

tional food crops wouldn't grow. They got into fights with hostile locals. I assume their leader was kind of a jerk.

Eventually, they starved to death.

That last bit takes me back to Eight, lying on our bed moaning about how he's digesting his own liver, and to Nasha, going up there probably expecting a fun time and instead getting him-as-me begging her to buy him something to eat.

Something to eat.

Where would they go to get something to eat?

I'm already on my feet before that thought has a chance to finish forming. Highsmith looks up from his tablet as my bench flips over behind me and I scoot over to the door. How long has it been? And how long would it take Eight to talk Nasha into coming down here? And how long would it take them to make the trip? I don't know the answer to any of those questions exactly, but I can't help but think that they're probably converging rapidly. I ping Eight.

<Mickey8>:Where are you?

<Mickey8>:On our way to the caf. Why?

<Mickey8>:Where, specifically?

<Mickey8>:Bottom of the central stairs. What the hell, Seven?

They'll be coming around the corner in ten seconds.

Maybe less than ten seconds.

It's okay. I've got time. I don't even need to run, really, just fast-walk down the corridor to the next intersection and take a turn. That done, I lean back against the wall, breathe in deep, and let it back out slowly. What if my brain hadn't kicked in when it did? What would have happened if Nasha and Eight had walked into the caf to find me sitting there staring at my tablet?

Come to that, what's Highsmith going to think when he sees

me walking back through the door, twenty seconds after I left in such a hurry, with Nasha beside me?

Ugh. With Nasha, and wearing a different shirt. Hopefully he's not too observant.

Best not to think about that. More importantly, where do I go now?

Can't go back to my room. I think it's probably safe to assume that they'll be headed there as soon as Eight has something in his belly.

I give some brief thought to heading up to Nasha's rack. She shares with a woman from Agriculture named Trudy. Trudy's nice enough. She'd probably let me hang around if I told her I was waiting for Nasha—who would eventually actually show up, and probably wonder how I got from my rack to hers quicker than she did, and what the hell I was doing there anyway.

Yeah, that won't work.

There's really only one other public space in the dome. Fortunately, this one is pretty much guaranteed to be empty more or less all the time.

I sigh, and straighten, and head for the gym.

A WORKOUT CENTER is not standard equipment on a beachhead colony. That we have one is a testament to Hieronymus Marshall's enduring belief in the importance of physical fitness as a component of moral and ethical fitness.

The fact that it is the only space in the dome guaranteed to be empty at any time of day or night is testament to the fact that, despite what Hieronymus Marshall might feel on the topic, exercise is the absolute last thing anyone wants to do during a famine.

The truth is, I don't even know exactly where the gym is. I have to pull up a map of the dome on my ocular to figure it out. Turns out it's right down the corridor from the cycler, which strikes me as oddly appropriate in the moment.

I take the long route around, following one of the spoke corridors to the outer ring and then taking that halfway around the dome before cutting back in, with the idea that I'd be less likely to run into anyone on their way to the caf or to start the new shift in Agriculture. I still pass a half dozen people, though, and I feel like they're all looking at me strangely. Paranoia? Maybe—or maybe they all just saw Eight and Nasha passing by, they've figured out exactly what's going on, and they're pinging Security as soon as I'm out of sight.

We've only been at this for two days now, and I'm already losing it.

When I finally reach the gym, I crack open the door and duck inside like I'm being pursued. I slam the door behind me, close my eyes, and lean my forehead against the cool plastic surface.

"Is there a problem?"

My head snaps around and my heart lurches so hard that for an instant I'm afraid I might be dying. This isn't much of a gym—just a row of treadmills, a rack for pull-ups, and a half dozen dumbbells in a space maybe two or three times the size of my room.

It's not empty.

In fact, there's a woman on one of the treadmills. She's turned around now, feet on the side rails, mat running away beneath her.

It takes me a long second of heart-thudding panic to realize that it's Cat.

We stare each other down. She stops the treadmill, steps down onto the floor, and folds her arms across her chest.

"What are you doing here?" I manage.

She rolls her eyes. "You sure you're the one who should be asking that question?"

I close my eyes and breathe until my pulse settles down to something close to normal. When I open them again, Cat's expression is shading from confusion to concern.

"Sorry," I say. I cross the room in three steps, turn, and lower myself down to sit on the last treadmill in the row. "I'm having a weird day."

"Yeah," she says. "I know. Do you need to go back to Medical? You look a little crazed right now."

"No," I say, maybe a little too quickly. "No. I'm fine. I just wanted a little space to myself, I guess, and you kind of startled me. It never occurred to me that someone might actually be down here working out."

She smiles, drops her arms to her sides, and comes over to sit beside me. "That's fair."

I turn to look at her. Her hair is pulled back into a high ponytail, and she's dressed in the tight gray under-suit from her combat armor. Somehow, she manages to wear it well. She isn't really sweating, so I'm guessing she hasn't been here for long.

"Seriously," I say. "What are you up to down here? You know we're in the middle of a famine, right?"

"Yeah," she says. "I'm aware."

"So?"

She sighs. "Gillian Branch was my bunkmate."

"Oh," I say. "Who's that?"

She shoots me a sharp, angry look. "We're all just anonymous goons to you, huh?"

I lean back, both hands raised in surrender.

"No! No, it's definitely not a you thing. It's a me thing. I don't socialize much with anybody, Cat. A lot of people around here think I'm some kind of abomination, you know? And a lot of the ones who want to talk to me are just looking to play out some weird fetish fantasy. It's just easier most of the time if I keep to myself."

"Oh," she says. "Ghost chasers, huh?"

"Yeah," I say. "You're not . . ."

Her eyes narrow. "Excuse me?"

"Sorry," I say. "It's just . . ."

"I already told you I'm not a Natalist, if that's what you're asking."

"Right," I say. "I mean, that's good, I guess. Berto's told me more than once that being fetishized sounds fantastic—but trust me, it's not."

Her face softens, and I lower my hands.

"Yeah," she says. "I get that. You may not have noticed, but Maggie Ling and I are the only two women on Niflheim with epicanthal folds. I've gotten a little of that myself." She grins. "Tell you what. I won't objectify you if you won't objectify me."

I offer her my hand. "Done."

We shake. Her smile widens briefly, then fades when she drops my hand.

"Anyway," she says, "Gillian was part of the sortie yesterday."

"Oh," I say. "Right. *That* Gillian."

She nods, and looks away.

"Oh," I say. "Oh, I'm sorry. Afterward, you didn't seem . . . I mean . . ."

"I don't want to make this more than it is," she says. "She wasn't exactly my best friend. It's not the easiest thing, sharing a space that small with another person. If I'm being honest, most of the time we were barely friends at all."

"But still . . ."

"Yeah," she says. "But still. I went back to my rack after my shift ended today, and I just . . ."

"Couldn't?"

She rubs her face with both hands. "Right. I couldn't." She lets out a strangled laugh, then drops her face into her hands as it tails off into a sniffling sob. "You'd think I'd be psyched to have the place to myself, right?"

I reach out to touch her shoulder. She lifts her head to look at me, then scoots over until she's half onto my treadmill and our hips are touching. I slide my arm around her, and she leans her head against my chest.

"I'm sorry," she says. "You didn't come here to be my grief counselor." She straightens, and turns to look at me. "Why did you come here, really? You've got a solo rack, right? If you wanted privacy, why didn't you just go there?"

"That's a good question," I say.

She stares at me. I stare back. After what feels like forever but is actually probably more like ten seconds, she says, "Are you going to answer it?"

I sigh. "Nasha's there."

"Oh," she says. "Are you . . ."

"She's with someone else."

That stops her for a moment.

"In your rack," she says finally.

I shrug. She shakes her head.

"You know what? I don't want to know."

"Yeah," I say. "That's a good call."

We sit in silence then for a while. I'm starting to think that I'm going to have to go wander the corridors all night like the freaking phantom of Niflheim when she says, "I may regret this, but . . . I've got a double, you know."

I turn to look at her, one eyebrow raised. "Are you objectifying me right now?"

She laughs. "I am not. All I'm doing right now is offering an empty bed to a homeless person. I've gotta say, though—I'm kind of surprised that you and Nasha are open. Sure didn't seem like she thought so yesterday."

I shrug. "It's complicated."

"Okay," she says. "Is it the kind of complicated where I wind up getting gutted tomorrow?"

"No," I say. "I mean, probably not. Worst-case, I might get shoved down the corpse hole at some point."

She brings one finger to her chin and pantomimes deep thought.

"You know," she says finally, "I think that's a chance I'm willing to take."

"Hey," Cat says. "Wake up."

I open my eyes. It takes me a disoriented minute to realize where I am. We pushed Cat's bed and her former roommate's together last night, but we both wound up sleeping on her side— Cat out of habit, I think, and me out of a vague sense that there's something disrespectful about crashing in a recently deceased person's bunk. Cat's propped up on one elbow now, with her arm pressing down on my shoulder and her face almost touching mine.

To be clear: nothing remotely sexual happened between us last night.

It may sound strange to hear that when I just said that we basically slept on top of one another, but when it came down to it I couldn't untangle what I was feeling about Cat from what I was feeling about Nasha and Eight, and Cat . . . I think she just needed a warm body to keep the monsters away.

I was okay with that. I know how she feels.

"It's almost nine," she says. "Do you need to be somewhere?"

That's actually a good question. I blink to the day's duty roster.

Looks like I'm supposed to be in Hydroponics today, trying to coax a bunch of half-dead vines to squeeze out a tomato or two. In fact, I was supposed to be there an hour ago. I haven't received a no-show, though, so Eight must be down there now, pinching off buds and checking pH levels.

Apparently I take duty on eaten-by-creepers days, and he takes duty when it's time to babysit plants. This is something we're going to need to discuss.

In the meantime, though, it looks like I've got a day to myself, for pretty much the first time since we made landfall. All I have to do is make sure I don't go anywhere near Eight, or bump into anyone else who might have seen him today.

This would be easier to accomplish if we didn't live in an inverted salad bowl less than a klick across.

"I'm off today," I say. "What about you?"

She shrugs. "I almost got killed in the line of duty twice in the past two days. In Security, I guess that earns you a half shift. I don't have to report until noon."

I wriggle out from under her arm and sit up, taking care not to jar my still-swollen left wrist any more than I have to. She rolls away and gets to her feet. We're both still wearing our underclothes, gray shapeless shirts and shorts covered in discolored patches from too much sweat and too many washings. They're so ugly that in a weird way seeing her like this feels almost more intimate than being naked.

"So?" Cat says. "What's your plan for the day?"

I rub my face with both hands and push my hair back from my forehead. She opens her locker and digs out a clean shirt.

"Not sure," I say. "It's been a while since I've had an off day."

The truth is that my plan is to slink around the dome hoping nobody sees me and realizes that I'm also down in Ag using an eyedropper to hand-feed baby tomatoes, but I can't really say that. Cat steps into her pants, then sits back down on the bed to pull on her boots.

"Well," she says, "my plan at the moment is to get something to eat. You interested?"

I grin. "Sure. You buying?"

She looks back over her shoulder with narrowed eyes. "No, I'm not buying," she says, "and just so you know, if you try touching my food again, you're gonna have two mangled hands instead of one."

Yeah, that's fair. I pull on my clothes, and we go.

THE HALLS ARE mostly empty at this time of day, and the few people we pass don't pay us much attention. Cat gets a few hellos, but even those folks mostly stare right through me. Especially since landfall, my job has been a pretty isolating one. For some reason, even most of the people who don't think I'm a soulless monster don't seem to want to associate with someone who's under what amounts to a perpetual death sentence.

At the moment, that seems to be working to my advantage.

Nobody wants to associate with someone who smells like a giant sweaty foot either, though, so we stop by the chem shower on the way down. Cat gives me an unreadable look when we get there. Is she asking if I want to share? I grin, give her a half bow, and wave her in. She shrugs, steps into the cubicle, and closes the door behind her. When she comes back out a few minutes later, I take my turn. I strip and scrub and dust-dry, and then climb back into my dirty clothes because even if I wanted to go back up to my rack, Eight is wearing my only clean change.

This reminds me that, while I miss a lot of things from Midgard to varying degrees, actual factual hot water is really close to the top of the list. The annoying thing is that there's clearly plenty of water lying around in drifts outside the dome. The systems *inside* the dome come straight from the *Drakkar,* though, so we still conserve water as if we're stuck in the interstellar desert. That won't change until we start doing local construction, and that won't happen unless and until a whole list of other things do, starting with metal fabrication and ending with resolving our issues with the creepers.

In the meantime, the chem shower is fine for sanitation, and it definitely keeps your body odor under control, but there's nothing remotely luxurious about it.

Not when you're in there by yourself, anyway.

That thought leads me to Nasha, and to Eight.

Best not to think about that now.

THE MAIN CAFETERIA is almost empty when we get there—just a couple at a table on the opposite side of the room from the food counter, heads close together, talking in whispers, and a lone Security goon near the entrance working his way through a pile of fried crickets. He nods to Cat as we pass him, and she gives him a finger-wave in return. I step to the counter and show my ocular to the scanner. It beeps, and my daily ration balance pops up in the upper left corner of my field of view.

It says I'm down six hundred kcal on the day. Looks like Eight had a big breakfast.

I'd like to be mad, but I can't blame him. The first couple days out of the tank really are a bitch.

I'm standing there, arms folded across my growling belly, trying to decide whether to splurge on a little mound of chopped yams to go with my mug of cycler paste and make this my only meal of the day, when Cat steps up beside me, close enough to brush against my shoulder.

"Are you going to order something?"

I scowl and tap the icon for the paste dispenser.

Cat smiles, shows her ocular, and orders a yam-tomato scramble. I can feel my mouth start to water, but that mound of yams I'd been eyeing might as well be a filet of beef given what's left on my balance. I grimace, gulp down a mouthful of paste from my mug, and then top it off before turning away. Three hundred kcal. That means I can have at least another half of a mug before bed tonight.

"I don't know how you stand that stuff," Cat says as her food slides out of a slot on the far side of the counter.

I glance over at her, open my mouth to say something rude, then think better of it and shake my head.

"If our friends in the Agriculture Section don't get their shit together soon," I say, "I think you're likely to find out."

She smirks. I pick up my mug of goo and take it to a table near the center of the room. Cat follows.

"You know," I say as she sits down, "you're kind of shoving your fancy-ass rich-person food in my face right now."

She laughs, but in a hesitant way that makes it clear that she's not entirely sure I'm kidding.

I am not, in fact, kidding.

None of my problems are her fault, though. I smile, and she visibly relaxes.

"Anyway," I say, "what's up in Security today? Anything new since that fiasco with the perimeter patrols?"

She takes a fat bite of her yams, chews, and swallows. I grimace and sip at my mug of paste.

"Well," she says around a second mouthful, "Amundsen is pretty worked up about this whole creeper issue. He's got us on a twelve-on-twelve-off duty cycle, which is a gigantic pain in the ass, and everyone who's on has to carry a linear accelerator at all times, which is also not great, because they're awkward and heavy and they leave you with sore shoulders at the end of a shift.

On the plus side, after what happened over the past two days, we're confined to the dome, so no more wandering around outside getting frostbite." She pauses to swallow. "I'm not even sure what he thinks we're supposed to do with an accelerator on the inside. Do you have any idea what kind of damage a ten-gram slug could do ricocheting around in here?"

She looks at me expectantly. It takes me a solid five seconds to realize that this wasn't a rhetorical question.

"Um," I say. "No?"

"A lot," she says. "That's what kind."

I'm most of the way through my paste by now. My belly still feels empty.

"Anyway," she says, "that's my jam. What about you? Have you had any more thoughts about how you're going to spend your day off?"

"Oh," I say, "you know. Hanging around. Sucking down cycler paste. Waiting to hear how Marshall's gonna kill me next. Just another day in paradise, I guess."

She laughs. Cat's laugh is not delicate. It's the sort of laugh you might expect to hear from someone who's just watched you slip on an ice patch.

"So tell me," she says as she scrapes up the last of her brunch, "what made you decide to get into the Expendable business?"

I think about making up some nonsense about service and duty, but for some reason I don't feel like I should be feeding self-serving lies to Cat. In the end I just shrug and tell her the truth.

"I wanted off of Midgard. This was the only way to make it happen."

"Ah," she says. "Got it."

I nod, turn up my mug, and let the last gritty dregs drain into my mouth.

"Wait," I say. "Got what? What do you got?"

"Why you signed on," Cat says. "You were a criminal, right? Killed somebody or something?"

This again.

"No," I say. "I didn't kill anyone."

"Huh. So what, then? Extortion? Armed robbery? Sex crimes?"

"No, no, and no. I'm not a criminal. If I were, do you really think they would have brought me onto Midgard's first colony mission?"

"As our Expendable? Yeah, maybe. During training I heard they were talking about conscripting someone."

"Yeah," I say. "I heard that too. Kinda raises questions about your judgment, doesn't it? You just let a murdering extortionist sex criminal spend the night in your room."

She grins. "I never said I was the brightest."

I run my finger around the inside of my mug to scrape up the bits of goo stuck to the bottom.

"Wow," Cat says. "You really like that stuff, huh?"

I scowl. "Oh yeah. It's the best."

She scrapes at her tray to get up the last burned bits of yam. "I never actually thought you were a murderer," she says. "I didn't believe they'd send someone like that on a colony mission, if only because they wouldn't want to screw up the gene pool. Most of the people I talked to, though, thought it was a lie when we heard that we'd gotten a volunteer. It's kind of hard to imagine someone just agreeing to . . . you know . . . do what you do. Gillian was sure you were a prisoner or something, and that they were feeding us a line about you volunteering so that we wouldn't ostracize you or whatever."

"Huh," I say. "That worked out great."

She rolls her eyes. "Oh come on. You've got friends. I've seen you around with Gomez, and Nasha seems to like you well enough. You still haven't answered my question, though. What were you thinking when you signed on to be the official crash test dummy for a beachhead colony?"

I could go into what actually got me into Gwen's office now.

I could, but I won't. Maybe a few self-serving lies wouldn't be so bad.

"Who knows?" I say. "Maybe I'm an idealist. Maybe I was just looking for a way to do my part for the Union."

She laughs again, harder this time. "Wow," she says. "How's that working out for you?" She sobers then, looks down at her empty tray and then back up at me. "Actually," she says, "it's working out pretty well for you, isn't it? Better than for Gillian or Rob or Dugan, anyway."

I'm not sure where she's going with this, but for some reason a chill runs down the back of my neck.

"What I mean," she says, "is that there are some definite advantages to being unkillable in a place like this, aren't there?"

"I'm not unkillable," I say. "I get killed all the damn time. That's the entire point of being an Expendable, isn't it?"

"And yet," she says, "here you are. Where's Gillian today?"

I don't have an answer for that. We sit in silence as Cat grimaces and downs a shot of cycler paste that she's gotten to supplement her meal. Medical says we all ought to be drinking a few hundred milliliters of paste per day for the vitamins. Apparently yams and crickets aren't actually a completely balanced diet. When she's done, Cat leans back in her chair and her smile returns.

"Anyway," she says, "totally unrelated, but I wanted to say . . . I guess . . . thanks, Mickey. I know last night was a little weird, but . . ."

"It wasn't weird," I say. "I get it."

She looks away. "Yeah. I just . . . I needed that, you know?"

I'm not sure what to say to that, so I reach across the table and touch her hand. She puts her other hand over mine for just a second before pulling away.

"Hey," she says, "what's your duty cycle look like tonight?"

I hesitate, but I can't come up with a good reason to lie about this. "I think I'm off tonight?"

She leans forward again, pushes back from the table, and picks up her tray. "Really? You're off now, right? How does that work?"

"You know," I say. "They make allowances when I'm fresh out of the tank."

"Wow," she says. "No kidding. The benefits just keep on coming, huh?"

I can't tell if she's smiling or not as she walks over to the refuse bin and drops her tray.

"Anyway," she says, "ping me around twenty-two hundred if you're free. Maybe we can do something fun together."

After Cat's gone, I dig out my tablet and run a search on the history of Expendables in colony expeditions. I'd always assumed that they were a standard part of the process, but in fact the technology has only been viable for the past two hundred years or so—and even in that span a lot of missions haven't made use of them. That seems crazy from a practical standpoint. When you're a half dozen lights from the nearest resupply, with a tiny pool of adults and a bunch of embryos that are going to take years of growing before they become useful, the ability to make new colonists more or less on demand ought to be compelling.

Turns out there are a lot of objections, though. The religious ones are obvious, even if they don't quite mesh with me. Apparently there are also some ethical issues with pulling someone off the streets or out of prison and forcing him to die for you over and over and over again. Landing a volunteer changes some of those considerations, obviously, but what are the odds of that happening?

It's possible I should have done some of this reading before giving Gwen my DNA. I'm not sure it would have dissuaded me—that torture machine was a powerful motivator—but I could at least have asked for a bigger signing bonus.

It's closing in on noon by the time I finish my reading, and the caf is starting to fill up. My stomach is already empty and rumbling, and watching my fellow colonists loading up their trays is not helping. I blink to my ration card. I've got four hundred and fifty kcal left for the day.

Correction. *We've* got four hundred and fifty kcal left for the day. If I'm going to stick to my deal with Eight, he's got a claim on three hundred of those.

That's a big if.

What's the worst that could happen if I went ahead and tanked our ration? It's not like Eight can go to Command with a complaint.

Of course, it's not like I can either. If I'd reported this mess two days ago, I probably would have been the one who didn't get disassembled. At this point, though, I'm confident that if Marshall gets wind of us, we're both in the slurry.

Also, Eight did say something this morning about murdering me in my sleep. I should probably just stick to the agreement.

That still leaves me with one-fifty to spend, but I can't imagine choking down another cup of slurry at the moment, so I decide to head back up to my rack and maybe take a nap to save energy.

On the central stairs, I have to edge past a man and a woman in Bio togs who are arguing about something in a loud, hand-flapping kind of way. I'm two steps past them when the man says, "Hey. Barnes?"

I turn, racking my brain for his name. Ryan? Bryan?

"Hey," I say. "What's up?"

"Not your shift," he says. "Where are you going?"

Uh-oh.

"I need to grab something from my rack," I say. "I'll be back down in five."

He scowls. "Make it three. We've got a new phage to test on the tomatoes this afternoon. It might be dangerous. They'll need you to help with the application."

"Sure," I say. "I'm on it."

They go back to arguing. I hesitate, then turn and continue, taking the stairs now two at a time.

After that, the whole nap thing turns out to be a bust. My heart is thudding in my chest by the time I get back to my rack, and it takes the better part of an hour for me to settle down enough to fall asleep. When I finally do, I wind up in the caterpillar dream again, but this time it's just a regular dream, and instead of talking he grows giant mandibles and feeding legs and starts chasing me through the forest. Pretty soon the forest fades and I'm back in the tunnels, running blindly, stumbling over loose stones while the skittering of a thousand tiny feet gets closer and closer behind.

I wake up to the sound of the door latch turning. It's Eight, back from his day playing farmer.

"Hey," I say once I've shaken off the nightmare and my heart has settled down into an almost-normal rhythm. "How are the tomatoes?"

He shakes his head. "Honestly? Not great. Most of the vines are dying, and the ones that aren't are squeezing out tomatoes that look more like overweight red raisins. Martin thinks there's something in the air—a microorganism, maybe, or some kind of trace gas—that's interfering with photosynthesis somehow. He doesn't have any actual candidates, though, so right now it's all speculation. The only thing we really know is that our tomatoes are sick." He pulls his shirt off over his head, then uses it to wipe a light sheen of sweat from his forehead. "Truth, though, it took everything I had not to shove the damn things into my mouth anyway."

"Yeah," I say. "I get that. Thanks for restraining yourself. If we wind up with another disciplinary ration cut, we're definitely going to starve to death."

He laughs, but there's no humor in it. "Pretty sure that's gonna happen anyway, friend-o. I used two-thirds of my ration this morning at breakfast, and I'm so hungry now that I could eat my own arm." He drops onto the bed. "Scoot over, huh?"

He pulls off his boots, and then lies back with a sigh.

"By the way," he says. "Have you been hanging around with Cat Chen?"

Uh-oh.

"Yeah," I say. "Sort of. Why?"

"Not sure. I ran into her on my way back up here, down near the main lock. She told me not to forget to ping her." He turns his head to look at me. "We're not screwing around on Nasha, are we? Because if we are, I have to tell you, I think that's a really, really bad idea."

"We are not," I say, and it's technically true. "Trust me—I'm just as interested in keeping all our pieces attached as you are."

"Good," he says. "Glad to hear it. Even putting Nasha aside, Chen seemed a little off, to be honest. She said something about my hand looking great, and she looked really confused when I said I didn't know what the hell she was talking about."

He glances down at my left hand lying across my belly. I've got it wrapped tight, but you can still see the purple bruise peeking out around the base of my thumb.

His wrap is slung across the back of our desk chair.

"Oh," he says. "Oh, right. That. Sorry."

SORRY.

Once again, thanks for that, asshole.

If you're not a member of the Natalist Church and you're not a student of Union history, you're probably wondering: Why am I so worked up about this? What's the big deal with multiples? I mean, on the surface, the idea of making a bunch of copies of your Expendable at once seems like a useful concept, doesn't it? For example, what happens if you've got a suicide mission that's a two-man job? Wouldn't want to risk an actual *person* for something like that, would you?

To understand the visceral reaction that most citizens have to the idea of multiples, you have to understand Alan Manikova, and you have to have at least a passing familiarity with what he did to Gault.

We've only had Expendables for a couple hundred years, but the bio-printer was actually invented long before that, even before the launch of the *Ching Shih*. Until Manikova came along, though, it wasn't much more than a curiosity. The systems they had then could scan a body, store the pattern, and re-create it down to the cellular level on demand, just like the bio-printer I pop out of every time Marshall gets me killed. Eventually they even figured out a way to reproduce synaptic connections, which modern systems don't bother doing. Theory at the time said that should be enough to accurately reproduce behavior if not consciousness, but repeated experiments, first with animals and later even with humans, demonstrated pretty clearly that their theory was fundamentally flawed. The things that came out of the bio-printers then were empty, tabula rasa bodies with less awareness or physical competence than a newborn baby. They were okay for creating fodder for medical experiments if you could overlook the obvious ethical issues, but they were not in any way a path to immortality.

To be fair, the old bio-printers weren't completely useless. People did occasionally use them to bring back babies who'd died in childbirth or shortly after—but even in those cases it usually didn't work out. The babies mostly came out of the tank breathing and with beating hearts, but they couldn't suck, couldn't swallow, couldn't cry. Sometimes, with a lot of intensive care, they made it through. More often, though, the parents just wound up burying another baby a few days or weeks after the first.

Then came Manikova.

Alan Manikova started life as the sole scion of a fantastically wealthy political dynasty on Eden. If he'd wanted to—and honestly, wouldn't you have wanted to?—he could have finished life that way as well. Most people in his position would have partied their way through school, maybe slipped into a mid-level government position at some point or maybe not, and either way spent their lives rich, fat, and happy.

Alan Manikova, though, wasn't most people. He was an epoch-defining genius, a mind so active and restless that he'd acquired doctorates in three seemingly unrelated fields before he turned twenty-five.

He was also a sociopath. That will become relevant later in the story.

Right around the time Manikova decided he was finished collecting graduate degrees, his parents both died suddenly, of unexplained causes, within a few days of one another. Six months later, after the local authorities had tried and failed to link Manikova to their deaths, he became one of the ten wealthiest people in the Union. Within a year, he'd plowed every penny of his inheritance into a venture he called Universal Eternity, Inc.

The popular press on Eden at the time thought that Universal Eternity was a boondoggle, or maybe some kind of tax dodge. Manikova didn't treat it that way, though. He could have kept the company virtual if the idea were to pull off some kind of financial scam, but he most definitely did not. Universal Eternity built a hulking research facility two hundred kilometers from the nearest town, hired huge numbers of engineers and scientists, and then . . .

Well, and then nothing. People came and went from the campus, but nobody said a word to anyone about what went on there. There was speculation that the company was engaged in aging research, or maybe in cryo-storage, but there was never any actual evidence for either theory. After a year or so, the press got bored, and people stopped paying attention to whatever Manikova was doing out there.

Five years later, he showed up on a talk show to announce that he'd finally uncovered the secret to recording and replicating a human mind.

Here again, we see the difference between Alan Manikova and most people. Immediately following an initial demonstration, in which he produced a duplicate of his company's HR director, had her say a few words to the assembled dignitaries, then immediately tranquilized her and broke her back down into slurry, the stock price of Universal Eternity skyrocketed, and Manikova went from being one of the ten richest people in the Union to far and away the richest, and in the public mind on Eden from a creepy possible parent killer to a creepy celebrity genius—maybe the greatest genius humanity had yet produced. Most people at this point would have acquired a palatial estate, maybe found a trophy spouse or two, and then spent the rest of their lives basking in the adulation.

Once again, Manikova didn't do any of that. Instead he liquidated everything he had, including Universal Eternity, Inc. The transactions involved so much cash and so many shell companies that he's one of the few people in history who can be credited with single-handedly causing a planetary economic recession. A year later, he boosted out of orbit alone in a custom-built interstellar transport packed with equipment, supplies, and the same prototype replication unit he'd used in his demonstration. He didn't tell anyone where he was going. Speculation was that he planned to become the first person to cross the galactic plane, reproducing himself as needed so that he'd still be alive at the end of the journey.

It would have been better for everyone if that had been the truth, but in fact he was bound for a recently established beachhead colony about seven lights anti-spinward from Eden that the founders had named Gault.

Even before Manikova showed up there, Gault was an interesting place. Unlike nearly every other successful colony in Union history, the expedition that founded it wasn't pulled together by Eden's planetary government. It was funded by a private group made up mostly of incredibly wealthy people who weren't happy with the fact that Eden, like Midgard and most other Union worlds, taxed the owners of the automated systems that produced pretty much everything in order to make sure that the people who didn't own those systems didn't starve in the streets.

The foundational principle on Gault was supposed to be Radical Liberty and Self Reliance, which in practice meant that none of the hundred and twenty colonists who made landfall there had the least interest in contributing anything whatsoever to the common good. They immediately broke into twenty-odd family groups, set up their own little fiefdoms, and tried to make do on their own. They'd all been pretty well resourced at the outset, and Gault was, all things considered, a pretty hospitable place, so most of them actually managed to establish themselves. The ones who had problems, though, didn't get any help from their neighbors. Apparently the Radical Liberty answer to, *Help, I'm dying*, is, *Well, you should have packed better.*

The upshot of all of this was that when Manikova arrived, he found a fragmented society of about ten thousand people, most of whom were reasonably well settled and not in immediate danger of starving to death, but none of whom were doing particularly well. At first he was greeted as a bit of a savior. He'd brought a lot of stuff with him, stuff that none of the individual groups on Gault had yet gotten around to being able to produce for themselves. He ingratiated himself with one of the smaller clans, gave them food and seeds and some shiny new tech that had been developed on Eden in the two hundred years or so since they'd boosted out. They gave him a place to live and a base of operations.

Once he was safely established, he set himself single-mindedly to making more Alan Manikovas.

As Marshall has emphasized to me more than once, building a human being from scratch takes a lot of resources. In particular, you need a lot of calcium and a lot of protein, but there are a bunch of other things that go into the mix as well. You can feed the hopper of a bio-printer with basic elements, but it takes a huge pile of wheat and beef and oranges to get everything you need for the job, and the process produces an ungodly amount of waste if you're not interested in churning the leftovers into food for a starving colony.

The ideal source of raw materials, obviously, is an already-existing human body.

It took Manikova about nine months to run through the supply of feedstock he'd brought with him to Gault. By that time he had close to a hundred copies of himself running around, and had built two additional replication units. It was another few months after that before anyone noticed that people were going missing. He'd begun the project by snatching up indigents and loners, of which Gault, by its nature, had a ton, but eventually he ran out of those and had to start grabbing people who had family and friends to miss them. Suspicion, as it always does, fell immediately on the new guy in town. The clan that had been hosting him sent Security forces to his compound to bring him in for some polite questioning.

This is when they learned that, while Manikova had been generous with seeds and trinkets, he hadn't shared the advanced military tech that he'd brought along.

On a more reasonable world—not even one with a single unified government, necessarily, but maybe one where the different polities at least talked to one another occasionally—Manikova might have been stopped. When it became apparent what he was up to, he was still outnumbered on the planet by a factor of twenty-to-one. Gault, unfortunately, was not a reasonable world. Manikova shoved every citizen of his host clan into the hopper, cranked them back out as copies of himself, armed them, and then launched an assault on his nearest neighbor. It was nearly a

year before the surviving clans even considered mounting a unified response to him. By then, Manikova was an absolute majority of the humans on the planet. The last few clans did eventually
pull together, but it was much too late by then. The only useful
thing they really accomplished was to get a last, desperate message back to Eden, describing what had happened to them and
begging for help from the home world.

Help wasn't coming anytime soon, of course. It took seven
years for their message to reach Eden, and once it did, it took the
authorities there almost two years to decide what, if anything, to
do about it. The folks who had left to found Gault had not been
particularly well thought-of on Eden when they boosted out, and
the ensuing years hadn't improved their reputation. Public sen-
timent tended pretty heavily toward *not our problem* and *serves
them right*. In the end, though, Eden's parliament decided that
Manikova might at some point actually pose a threat to other
worlds, and so would need to be dealt with.

This was the origin of the Union's first, and so far only, interstellar military expedition.

A lot of thought went into what, exactly, an invasion across
seven light-years ought to look like. The idea of ground forces
was obviously absurd. Eden was an immensely rich world, but
its budget would be stretched close to breaking just putting
together and fueling something similar to a colony ship. They
didn't need to worry about carrying terraforming equipment or
fetuses, obviously, but military equipment is heavy too. In the
end, they settled on a slightly up-armored colony ship that they
called *Eden's Justice*. It boosted out of Eden's system four years
after Gault's message arrived, carrying a crew of two hundred, a
half dozen orbital bombardment craft, and an enormous number
of fusion bombs. The thought was that they would settle into orbit
around Gault, make contact with Manikova, determine what his

intentions were *vis-à-vis* the rest of the Union in general and Eden in particular, and then, if necessary, glass the planet over.

You're probably already seeing the flaws here.

First, by the time they got to Gault, Manikova had had almost eighteen years to consolidate his hold on the system, create ever more copies of himself, and dig himself in.

Second, stealth was simply not an option for *Eden's Justice*. A starship's deceleration torch is visible from a light-year out, and there's not really a way to disguise it.

Third, and probably most importantly, Alan Manikova was not the sort of person who was inclined to wait for the fight to come to him.

The upshot of all this was that the Battle of Gault lasted something on the order of twelve seconds. *Eden's Justice* was still decelerating, blinded by her own torch to what was coming, when a dozen or so nuclear-tipped missiles slammed into her from a base Manikova had built on Gault's second moon. Her commander never even managed to get off a retaliatory shot.

Unfortunately for Alan Manikova, but probably fortunately for the rest of the Union, Eden wasn't the only world that had received Gault's last messages. They were also picked up by Gault's next-closest neighbor, a much younger, poorer, second-gen colony called Farhome. The government there was, if anything, more alarmed than the one on Eden. They didn't have either the ambition or the resources to mount the sort of expedition that Eden had attempted, though.

Their response was much simpler, more direct, and much, much cheaper. They called it *The Bullet*.

The critical thing about interstellar travel is this: kinetic energy is equal to the mass of an object times its velocity squared. That makes the process very expensive. It also makes it very dangerous. *Eden's Justice* was betrayed by her deceleration torch. *The*

Bullet avoided that problem by never attempting to decelerate. When an object is moving at 0.97 *c*, as *The Bullet* was when it slammed into Gault three months after the destruction of *Eden's Justice,* it doesn't have to be all that massive in order to crack a planet open like an eggshell. Even better, there's no practical way to defend against a relativistic attack, or even really to know that it's coming, because the light waves announcing its arrival reach its target a bare fraction of a second before it does. *The Bullet* delivered the energy equivalent of two hundred thousand fusion bombs to Gault's ecosystem over a period of roughly a picosecond.

You just don't come back from something like that.

As the fact that we're trying to make it work on Niflheim shows—there just aren't a lot of habitable planets hanging around waiting for us out here. Turning one of them into a ball of molten slag is widely considered to be the single greatest crime in the history of the Union.

Nobody blames Farhome for it, though. They blame Manikova—and ever since, in most parts of the Union you're better off in most people's minds being a child stealer or a human head collector than you are being a multiple.

Twenty-two Hundred comes. I don't ping Cat. Does she know for sure what's going on with me and Eight? Maybe not, but after her run-in with him this afternoon she definitely knows something's up, and somehow I don't think she's the sort of person to just let abominations slide. I'm starting to feel like my best chance at not getting converted into protein paste at this point is to avoid her for as long as possible, and hope that she gets eaten by creepers in the meantime.

That plan doesn't last long. Cat pings me at 22:02:

<CChen0197>: So. You free?

"So much for staying out of her way," Eight says. "You gonna answer?"

I turn to look at him. He's stretched out on the bed with his hands folded behind his head. I'm in the swivel chair, feet propped up on the desk. I'd been reading about yet another colonial disaster—this one a beachhead that died of insurrection and civil war before it even had a chance to earn a real name—but the

narrative wasn't really grabbing me. Mostly, I've been perseverating on the idea of getting shoved down the corpse hole.

"Yeah," I say. "I guess I have to, don't I?"

<Mickey8>:Hey Cat. I was just catching up on some stuff, but yeah,
    I'm free.

The more often I see myself tagged as Mickey8, the weirder it
feels. I imagine the foreboding that eight at the end of my name
calls down on me right now is kind of like what a regular person
might feel if she walked past a grave marker with her name on it.

<CChen0197>:Great. We should talk.
<Mickey8>:Meet at your rack?
<CChen0197>:...
<CChen0197>:I don't think so, Mickey. Let's go with the gym again,
    huh? Meet me there in ten.
<Mickey8>:Uh ... sure. See you then.

"The gym?" Eight says. "What's up with that?"

I shrug.

"Seriously," he says. "Who works out during a famine?"

"It's a thing," I say. "I ran into her there last night, when I
was afraid to come back here because I thought you might have
Nasha with you."

"I did, just FYI."

I shoot him a glare. He crosses his legs at the ankle and grins.

"Anyway," he says, "be careful. There's something off about her."

"Whatever," I say. "If she murders me, you get to go to full
rations, right?"

His grin widens. "Good point. Hey—what are you gonna do
about that hand?"

I look down. The swelling is mostly gone, but I've still got it wrapped.

"Dunno," I say. "I could take off the bandage, I guess?"

"I wouldn't. It's still purple. Just . . . I don't know . . . keep your hand in your pocket?"

I shake my head. "I don't think so. Honestly, it hurts just thinking about doing that. Maybe you should go instead of me?"

"No," he says. "No chance. You two have a history. What if she wants to talk about whatever went down between the two of you last night?"

Unfortunately, that's a fair point.

"Anyway," he says, "I actually worked today, and I'm tired. Have a fun time."

He closes his eyes. I open my mouth to reply, but I've got nothing. I get to my feet, and I go.

I'M HALFWAY TO the gym when my ocular pings.

<Mickey8>:Ar chi** ?

What the hell?

<Mickey8>:Eight?
<Mickey8>:What?
<Mickey8>:Co m . . . ren?
<Mickey8>:What the hell, Seven?
<Mickey8>:Go back to sleep, Eight. I don't have time for this.
<Mickey8>:Mol**an inv?

Whatever. I cut the connection.

"HEY," CAT SAYS. "Why didn't you ping me?"

She's sitting on one of the treadmills. She doesn't look like she's dressed to run this time.

"I was going to," I say. "You didn't give me a lot of slack."

She shrugs. "Doesn't matter. It's fine. Have a seat."

She pats the other treadmill. I hesitate, then decide that if she plans to kill me, she doesn't need to trick me into sitting on a treadmill to do it. I sit.

"So," I say. "Um . . . are we working out?"

She stares at me for what feels like a long while.

"No," she says finally. "We are not working out. We're in the gym because I wanted to speak with you privately, and this is the last place that anyone in this colony other than me would come voluntarily."

"We could have met in your room."

She looks away. "I don't think that's a good idea. Not until we get some things sorted out, anyway. Clear?"

"Yeah," I say. "Clear. So. What are we talking about?"

She gives me another long look. "How's your hand, Mickey?"

I sigh. "Getting better. Thanks for asking."

She nods. "It was all the way better this afternoon."

No point in dragging this out. "Look," I say. "Tell me what we're here for."

"Okay," she says. "Cards on the table. There's two of you, Mickey. You're the one I had breakfast with this morning. You're the one who was in my bed last night. You've got a busted hand, and you were off shift today. The other one, who I ran into in the corridor a few hours ago, has an unbusted hand, and spent the day growing tomatoes. I don't know how or why, but you're a multiple."

And I knew she knew this, but still my stomach knots, and I can suddenly feel my heart pounding in my throat. "Have you talked to Command?"

She manages to look offended. "Seriously? You sort of saved

my life two days ago, and yesterday I saved yours. *You slept in my bed.* After all that, do you really think I'd just turn you in without talking first?"

I close my eyes, and the clench in my belly relaxes slightly.

"Don't get me wrong," she says. "I definitely have a serious problem with what you're doing. How the hell did you get Bio to make you a multiple, anyway? That's a capital offense for everyone involved, isn't it?"

I shake my head. "I didn't *get* them to make me a multiple. I know what the law says, and I don't have any interest in getting turned into slurry. It was a mistake."

She raises one eyebrow. "A mistake? Like somebody tripped and fell on the bio-printer, and you came squirting out the other end?"

"Sure," I say. "Something like that."

She opens her mouth, hesitates, then shakes her head. "You know what? I don't want to know. If the shit winds up coming down on you, I don't want to be implicated. That's the other reason I didn't want you in my room. I'll tell you, though—it won't be long before somebody who *does* want to know is going to figure out that something is up with you, and when they do, you'll want to have a better story ready than, 'It was a mistake.' "

"Yeah," I say. "You're probably right."

We sit in silence for a while. I'd like to ask her what she brought me here for. It doesn't look like she wants to kill me, and she hasn't indicated anything about blackmail yet. My only other guess was that she wanted to pick up where we left off this morning, but "I definitely have a serious problem with what you're doing" seemed to rule that one out. I'm thinking about wishing her a good evening and heading back up to my rack when she says, "Do you think you're immortal?"

Did not expect that.

"What?"

"Do you think you're immortal? You've been killed, what, seven times?"

"Six," I say. "It's only six so far. That's kind of the root of the problem."

"Whatever. Are you the same person you were when you boarded the shuttle off of Midgard?"

I have to think about that.

"Well," I say finally. "This isn't the same body, obviously."

"Right," Cat says. "That's not what I was asking."

"Yeah," I say, "I know. So, yeah, I remember being Mickey Barnes back on Midgard. I remember the apartment he grew up in. I remember his first kiss. I remember the last time he saw his mother. I remember signing on for this stupid expedition. I remember all of that stuff as if it was me who did it, not someone else. Does that mean I *am* Mickey Barnes, though?" I shrug. "Who the hell knows?"

She's staring at me. Her eyes are narrowed, and I feel that chill from this morning running down the back of my neck again.

"I looked up that Ship of Theseus thing. You did a terrible job describing it."

"Yeah," I say. "I know. That's one of those things that I thought I remembered from training, but then when I started talking I realized that, no, I didn't actually remember it at all."

"I'm surprised. It's a pretty tight analogy for your life. I'd think it would have stuck with you."

I shrug. "Sorry."

"It's a pretty airtight argument, don't you think?"

I start to answer, then shake my head and start again. "I'm confused, Cat. Where are you going with this?"

"Where I'm going is, I want to know if you're Mickey Barnes, or if you're just some other guy running around in his clothes."

"I told you," I say, "I don't know. I know what Jemma told me back on Himmel Station, and I know that I *feel* like I'm the same person I was back on Midgard, but . . . I don't know. That's the flip side of the argument, isn't it? The fact that it doesn't make any measurable difference in any way whether I'm the same person or I'm not means that there's no possible way for me to know for sure. It's an unanswerable question."

"Still," she says, "you don't know that you're *not* him, right?"

"No," I say. "I guess I don't."

She doesn't respond. We sit in silence for a while. I'm about to ask if we're done here when she says, "You know, I've been thinking a lot these past two days."

"Um," I say. "Okay. What about?"

"Dying. I've been thinking about dying. I'm only thirty-four years old. I shouldn't have to think about dying for another fifty years, but here we are."

Beachhead colonies are dangerous places. I wonder if they emphasized that as heavily in her training as they did in mine. I don't get a chance to ask, though, because apparently she's heard all that she needed to hear. She gets to her feet, and then offers me a hand up.

"Look," she says. "I like you, Mickey."

"Thanks," I say. "I like you too."

"You're a good guy, I think. If it weren't for this whole multiple thing . . ."

If it weren't for that, I would have been with Nasha last night instead of with her, but this probably isn't the time to say that. I'm standing there trying to come up with something that I *can* say when she rises up onto her toes and kisses my cheek. She steps back, gives me a sad smile, and opens the door.

"Tell the other you I said hello, huh?"

I stand staring, my jaw hanging slightly open, as she walks away.

* * *

THE DOOR TO my room is locked when I get there. I show my ocular, wait for the click of the latch disengaging, and then push it open. It's dark inside, but in the wash of light from the corridor I can see that there are two people lying on my bed.

Two naked people.

One of them is Eight. The other is Nasha.

I stand there, frozen. I have no idea what I'm supposed to be feeling right now. Jealousy? Anger?

Abject terror?

"Get in here," Eight says. "Close the door."

"But you're . . ." I sputter. "What the shit, Eight? What the actual shit?"

"Sorry," he says. "I thought you'd be spending the night with Chen again. That or be dead, anyway."

Nasha rises up on one elbow. "You slept with somebody else?"

"No," I say. "I mean, yes, I slept in her room, but we didn't . . ."

"Oh," she says. "You just cuddled?"

I open my mouth to protest before realizing that she's laughing at me.

"I'm sorry," I say. "You were with Eight."

"Eight?" Nasha says. "Is that what you're calling each other now? Seven and Eight?"

"Yeah," Eight says. "Got a better suggestion?"

"No," she says. "It's kind of cute, I guess."

"Eight," I say.

"Seven," he says. "Close the door."

I do. It's dark enough now that my ocular flips over to infrared. Eight shows up as dull orange. Nasha is bright, glowing red. I drop into the desk chair and lower my head into my hands.

"So," Eight says. "How'd it go with Chen, anyway?"

I look up at him. "What? Who cares about Chen? What are you doing here, Eight?"

"Seriously?" Eight says. "I thought that was pretty obvious."

"No!" I say. "What I mean is . . . fuck you! You know exactly what I mean!"

"What Eight is doing," Nasha says, her voice a low, feline rumble, "is stealing away your woman. What're you gonna do about it?"

"Eight," I say, "we talked about this. Why didn't you ask me before you brought Nasha into this?"

"Oh, relax," Nasha says. "I'm not about to turn you two pervs in to Command."

"We're not pervs," I say. "It was an accident."

"I told her what happened," Eight says. "She's just screwing with you. Seriously, though—what happened with Chen? Did she try to kill you?"

"Chen?" Nasha says. "Cat Chen, from Security?"

"Yeah," I say. "You said yesterday that you were gonna gut her like a fish, remember?"

"Only if she touched you. Did she touch you, Mickey?"

"No," I say. "I mean, yeah, sort of, but she's not interested in that, I don't think—especially not now. She seemed pretty put off by the whole multiple thing."

"Not surprised," Nasha says. "Security types all have rods up their asses."

"Back up," Eight says. "She knows?"

"Yeah," I say. "She knows. The whole miraculously healing and unhealing hand tipped her off. Also, you apparently told her you'd been in the Agriculture Section today, while I told her today was an off-shift."

"Huh," Eight says. "That's not good. How'd you leave it?"

I sigh. "Honestly, I have no idea. She didn't say she was turning us in, so I guess that's good. She didn't exactly say she wasn't either, though, so I guess that's not so great."

"Did you think about gutting her?" Nasha asks. "Leave her outside the main lock, say a creeper got her? Problem solved, right?"

Eight snickers. "If anybody was getting gutted tonight, it wasn't gonna be Chen."

"Truth," I say. "Not sure what you're giggling about, though. If I go down the corpse hole, you're going with me, remember?"

"Nobody's going down the corpse hole," Nasha says. "Chen won't turn you in."

"Really?" I say. "Why not?"

I mean, I don't think so either, but I'm assuming Nasha's reasons for thinking that are very different from mine.

"Because," she says, "she doesn't want to deal with the blowback."

"Blowback?" Eight says.

"Me," Nasha says. "I'm the blowback."

She makes a good point, actually. I wouldn't cross her.

Of course, I wouldn't cross Cat either. Security goons are spooky.

"Look," Nasha says, "everything's gonna be fine. You two just need to lie low until one or the other of you gets offed doing some dumbass suicidal thing. Then we can register whichever one of you is still alive as Mickey9, and everybody lives happily ever after."

"Well," Eight says. "Almost everybody."

"Right," Nasha says. "Almost."

"I don't know," I say. "It's only been a couple of days since Eight came out of the tank, and we've already got two other people who know about us. At this rate, the entire colony will be in on this in a couple of weeks. I'm not sure I can die that fast."

Nasha laughs. "You know what, Mickey? You think too much. Take off those clothes and get in here. You need to shift some blood away from your brain for a while."

I stare at her. "Come on, Seven," Eight says. "We're already perverts, right? And blowback or not, I'm not too confident that we're not both going down the corpse hole soon enough. Might as well have some fun while we're here."

THE NEXT TWO hours are weird. I don't think I want to talk about them.

Just to be clear, though: I regret nothing.

THE THREE OF us are just settling into that soft, calm after-place, with me hanging off one side of the bed, Eight on the other, and Nasha pressed in between us, when someone knocks on the door. Nasha had been saying something to Eight about how much fun we were going to have until one of us got recycled, but she cuts off midsentence with a hiss of indrawn breath.

The knock comes again.

"Should I answer?" I whisper. "I could try to get rid of them."

Eight reaches across Nasha to slap the side of my head. "Shut up," he hisses. "That's probably Berto. If we're quiet, he'll go away."

"Mickey? Are you in there?"

Oh shit. That's not Berto.

Nasha shifts around until her mouth is next to my ear.

"You did set the security lock, right?"

The latch disengages with a quiet *snick,* and a crack of light appears around the door.

"No," I whisper. "I did not."

"Mickey?"

Fuck. Fuck fuck fuck.

The door swings open.

"Hey," Eight says. "Chen, right? Good to see you."

Cat stares at us, her mouth working silently.

"Cat?" I say. "Close the door. We can talk about this."

She shakes her head.

"Cat?"

I sit up and reach out to her. She takes a half step back. "What are you doing, Mickey?"

"What does it look like?" Nasha says. "Get in or get out, Chen. Either way, close the door."

Cat turns on her heel and bolts, leaving the door standing open behind her.

"You probably want to close that," Nasha says.

I climb out of bed and swing the door shut. This time, I remember to set the privacy lock.

"This is bad," I say, and slump down into the desk chair.

"She already knew about us," Eight says. "You said that, right? So, nothing's changed."

That almost makes sense. So why is my heart trying to beat its way out of my chest?

"It's fine," Nasha says. "Come back to bed, Mickey."

I take a deep breath, hold it, and then let it out again. Maybe they're right?

They're not right. I know they're not.

Nothing to do about it now, though. I pull back the sheet, and climb back into bed. Nasha twists around to kiss me.

"Relax, Mickey. Let's get some sleep."

I WAKE IN the darkness to the *snick* of the privacy lock being overridden. After that comes a rush of light, and then a deep male voice saying, "You've got to be kidding me." I squint into the glare coming in from the corridor. Two Security goons have wedged themselves into my room. They're both carrying burners.

"Holy shit," the smaller one says. "What the hell is wrong with you people?"

The other shakes his head. "Doesn't matter. Get up, all three of you, and for shit's sake put some clothes on. You've all got a date with the cycler."

I'M LOSING IT.

The fact that I'm losing it makes me feel even worse than the actual losing it does.

Nasha has every right to be freaking out right now. She's never been marched off to her own execution before. I've got no excuse, though. This is practically routine for me. I once had three executions in two weeks.

A COLONY SHIP doesn't just land when it reaches its destination. Most of what gets us from one star to another is built strictly for space. It's too bulky and too fragile to survive entering an atmosphere or exposing itself to a gravitational field. A colony comes down from orbit in bits and pieces.

The first bit to come down to the surface of Niflheim, just a few hours after we made orbit, was a lander piloted by Nasha containing a biological isolation chamber, a team from Medical, a team from Biology, and me.

We already knew by then that we were more or less boned when it came to both the climate and the atmospheric composition of our new home. Marshall had actually considered trying to push on to a secondary target when he realized that we wouldn't be able to survive outside without rebreathers, but after a lot of discussion and a fair bit of yelling, Dugan and a few others from Bio convinced him that once we'd introduced some engineered algae into the ecosystem, we'd be able to get the partial pressure of oxygen in the atmosphere up to survivable levels within a reasonable time frame—reasonable in this case meaning not necessarily within the lifetimes of any of the adult members of the expedition, but possibly within the lifetimes of some of the embryos we were carrying in the hold.

As I think I mentioned, the odds of an expedition like ours ever reaching a secondary target are not-quite-but-almost zero, so in the end he decided to give Niflheim a go.

The first order of business for any new colony is determining whether there's anything in the local microbiota that might pose a hazard to human health.

For the record, there is always something in the local microbiota that not only might, but in fact definitely will, pose a hazard to human health.

The way this is determined, naturally, is by exposing the expedition's Expendable to anything and everything that can be isolated from the local environment, and then waiting to see what happens to him.

We'd been on the surface for less than a day when Nasha gave me a last kiss and a pat on the cheek, and then a tech from Medical named Arkady marched me into the isolation chamber. The last thing he did before he left me there was fit me with a scanning helmet for continuous upload. When I asked him what that was for, he said, "I guess they might want to ask you what you thought about this later."

"Seriously?" I said. "You're gonna give me super-herpes? Fine. That's my job. Do I really have to remember it?"

He shrugged, backed out of the chamber, and closed the door.

THE ISOLATION CHAMBER was a cylinder just wide enough that I could almost touch both sides if I stretched out my arms, and just tall enough that I could stand up without hitting my head. It had a metal chair in the center that doubled as a toilet if you slid back a lid on the seat, a vent in the ceiling, and a drawer set into the wall opposite the door where they'd left me some snacks, in case I didn't die right away. I'd just sat down when the vent began hissing.

"Take a few deep breaths," Arkady said through the intercom. "Breathe through your mouth, if you don't mind."

I actually didn't, because whatever was coming out of the vent smelled like dog farts.

It tasted like dog farts too.

After a minute or so of that, the vent closed with an audible click.

"Thanks," Arkady said. "Make yourself comfortable. This may take a while."

I had to bite back the urge to tell him that I hated to inconvenience him, and that I'd try to die as quickly as possible.

A few minutes after that, Nasha's face appeared in the door's tiny window.

"Hey," she said. "How's it going in there?"

I grimaced. "Great." I gestured to the drawer behind me. "They gave me snacks."

She smiled. "Lucky you. All we've got out here is cycler paste and water."

I turned around and rooted through the drawer, found a protein bar, and peeled off the wrapper.

"Well," I said, and took a bite. "Nothing but the best for the sacrificial pig, right?"

"Lamb," she said.

"What?"

"Lamb, Mickey. You sacrifice a lamb. Pigs are gross. You don't sacrifice them. You just eat them."

I sighed. "Either way, they end up just as dead."

NASHA TRIED. HONEST to God, she did. She'd probably known since we first kissed that someday she'd have to watch me die, but after eight years it was finally happening, and I don't think she knew what to do. I don't think she knew what to *feel*. So she stood outside that window for four hours, and she talked to me. She talked about what the planet looked like through the viewscreens. She talked about what a jackass Arkady was. She talked about some vid drama she'd been watching about a family of obscenely wealthy assholes on Midgard.

She talked about the stuff we could do together when this was over, when I came back out of the tank again.

I tried too, because she was trying, and I didn't want her to feel any worse than she probably already did. After a couple of hours, though, I wasn't feeling so well myself. At first I thought it must be psychosomatic. Who ever heard of a bug starting in on you that quickly, right? Before long, though, it was pretty clear that I was spiking a fever. Arkady came back to ask me a few questions about what I was feeling. I told him it felt like the early stages of the flu. He nodded and went away again. The coughing started at three hours. I first brought up blood at three and a half. Nasha had mostly stopped talking by then, but she was still there, watching me through the window, one hand pressed against the glass next to her face.

At the four-hour mark, I mustered up enough breath to tell her to go away. I didn't want her watching what came next.

She didn't go away. When it was clear what was happening, she arm-twisted Arkady into strapping her into a biohazard suit so that she could come into the chamber with me. I didn't want her there at first. When things got really bad, though, when I started coughing so hard that I cracked a rib and brought up chunks of tissue, she held my hand and cradled my head against her belly and talked me through it. It was awful, what she did then, and it was beautiful, and if I live another thousand years I will never stop being grateful for it.

It was only another hour or so after that. Just for future reference: If you have any choice in the way you leave this life, try to stay away from pulmonary hemorrhage. I think I can speak from a position of authority on this topic. This is not the way you want to go.

I WOKE UP naked and covered in goo, laid out on the floor next to the portable tank they'd brought down in the lander.

"Really?" I said when I'd coughed the last of the fluid out of my no longer bleeding lungs. "I don't even get a bunk?"

Burke, my friend from Medical, tossed me a towel. "You were covered in crap," he said. "I didn't want to wash the bedding."

I scraped as much gunk off of myself as I could, then climbed into the one-piece gray coverall he handed me.

"Get something to eat," he said. "You've got at least twenty-four hours before you go back in."

"So," NASHA SAID. "That was rough."

I looked at her across the common room table. She wouldn't meet my eyes.

"Yeah," I said. "That was rough. Thanks for staying with me."

She looked up at the ceiling, then down at her hands—anywhere but at me.

"Mickey . . ." she said.

I waited for her to go on, but when it was pretty clear she couldn't, I let her off the hook.

"You don't have to do it again," I said. "Nobody should have to watch someone they . . ."

"Love," she said.

In spite of myself, I smiled. We'd been together for eight years by then, but that was the first time either one of us had said that word.

"You shouldn't have to watch me die more than once."

"No," she said. "I'll be there. Dying . . . even if it's temporary, you shouldn't have to do it with nobody around for company but that little bitch Arkady."

I reached across the table. Our fingers intertwined.

"Anyway," she said, "somebody's got to be there to make sure you don't sneak away."

As it happened, it was almost a week before they sent me back into the chamber. I spent most of that time with Nasha. We talked sometimes, we played a few rounds of a card game she'd brought down from the *Drakkar*. Mostly, though, we held each other. There wasn't much else to do.

After four days, Burke came into the tiny, curtained-off nook where I'd been sleeping, had me pull up my sleeve, and gave me a half dozen injections with needles that looked like sawed-off water pipes. Halfway through he had to switch arms because my left shoulder was already turning purple. When I asked him what they were, he gave me a look that said clearly that he didn't think he should have to explain himself to the guinea pig. When

I asked again, though, he rolled his eyes and said, "The first two were immune boosters. The other four were vaccines against the microorganisms that killed your last iteration. We'll give it two days for them to take effect, and then try again."

"Great," I said. "So you think I've got a chance this time?"

He looked at me, then shrugged and turned away. "You never know," he said, then added after he'd let the curtain swing back behind him, ". . . but probably not."

I DON'T REMEMBER what happened to Mickey4. I know that he died in Nasha's arms, more or less just like Mickey3, because they made me watch the surveillance video later. I don't remember it, though, because the first thing he did when they opened the vents in the isolation chamber was to unplug the leads from the scanning helmet and take it off.

"Hey," Arkady said. "What the hell are you doing?"

He rolled his eyes. "What does it look like?"

"You need to put that back on," Arkady said. "You're breaking protocol."

Four shook his head. "Sorry, Arkady. If the inoculations work, we can do a full recording as soon as you let me out of here. If they don't . . ."

"If they don't, we'll be losing valuable data."

He rolled his eyes. "Valuable data? What the hell are you talking about? You didn't ask me a single question about what happened to Three."

"We know what happened to your last iteration, Barnes. He bled out through the lungs. We didn't need to ask any questions about that. What if what happens to you is more interesting?"

Four stared at him through that little window for a solid ten seconds, then burst out laughing.

"Interesting?" he said when he'd finished. "Interesting? I'll tell you what, asshole. If anything *interesting* happens to me while I'm in here, I'll be sure to let you know. Fair enough?"

"Barnes," Arkady said. "Put the helmet on. Now."

Four folded his arms across his chest and smirked out at him.

"Those biohazard suits are fragile," he said. "It'd be pretty easy to knock a hole in one of them, wouldn't it? Give that some thought, and then come in here and make me."

AS IT TURNED out, what happened to Four was not particularly interesting. He lasted a lot longer than Three did—over twenty-four hours before he started showing any symptoms. When the bug that killed him got going, though, it worked quickly. It cleared out his GI tract first, with fluid pouring out of both ends in great, bloody torrents. When there wasn't anything more to be done on that front, it went to work on his liver and his kidneys. He was septic at thirty-two hours, and unconscious at thirty-six. By hour forty, he was dead.

I WOKE UP on the floor again. This time, there were eleven needles waiting for me.

"Wow," I said. "That was quick."

"Not really," said Burke. "It's been eight days since the last trial. Dugan told us not to bring you back this time until we were ready with the next round of inoculations. No point in wasting resources feeding you when you're just going back in the hopper anyway, right?"

He worked his way through the injections. Four in the right shoulder, three in the left, and the rest in my right thigh.

"Oh," he said when he was done. "Dugan also said to tell you that Marshall says you're wearing the helmet this time."

"No," I said. "I'm not."

"Yeah," he said. "He thought you'd say that. He also said to tell you that if you don't, we're authorized to throw your next iteration into the chamber without any shots, and to keep doing that as many times as we need to until you get with the program."

He walked away then, and left me sitting naked on the edge of the tank to ponder which is worse: an infinite loop of torment that you don't remember a bit of, or a single bad death that's stuck in your head forever.

IN THE END, I put on the helmet. Nasha came to see me off again. This time, when she kissed me, she wrapped her arms around me and didn't let go until Arkady pulled her away.

"This is the one," she said as I stepped into the chamber. "You're coming back out this time."

"What do you think?" I asked Arkady as he was hooking up the leads to the helmet. "Is this the one?"

He shrugged. "Stranger things have happened."

AFTER A DAY in the chamber, I felt fine.

AFTER TWO DAYS, I felt fine.

AFTER THREE DAYS, I was cranky and stiff from trying to sleep in that stupid chair, and my snack drawer was running low. Otherwise, though, I felt fine.

ON THE MORNING of the eighth day, Arkady told me to strip naked, stand spread-eagled, hold my breath, and close my eyes. For the next thirty seconds, I was doused in a series of increasingly caustic and almost definitely toxic sprays.

"Breathe," Arkady said when that was done, "but keep your eyes closed."

Even through my tight-clenched eyelids, the glare of the UV disinfectant was painful.

That cycle repeated three times.

By the time it was done, I was bloodred from head to toe and felt like I'd been flayed alive.

But I was alive.

For the first time, I walked back out of the isolation chamber.

"Get dressed," Arkady said, "and get down to Medical. You're not out of the woods yet, friend."

"Hey," Nasha said. "Can I go with?"

Arkady looked at her for a long moment, then shook his head. "Best not. If he checks out there, you can have at him. Until then, he's still a potential vector."

My exam was almost perfect.

Almost.

Blood work, physical exam, skin cultures, throat cultures, sinus cultures—everything came out clean. The last thing they did was a whole-body magnetic resonance scan.

"Just to be sure," Burke said.

Famous last words.

I was back up in the mess, sitting across from Nasha while she sipped a paste smoothie and went over in glorious detail all the things she was going to do to me once she was allowed to touch me again when she stopped midsentence to look over my shoulder. I turned. It was Burke. He was holding a tablet.

"Have you two exchanged fluids yet?"

"Not yet," Nasha said. "We're definitely going to, though."

"No," Burke said. "You're not."

He turned the tablet around so that we could both see it. There was an image there, a picture of a walnut cut in half, gray matter wrapped around white matter wrapped around . . .

"What is that?" I asked, though I was pretty sure I already knew the answer.

"It's your brain," Burke said.

"No shit," Nasha said. She leaned across the table and poked the dark curl in the center of the image with one finger. "What the fuck is *that*, asshole?"

"It's a tumor," I said. "I've got a brain tumor, right?"

"No," Burke said. "You definitely don't have a brain tumor. Your body is barely a week old. Brain tumors don't grow that fast."

"Fine," I said. "So what is it?"

"I don't know," Burke said, "but you're going back in the chamber until we find out."

So you remember I said that you don't want to die of a pulmonary hemorrhage? Well, here's another thing to add to your list of deaths to avoid: having your brain eaten from the inside out by parasitic worms.

It took the better part of a month for them to finish me off, but for the last week or so of that I was basically an empty shell. Weeks two and three, though, were not fun. It started with headaches, then seizures, then progressive dementia. By the end, the walls were talking to me, telling me that Nasha didn't really love me, that all my other iterations were in hell waiting for me, that the parasites were going to just keep eating and eating and never let me die.

That was a lie, anyway. They did let me die.

When it was over, the larvae came pouring out of my mouth and nose and ears, ready to move on to whatever the next stage of their life cycle was. We never found out what that might be, because Arkady sterilized the living shit out of them and then tossed the whole mess into the hopper to make a new me.

SO YEAH, AFTER all that, you wouldn't think whatever Marshall has planned for me now would scare me, would you?

You wouldn't think so—but for some goddamned reason, it does.

THEY MARCH US down the spoke corridor toward the hub in a single-file line, with the smaller goon leading, the bigger one trailing, and Nasha, Eight, and me strung out in between. When we start down the central stairs my stomach knots as I suddenly wonder if we're actually going straight to the cycler. Apparently Nasha has the same thought, because when we pass the second level she says, "You know you can't take any disciplinary action against us until you have a judicial finding, right?"

"Oh please," the bigger goon says from behind us. "After what we just saw, you're lucky we didn't burn you down on the spot."

"Fuck you," Eight says. "What are you, a Natalist?"

"Yeah," he says, "and so is Marshall. You guys are screwed."

"He's not wrong," the one in front says without turning around.

"This colony wasn't chartered as a theocracy," Nasha says. "You can't just burn us at the stake."

The goon shrugs. "Guess that's up to Marshall."

When we get down to the ground level, they don't take us to the cycler. They don't take us to the dungeon either, because we don't have one. We don't even have a jail, as far as I know.

Instead, they take us to the Security ready room. It's an odd choice, because there are lockers there filled with body armor and weapons. There's also a miniature auto-caf. We could start an armed insurrection, and also have a nice snack. This seems like really poor planning on Security's part.

"Wait here," the bigger one says before closing us in. "Keep your hands off the equipment, and don't even think about ordering food."

"Or what?" Nasha says.

He stares at her for a long moment, then shakes his head and says, "Just wait here."

After he's gone, Nasha walks over to one of the lockers and shows her ocular to the scanner. The light on the display flashes red.

"Oh well," she says. "Worth a try."

"Nice," Eight says. "What would you have done if it'd opened?"

She shrugs. "Shot my way to freedom, I guess."

If we could get into the lockers, what would we do? It's an interesting question, actually. We're not even locked in here. Even without being able to get at weapons, we could run. We could try to jump one of the goons when they come back for us. We could do lots of things. What would it get us, though? This dome is the only place on this planet that won't kill us in short order. When I actually think about it, I start to realize that in some sense Niflheim itself is just a really big, really cold jail.

There's a couch in the center of the room, and a low coffee table. Eight drops down on one end, leans his head back, and closes his eyes. After a minute, I take the other. Nasha sits between us, pulls us toward her, and slings her arms around both of our shoulders.

"You know," she says, "if you'd asked me before we left Midgard how I thought I was going to die, shoved down the corpse hole for sex crimes wouldn't have been at the top of my list."

"You're not going down today," Eight says without opening his eyes. "We've only got two atmospheric pilots, and you're one of them. Marshall will find some way to make you miserable over this, but he can't kill you."

"I don't know," Nasha says. "He may think that way now, but what about after I murder Chen?"

Eight shrugs. "Depends on how hard you try to make it look like an accident, I guess."

We're quiet for a while then, the three of us, eyes closed and heads touching. Eight's probably right that Marshall won't kill Nasha. He definitely will kill the hell out of us, though, and at this point I'm pretty confident that when Nine comes out of the tank afterward, it won't be me looking out through his eyes, Ship of Theseus be damned.

Oh well. At least I'm in good company.

It's maybe an hour later when the smaller of the two goons who brought us here comes back.

"Barnes," he says, "let's go." He grimaces. "Both of you. Adjaya—you stay here for now."

Nasha still has her arms around us. She kisses Eight, then turns to kiss me. The goon turns away.

"What the hell, Adjaya? Seriously. What the hell?"

"Suck it," she says.

Eight sighs. "You know," he says, "you're not helping things here."

He's probably right. On the other hand, from our perspective at least, there's almost certainly no way to make things worse. We get to our feet, and we go.

HE DOESN'T TAKE us to the cycler. He takes us four doors down the corridor, and sticks us in another room about the size of a storage closet.

"What's this?" I ask.

He shrugs. "A storage closet."

He shoves us inside, then closes the door behind us. The room is dark. My ocular flips over to infrared, but I'd just as soon get some sleep at this point, so I flip it back. I hunch down in one corner and rest my forehead on my knees. I'm just drifting off when a chat window opens.

<Mickey8>:Ab**st nder**nd?

I flip my ocular back to IR and look up at Eight. He's in the opposite corner, hunched over just like me. He's already snoring.

<Mickey8>:Un***st**d

Ugh. He's sleep-texting. I blink the chat widow closed, shut my ocular down, and close my eyes.

I HAVE NO idea how long it's been when I wake to a flood of light from the open door. A new goon has come for us. This one I recognize. His name is Lucas. I used to see him in the carousel during transit, practicing some sort of martial art in extreme slow motion. I once asked him what the point of that was. I mean, isn't the whole key to winning a fight being faster than the other guy? He smiled and shook his head, and proceeded on to the next form.

He's always struck me as a decent sort, but he doesn't look happy to be dealing with us this morning.

"Hey," he says. "You're in some trouble here, Mickey."

"Yeah," Eight says. "We gathered."

"What happened to you, homes? How the hell did you wind up a multiple?"

"Long story," I say. "The short answer, though, is that this is all Berto's fault."

He laughs. "Should have known. Gomez is a piece of work. I never understood why you spent so much time with him."

"Yeah," Eight says. "I've been wondering that myself lately."

"Oh well," Lucas says. "Best get to your feet now. The big man wants to see you."

"GOOD LORD, BARNES," Marshall says. "Despite everything, I didn't want to believe it."

I decide not to ask what he means by "despite everything."

We're back in his office again, sitting in the same little chairs Berto and I were in a couple of days ago. The past forty-eight hours don't seem to have improved Marshall's mood.

"Look," Eight says. "I know this seems bad, sir, but it doesn't have to be the end of the world. I get that there shouldn't be two of us right now, but you know we didn't do it deliberately. And anyway, in some ways this is a good thing. The colony is barely at viability as it is, and the two of us can be twice as useful. At the end of the day, you need us. You need to let this slide."

Marshall's face reddens, and his jaw works silently for a long two seconds before he surges to his feet and slams his fists down onto his desk.

"Listen to me, you goddamned abomination! I don't give a *shit* about deliberately! Set aside the fact that you've stolen seventy kilos of vital calcium and proteins from a colony that's on the brink of starvation. Set aside the fact that one of you should have gone back into the cycler the goddamned *second* that you realized that you'd become a multiple. For the love of all that's holy, Barnes, you were having *relations* with one another. I don't . . . I . . ."

He sputters to a stop, then drops back into his chair. He takes a deep breath in, closes his eyes, and then lets it out slowly. When he opens them again, his expression is as blank as a mannequin's.

"You are a monster," Marshall says, his voice low and even, "and you are both going into the cycler. The only point of this discussion, the only questions we are trying to answer, are whether there will ever be a ninth iteration of you, and whether Adjaya should go down the corpse hole with you."

Eight's face goes slack at that, and I can feel my eyes widen.

"Sir," Eight says. "Please—"

"Nasha didn't know," I say. "I mean, she didn't know until I walked in on her with Eight, just before Security showed up to haul us away. You can't blame her, sir. This wasn't her fault."

"I've already spoken with Adjaya," Marshall says. "She claims that she did know, in fact. She claims that she realized something was off with you two days ago. She also let me know that what she was doing with the two of you is none of my goddamned business, and that I can shove my bullshit Natalist morality all the way up my ass sideways." He pauses for another deep, cleansing breath. "If she weren't one of our two qualified combat pilots, and if we were not currently facing the possibility of combat against hostile native sentients, she would have been gone already."

"Wait," Eight says. "What?"

"The prize you brought home from your snipe hunt two nights ago," Marshall says, "was not fully biological. The things you've been calling 'creepers' appear to actually be some sort of hybrid miltech. We suspected as much, of course, based on what they were able to do to the decking in the main lock, but our examination of the specimen has confirmed it. We are now on a war footing, which means that I'm going to have to think long and hard about what to do about Adjaya." He leans back in his chair, squeezes his eyes shut, and pinches the bridge of his nose. "Fortunately, I have no similar issues with the two of you." He gestures toward Lucas, who's been waiting just inside the door. "Take them to holding, please. I have a few more people I need to speak with. We'll sort them out when I'm done."

So, FUN FACT: it turns out we do have a jail.

"WELL," EIGHT SAYS. "It's been a nice few days, anyway."

I get to my feet and walk the two steps from the bench to the bed. I had no idea until they tossed us in here that this colony even had a holding cell—apparently the goons who dragged us out of our room didn't either, or they wouldn't have risked their snack machine with us—but I guess it does. We're in a standard three-by-two room. The only difference between this place and all the other standard three-by-two rooms under the dome is that the door on this one locks from the outside.

As far as I can tell, we're the first two occupants it's had since we left Midgard.

"I guess our original plan was right, huh?" I drop onto the bed, lie back, and close my eyes. "You should have shoved me down the corpse hole when you had the chance. At least you would have done it headfirst."

"Yeah," he says. "I guess you're right about that. You think he's really gonna kill us both?"

"Seems like it."

We sit in silence for a while then. It's strange—in a way, this all almost comes as a relief. Ever since I walked into our room to find Eight in my bed covered in tank goo, I've had this knot of visceral dread hanging around in my stomach. I knew we wouldn't be able to keep this a secret forever, and I was terrified of what would happen when it came out. Now that it has, and I know more or less what's going to happen and when, I actually feel a little calmer. In fact, I'm almost dozing when Eight speaks again.

"He said he might not pull Nine out of the tank. You don't think he'd do that, do you? I mean, the colony needs an Expendable."

I open my eyes, and turn my head to look at him. "Did it look like Marshall cares?"

He starts to reply, hesitates, then shakes his head. "No. I guess not."

I close my eyes again. "Here's a better question: Does it matter?"

"What the hell is that supposed to mean?"

I sigh, sit up, and turn to face him. "You're not me, Eight. Isn't that obvious?"

He stares at me for a long five seconds before saying, "What's your point?"

"My point is that all that stuff Jemma crammed into our head back on Himmel Station—all the bits about immortality, anyway—that was all bullshit. This is it. The past six weeks are the only life I get, and the last few days are the only life you get. We're fucking mayflies, and when Marshall shoves us down the corpse hole, that's it for us. I don't care if he pulls Nine out of the tank or not, because even if he does, *Nine won't be me.* He'll just be some other guy who sleeps in my bed and eats my rations and gets his hands all over my stuff."

Eight shakes his head. "No. I don't buy it. Remember that Ship of Theseus thing? Remember Kant? If he thinks he's me, and everyone around him thinks he's me, and there's no way to prove that he's not me, then *he's me.* This stuff you're doing right now? This is exactly why they don't allow multiples."

I roll my eyes. "They don't allow multiples because Alan Manikova tried to take over the universe."

"Whatever."

He slouches down on the bench then, folds his arms across his chest, and closes his eyes.

Time passes. I doze and wake, doze and wake. Eight stays upright on the bench, eyes half-open mostly, hands folded in his lap. It occurs to me at one point that I'm sleeping away my last hours of existence, but I can't bring myself to care.

Eventually, the lock disengages with a *snick,* and the door swings open. A goon named Garrison steps inside. He's short and skinny and not carrying a burner, and for one stupid second I think about jumping him, overpowering him, busting out, and running.

Running where, though? Idiot.

"Hey," he says. "Which one of you is Seven?"

I glance over at Eight. He shrugs. I groan, sit up, and raise one hand.

"Great," he says. "Let's go."

I stand. Eight gives me a half smile. "See you on the other side, brother."

"Yeah," I say. We both know that the other side for us is somebody's mug of slurry, but at least it seems like he's forgiven me for pricking his immortality bubble. Garrison steps back and gestures down the corridor. I follow him out.

The cycler is on the bottom level, at the center of the dome. It quickly becomes obvious that's not where we're going. By the time we get to Marshall's office, I've started to wonder whether I might live another few hours after all.

It only occurs to me as Garrison is knocking on his door that maybe Marshall just wants to shoot me himself.

"Come," Marshall says. The door swings open, and Garrison waves me in. I step past him. The door closes behind me.

"Sit," Marshall says.

I shake my head. "I think I'd rather stand."

He sighs, lets his bloodshot eyes sag closed in a long blink, then opens them again. "Suit yourself, Barnes."

He leans back in his chair, drops his hands into his lap, and looks up at me. "I've been talking to Gomez. I need you to tell me what you know about those things out there."

"Things, sir? You mean the creepers?"

"Yes. In his initial report regarding your presumed loss, Gomez said that you'd been killed by them. In his amended report subsequent to our interview three days ago, he said that you were killed in a fall. An hour ago, he amended that explanation further to state that you did in fact fall through the ice into some sort of tunnel or cave system, but that you were still alive and conscious when he left you there. He estimated that you may have been as much as a hundred meters below the surface. He thought you'd died there, but clearly you managed to find your way back out, didn't you?"

I nod. "That's what caused this mess, sir. Berto reported me lost, and by the time I made it back to the dome, Eight was already out of the tank."

He cuts me off with a wave of his hand. "I don't care about that right now, Barnes. I care about these tunnels. They shouldn't be there. Our orbital surveys indicated that this entire area was completely geologically stable. No volcanism, no fault lines, no mountains, no soft rock. There's nothing here that would explain an extensive cave system."

"Yes, sir," I say. "I thought the same thing."

"Right. What was your impression when you were down there? Did it appear to be a natural geologic formation? Was there anything about what you saw that seemed artificial?"

I hesitate. How much to tell? How would Marshall react to knowing that there are creepers down there big enough to tear straight through the wall of the dome if they wanted to?

I don't have to wonder about that, actually. I know how he'd react. He'd kill them all, if he could think of a way to do it.

Marshall controls the output of a starship engine.

He could definitely think of a way to do it.

I wonder if someone on Roanoke had similar thoughts at some point.

"The tunnels did not appear natural to me, sir. They appeared to be deliberately structured."

His eyebrows come together over the bridge of his nose. "I see. And when, exactly, were you planning on mentioning this to someone?"

I don't respond. He obviously knows the answer. After an awkward five seconds, he waves the question off.

"Fine. I suppose I understand your hesitance to come forward, given your circumstances. Did you see anything alive down there?"

And this is the moment of truth, isn't it? I think about the giant creeper pushing me up that tunnel, setting me free in the garden. I think about the visions I've been having, about the caterpillar's Cheshire grin.

I think about Dugan, being pulled under the snow.

I think about Roanoke.

I close my eyes and breathe in, breathe out.

I tell him everything.

EIGHT'S HEAD SNAPS up when the door swings open. His jaw sags when he sees it's me.

"Hey," I say. "Did you miss me?"

Garrison locks us in again. I sit down on the bed.

Eight tilts his head to one side. "Explain?"

I shrug. "For the moment, it seems like Marshall is more worried about having his colony eaten by creepers than he is about having a perverted multiple hanging around."

"Huh," he says. "That's surprisingly sensible."

"To be clear, I didn't say he's not going to kill us. He's still pondering, I think. I told him what happened to me after Berto abandoned me. I think it spooked him."

"What *did* happen to you? You never told me."

"Let's just say that I wasn't surprised when Marshall told us that we're dealing with sentients. Also, just FYI, the kind we've seen aren't all there is. There are creepers out there that are big enough to eat a flitter and have room left over for dessert."

"And they've got miltech."

"Apparently."

"And we're moving to a war footing."

"That's what Marshall says."

He leans forward, rests his elbows on his knees, and rubs his face with both hands.

"This isn't good, Seven. We're not equipped for a ground war with a technological species. There's only a hundred and eighty of us."

"One-seventy-six. We're down five of everyone else, and up one of us."

He looks up at me and scowls. "Whatever. We needed to know this before we dropped the colony."

So that we could have bombarded the creepers from orbit, he means. So that we could have committed genocide before putting any of ourselves in harm's way.

I have to remind myself at this point that Eight is me, six weeks or so removed. How can I be so horrified at what he's saying? Have the creepers really gotten that far into my head?

"Doesn't matter," I say. "We didn't know, and it's too late to do anything about it now."

He leans back and folds his arms across his chest. "Is it?"

And that's it, of course. It might not be. As I said before—Marshall has the full energy output of a starship engine at his disposal. We may not have the high ground anymore, but we still have an insane amount of power available.

"Anyway," I say, "whatever winds up happening, I don't think either of us is going to be around to worry about it."

"I don't know," Eight says. "He hasn't killed us yet, right?"

I lie back on the bed again, fold my hands behind my head, and close my eyes.

"Don't get too excited, Eight. I'm pretty sure this is a temporary reprieve."

FOR SOME REASON, while I'm lying there in the holding cell waiting for Marshall to make up his mind about what to do with me and hoping that if he does decide to cycle me he at least has the decency to kill me first, I find myself thinking about Six.

I don't remember all of my deaths, obviously. Four refused to upload before he died, and I don't remember being Two at all. I know exactly what happened to both of them, though. I saw surveillance video of each of their endings. I'm still not sure which is worse, honestly—remembering your own death, or watching it on video. Six, though . . . I thought I knew what happened to him. Berto told me he got torn apart by creepers.

Berto told me *I* got torn apart by creepers.

Berto has demonstrated pretty clearly that he can't be trusted when it comes to me and dying.

I wonder now—did Six wind up abandoned in the tunnels too? Did he just never manage to find his way back out? If I ever get the chance to see Berto again, I'm gonna squeeze the truth out of him.

Even if it kills me.

I'm still contemplating that when my ocular pops open a chat window.

<Mickey8>:In**stan* cl**r?

I turn my head to look at Eight.

"Come on," he says. "Again with this shit?"

<Mickey8>:C*e*r? S**nder?

I sit up. "What are you doing, Eight?"

"Me? What are *you* doing? What's with the gibberish?"

I shake my head. "That's not me. I thought you were sleep-chatting."

His face shifts from annoyed to confused. "Sleep-chatting? Is that a thing?"

"Maybe?"

<Mickey8>: Un*r**nd? C***r?

I blink the window closed. "If that's not you, and it's not me, then who is it?"

Eight shrugs. "It's a glitch, obviously. There's not supposed to be two separate nodes in the system with identical handles. There must be some kind of feedback thing going on between us."

"Oh please," I say. "You're making that up. You don't know any more than I do about the network, and I don't have any idea whether what you're saying is even plausible."

"Tell you what," he says. "After Marshall shoves you down the corpse hole, I'll see if he'll hold off on me for a while so I can check to see if it's still happening. Should be an interesting experiment."

I sigh. "Thanks, Eight. You're a pal."

YOU MIGHT HAVE the impression at this point that every colony that's ever been attempted has failed miserably. That's not remotely true, obviously. I've been perseverating on the failures because that's where my head has been pretty much ever since we entered orbit around Niflheim, but there have been tons of rousing successes. Take Bergen's World, for example.

Bergen's World was jungle from pole to pole when the first colony ship arrived. It had two continents, one huge and one smaller, both straddling the equator on opposite sides of the planet, with warm blue oceans, a whole mess of jungle islands, an atmosphere rich in oxygen and thick with CO_2, and a biosphere that could best be described as maniacal. There weren't any sentients and there wasn't anything alarmingly large, but the animals were fast and strong and bad-tempered, the trees were semi-motile and carnivorous, and the microbiota was adaptive, infectious, and omnipresent. Command dropped a small exploratory party from orbit, just to get the lay of the land.

Even with armor and heavy weapons, they didn't last a day.

The inhospitality of the place put the Bergen's World Command in a bit of a pickle. As I've mentioned, colony ships don't really have the option of packing up and heading to a new destination once they've settled down. So they made the best of it.

They sterilized the smaller continent. Burned it down damn near to the bedrock.

It's a beautiful place now. Practically a paradise, from everything I've read.

So, yeah, it's not true that every time we make landfall on a new planet we wind up dying.

I mean, *somebody* almost always does.

It's just not necessarily us.

IT'S CLOSING IN on noon when the door opens again. It's a different goon this time—a bigger guy, with dark skin and a clean-shaven head. His name is Tonio. I'm pretty sure he was the one who tased me in the cafeteria two days ago.

"On your feet," he says. "Let's go."

"Which one of us?" Eight asks.

"Both."

I look over at Eight. He shrugs. We get to our feet, and we go.

It's funny how expectations work. Four hours ago, I left the cell expecting to go to the cycler. I wasn't afraid, really. I knew what was going to happen, and I knew there was nothing I could do about it. There's a certain peace that comes with that.

This time, I leave the cell assuming that we're headed back to Marshall's office to talk about creepers. We're not, though. We pass that corridor and keep walking. My heart lurches, and my stomach twists itself into an aching knot.

This time, we really are going to the cycler.

Marshall is there waiting for us when we arrive, along with Nasha and Cat and two other goons. These ones are carrying burners.

The corpse hole is open. Tiny flashes of light dance across its surface.

"So," Marshall says. "Before we get started, I have a few questions."

"Oh, for shit's sake," Eight mutters.

Marshall's eyes narrow. "Excuse me?"

"Look," Eight says. "I know you, Marshall. I've been getting myself killed for you for nine years now. Despite that, for the most part you're a decent guy. You've got a stick up your ass most of the time, but you're not some kind of villain from a vid drama, and I don't know why you're trying to act like one now. You don't want a multiple hanging around your colony. Fine. Kill one of us, and shove him down the hole. Problem solved. Or kill both of us and pop a new one out of the tank, if that's the way you want to go. Just do it, and quit dicking around."

"Well," Marshall says. "Just to be clear—if the two of you wind up going down the hole today, there will never be another of you. Your personality will be wiped from the server, as will your body template. You're not looking at a trip to the tank right now, Barnes. You're looking at a death sentence."

Eight shakes his head. "Bullshit. There are only a hundred and seventy-six of us left, and we're moving to a war footing. You need every body you can get right now. You sure as shit can't throw away your only Expendable."

"This is true," Marshall says, and his face breaks into a tight-lipped smile. "What is not true is that you are the only person in this colony who is willing and able to fill the role of Expendable. In fact, Corporal Chen has graciously volunteered to take your berth, if and when that becomes necessary."

Eight opens his mouth, closes it, then opens it again, all without speaking. I turn to look at Cat and her Security pals. The other two are eyeing me, fingers tickling the triggers of their burners, but Cat's staring down at the floor in front of her.

"Cat?"

"I'm sorry," she says without looking up. "It's nothing personal, Mickey. It's for the good of the colony."

I bark out a short, sharp laugh. "The good of the colony. Right. This is what you were on about the other night, isn't it? Do I think I'm immortal? I guess you've got your answer to that now, huh?"

She meets my eyes. The anguish in her face drains the anger out of me.

"Please, Mickey. I didn't mean for all of this to happen."

"You *made* all of this happen, Cat."

A tear leaks from the corner of her eye and trails down her cheek. "I'm sorry," she says. "I just . . ."

"Shut up," Nasha says. "Seriously, Chen. Just shut the fuck up."

"Enough!" Marshall says. "There's no point in acting as if this is some kind of betrayal, Barnes. As I understand it, Chen became aware of your situation through your actions, not hers. Once that happened, she was bound by duty to report to Command. If she hadn't done so, she'd be standing beside you right now, waiting to go down the hole. Moreover, her decision to volunteer to replace you has no bearing whatsoever on what eventually becomes of you. If I decide to wipe you, we'll either find a volunteer to replace you, or we'll draft one." He pauses to wait for that to sink in before continuing. "The salient point right now, however, is that you still have an opportunity to make sure that doesn't happen."

The room falls silent. Behind us, one of the goons resets the safety on his burner with an audible click.

Eight is the first one to speak. "What do we have to do?"

"Nothing out of the ordinary," Marshall says. "All you need to do to avoid going down that hole is to fulfill your duty. I have a mission for you."

I roll my eyes. "A mission which will result in both of us being killed, I assume?"

Marshall turns to me, and his smile turns into a smirk. "Do I need to refer you back to your job description, Mr. Barnes?"

I sigh. "Tell me."

And so, he does.

ANTIMATTER, IN CASE you were wondering, is a hell of a thing.

When it's kept to itself, it basically behaves like regular matter. If there had been a hair more antimatter created during the Big Bang and a hair less normal matter, we could have a perfectly functional antimatter universe right now. There wasn't, though. Because of that, we have a normal matter universe, and when antimatter is brought into it, bad things happen. It's not quite true that you get a pure conversion of mass to energy when normal matter and antimatter interact, but depending on exactly what kind of particles are interacting, what their energy states were before they met one another, and what sort of environment they're in, you can get anything from a barrage of gamma rays to a massive spew of subatomic particles ricocheting around at a significant fraction of the speed of light.

As either One or Two would have been happy to tell you, as a living organism, you really don't want to be anywhere near any of those things.

Antimatter was discovered back on old Earth, pre-Diaspora, well before the *Ching Shih* was even a gleam in someone's autoCAD. For a long time, though, it was mostly just a curiosity. They didn't figure out how to synthesize and contain it in any significant quantity until just before the breakout. In fact, most people would argue that the Chugunkin Process was the singular advancement that led most directly to the Diaspora.

Partially that's because antimatter is absolutely critical for interstellar travel. Nothing else that our physics has yet discovered contains enough energy in a compact-enough form to get us anywhere near the speeds that we need to cross the gulfs between stars. Still, even if that weren't true—if, for example, some of the reactionless thrust concepts they were playing with before Chugunkin did his thing had actually paid out—it seems pretty likely that the Diaspora wouldn't have happened without the ability to create antimatter in bulk.

It should be pretty clear by now that launching a colony mission is in most ways a desperate act. It's expensive, it has a high probability of failure, and even if it succeeds, the place you're going to will probably be significantly worse than the place you came from for at least a few lifetimes. In order to make a leap like that, you have to either be running *toward* something great, or running *away* from something truly terrifying. For the ancient Micronesians, the thing they were running from was resource depletion and starvation.

The thing that we're running from is the Bubble War.

It's a truism that every new technological advancement in human history has been applied first to advance the interests of the horny. The printing press? Some Bibles, mostly porn. Antibiotics? Perfect for treating STIs. The ocular? Don't get me started on what those were first used for. Large-scale antimatter production didn't really fit that model, though. There's nothing remotely sexy about a rapidly expanding cloud of high-speed quarks and gluons.

The second area where every new technology is applied, of course, is war.

In that space, antimatter worked out heinously well.

In fairness, our ancestors did spend about ten seconds or so thinking about how antimatter could be used for things like energy production and starship propulsion before they turned their attention to the ways it could be used to convert their fellow humans into radioactive dust. I'm guessing, though, that the main reason for that was that until the invention of the magnetic monopole bubble, there wasn't any practical way to use antimatter as a tool of genocide. You can't just make an antimatter bomb the way you can a thermonuclear bomb, for example. You need a way to keep your antimatter core completely isolated from any interaction with normal matter until you want it to do its thing, and absent a five-thousand-kilo magnetic torus and a vacuum chamber to keep it in, that's pretty difficult to do.

The magnetic monopole bubble solved that problem neatly. As Jemma explained it to me, each one is a kind of knot in space-time, with the interior and exterior essentially existing in separate universes. Wrap a little dollop of antimatter up in one of those, and you've got a whole lot of potential energy stored in a compact and relatively safe-to-handle package. That's how the *Drakkar* stored her fuel. When she was under acceleration, a steady stream of monopole bubbles filled with antimatter were passed through from containment into the reaction chamber, where they were mixed with opposite-polarity bubbles filled with normal matter.

Then, two by two, the bubbles popped. Annihilation occurred, and off we went.

You can probably see where this is going.

The bubble bomb is a very simple thing. You just pack a bunch of monopole bubbles full of antimatter into some kind of delivery device. When that device bursts over the target, the bubbles drift with the wind, forced apart from one another by their mutual magnetic repulsion. After a fixed amount of time, they pop.

Depending on how much dispersion you've allowed and what specific type of antimatter you've packed into your bubble, the result can range from an explosion that blows a hole through the stratosphere, to a rain of hard radiation and quantum particles that kills every living thing in the target area down to the viral level, but leaves the buildings and other infrastructure completely intact.

It was that bit that caught the attention of old Earth war planners. They'd had thermonuclear weapons for a long while by then, but they hadn't figured out a way to make them useful for anything other than an apocalyptic suicide pact. The problem was that if you ever used enough of them to deliver a knockout blow, the environmental blowback in terms of fallout, garbage thrown into the stratosphere, lingering background radiation, etc., etc., meant that you'd wind up killing not just your target, but also their neighbors, their neighbors' neighbors, their neighbors' neighbors' neighbors, and so on back to probably yourself—and that's assuming that your victims didn't have their own doomsday arsenal to throw back at you, which they probably did if you were contemplating that kind of escalation against them in the first place.

The bubble bomb solved all of those problems. Structured and deployed correctly, it allowed you to sterilize wide swaths of your enemy's landmass with almost no lingering side effects. You could make the bombs small and light and deliver them stealthily enough that the enemy wouldn't know they were coming until they were already dead. You could kill everyone and everything, and then move right in and take over the next day if you wanted to. You didn't even need to worry about the bodies stinking, because there wouldn't be any viable bacteria around to make them decay. From a warfighter's perspective, it was the perfect weapon.

From an actual human being's perspective, of course, it was a nightmare.

The critical context here is that old Earth was undergoing a bit of an environmental crisis at the time that all this was going on. Their population density was almost a hundred times greater than Eden's is now, which is more like a thousand times the average density of most of the Diaspora, and their industry and agriculture were a lot more inefficient and messy than ours are. As a result, they were basically choking on their own waste. Over the course of a few hundred years they'd altered their atmospheric chemistry to the point that whole chunks of the planet that were once heavily populated were rapidly becoming uninhabitable, and they were having serious issues with distribution of both food and water. Combine this with the fact that they were also completely fractured politically—there were nearly two hundred independent political entities claiming sovereign rights over one part of the planet or another—and then throw in the sudden appearance of a weapon that allowed one of those entities to eliminate the population of another completely, and subsequently to move into their newly empty territory, and you've obviously got the makings of a very bad situation.

Records of the Bubble War are probably not particularly reliable, since they were almost entirely written by the folks who struck first and hardest and therefore survived, but there are a few things that we know for certain. The war lasted, in total, less than three weeks. Only a half dozen or so of those independent political entities participated. It ended only when the planet's existent supply of antimatter was exhausted.

Most importantly, it left more than half of old Earth's population, which at the time was all there was of us, dead or dying.

Most historians think that the launch of the *Ching Shih,* which took place less than twenty years later, was a direct reaction to the Bubble War. What else could explain the Diaspora? What else could explain the fact that we left the one planet in all of creation that we were actually evolved to inhabit, the one that didn't require any terraforming or inoculations or wars with native sentients, for . . . well, for places like Niflheim? It was clear to those people that if humanity stayed in one place, we'd eventually kill one another—and they were almost certainly right. Nobody has heard a peep out of old Earth in over six hundred years.

Our only hope for long-term survival was to spread.

It was also clear to them that the Diaspora would be futile if antimatter weapons came with it. We've ostracized old Earth from the start of the Union, and at this point we don't even know if there's anyone left alive there. We like to think that we're different from them, that we're more enlightened or evolved or some such bullshit.

It's not true, though. The people of the Union are no different, at the end of the day, from the ones of old Earth. We still argue with one another. We still sometimes fight.

We don't do it with antimatter, though. That's the one hard and fast rule, even deeper-seated in our psyches than the ban on multiples, that every world in the Union abides by.

That's the one rule that, if it's broken and one of the neighboring worlds finds out about it, will buy you a *Bullet.*

"THIS IS THE place, right?" Berto asks from the cockpit.

The bay door slides open, and I look down. We're hovering over a crevasse. It looks pretty much like every other crevasse in this godforsaken place. Is this where I fell?

"Maybe," I say. "Who knows?"

"I'll take that as a yes," Berto says.

The drop winch deploys two meters of cable. Eight shoulders his pack and clips in.

"See you down there," he says, and steps into space.

I lift my own pack as the cable plays out. It's not as heavy as I expected.

Hard to believe it carries enough destructive force to sterilize a city.

Soon enough, the winch reverses. When the end of the cable appears, though, I hesitate.

"Hey," I say. "Berto? Before I do this, there's one thing that I'd really appreciate you clearing up. What actually happened to Six?"

Berto sighs. "Creepers took him, Mickey. I told you that the first time you asked, right after you came out of the tank."

"I don't believe that," I say. "You told me that creepers ate me, remember?"

"I didn't say they *ate* him," Berto says. "I said they *took* him. You inferred the eating thing. He was working another crevasse, not too far from here. They came up out of the snow, just like I said. They didn't rip him up, though. They dragged him down a hole. It was fifteen minutes before I lost his signal. He was incoherent for the last ten. I got the impression . . ."

"What?" I say.

"I'm pretty sure they were doing what we did to that creeper you hauled in," Berto says. "They were taking him apart to see how he worked."

"They took his ocular," I say. "They took *my* ocular."

"Maybe," Berto says. "Not like they could do anything with it."

Until the last few days, I would have agreed. Now, though?

"You lied to me," I say. "You lied to *Command*. You must have known the creepers were sentient before I did. You could have gotten cycled for that, Berto. What were you thinking?"

He doesn't answer. I wait through a long ten seconds, then shake my head and reach for the cable.

"I was afraid," Berto says.

I turn to look at him. He won't meet my eyes.

"Afraid of what? Until you falsified your reports, you hadn't done anything wrong. What happened to me wasn't your fault."

"No," he says. "I wasn't afraid of Command. I was afraid of those fucking creepers. I could have saved you, probably. I could have pulled you back out of that hole. I could maybe even have saved Six if I'd gotten to ground quick enough, and brought along an accelerator. I didn't, though. I didn't, because I was afraid."

And now, suddenly, it all makes sense.

"You're Berto Gomez," I say. "You're the guy who flies a flitter through a three-meter gap at two hundred meters per second. You're not afraid of anything."

He sighs, and nods.

"You risked actually getting cycled because you couldn't admit to me, to Marshall . . . to yourself? You couldn't let anyone know that there was something out there that frightened you."

He turns back to the controls. "Eight is waiting for you, Mickey."

"You know," I say, "if any of me makes it through into Nine somehow, I'm gonna make a point first thing of kicking the crap out of you."

He doesn't have anything to say to that.

I clip in, and I go.

"So," EIGHT SAYS when I unclip at the bottom. "*Is* this the place?"

I look around. The floor of the crevasse is maybe a half dozen meters wide. Thirty meters of ice loom over us on both sides. Halfway up one wall, a boulder that looks a little like a monkey's head juts out of the ice.

"Yeah," I say. "I think so. Don't think it really matters, though. I'm pretty sure this whole area is undermined. If this isn't exactly where I went down before, we just need to find another entrance to the tunnels."

The cable disappears, and a few moments later we hear the hum of gravitics as Berto's shuttle accelerates away. We start walking. Just past the boulder, I see the edge of the hole. Apparently it hasn't snowed enough in the past few days to cover it over.

"There," I say. "That's where I fell."

We walk up to the edge and look down into a steep, slanting, rock-walled tunnel a bit more than a meter wide.

"Looks climbable," Eight says.

"Eight," I say. "We shouldn't do this."

He turns to look at me. "You think there's a better way in?"

"No," I say. "That's not what I mean. I mean that we shouldn't do this."

"Yes," he says. "We should."

"The creepers," I say. "They're sentients." I hook one thumb toward my pack. "And these things are war crimes. If Midgard finds out that we did this, they'll make us the next Gault."

Each of our packs, for all intents and purposes, contains a miniature bubble bomb: fifty thousand tiny nuggets of anti-matter taken from what's left of the *Drakkar*'s fuel stores, each one isolated in a magnetic monopole bubble. When we release them, they'll disperse, drifting through the air like will-o'-the-wisps.

Eventually, the bubbles will pop.

The fact of what I'm carrying on my back right now is making my skin crawl.

"I know they're sentients," Eight says. "That's why we have to do this—and it's only a war crime if we use these weapons on humans. Anything goes on a beachhead. Our terraformers have sterilized entire continents to make space for us where they had to. You know this." He sits down at the edge of the hole and leans forward. "Give me a hand, huh? It's a bit of a drop to the first ledge."

"One of them saved me," I say.

He looks up at me. "What?"

"Four days ago," I say. "When I got lost in these tunnels, and Berto gave me up for dead. One of the creepers saved me. It picked me up and carried me almost back to the dome. It let me go."

"So what you're saying," Eight says, "is that all of this bullshit that's happened to us is actually *their* fault."

Okay. I guess that's one way of looking at it.

"Anyway," Eight says, "it doesn't matter. You heard what Marshall said. If we don't do this, we go into the cycler, and we don't get to come back out. He wipes our personality off the server, and fucking *Chen* takes our place." He inches a bit farther forward, and looks down again. "You know what? I think I've got this." He braces one hand on either side of the opening, lifts himself up, and lets his legs dangle. "Meet me at the bottom, huh?"

He lowers himself down into the hole and disappears.

I stand there, staring down into the hole, for a long while. I could just walk away, I think—wander off into the snow, pop the seals on my rebreather, and be done with it.

Wouldn't make a difference, though, would it? They'd send Berto or Nasha out to find my body, retrieve the pack, and send Nine down into the tunnels with it, assuming that Eight hadn't already finished the job.

Eventually, my ocular pings.

<Mickey8>:Let's go, Seven. We've got things to do.

I sigh, tighten the straps on my pack, and follow him down.

"WE SHOULD SPLIT up," Eight says. "Get as far away from one another as we can, then pull our triggers simultaneously. That way we get maximum spread, and we shouldn't have to worry about the blast from one of our weapons screwing with the dispersal pattern of the other."

"Eight—" I begin, but he shakes his head.

"No," he says. "I don't want to hear it. Start walking. Keep a voice channel open. When you're ready to do it, let me know. And if you run into your friend from the other day . . ." He turns away. "I don't know. Tell him we're sorry."

I stand there watching his heat signature fade long after he's disappeared down one of the side tunnels. Maybe I think he'll come back? He doesn't, though. Eventually, I pick a tunnel of my own, snug the straps of my pack down to my shoulders, and start walking.

"SEVEN. YOU THERE?"

"Yeah. I'm here."

"You seeing anything? These tunnels seem pretty empty."

"Nope. I've been hearing things off and on, though."

"Yeah, me too. Scratching behind the walls, right?"

"Right. That's our friends, I'd guess."

"Think they know we're here?"

I roll my eyes, though I know he can't see it. "This is their house, Eight. How long would it take us to figure out that one of them had gotten into the dome?"

The silence stretches on, until I begin to wonder whether he's cut the connection.

"Think they know what we're here to do?"

IT'S TEN MINUTES later, and I'm standing at a crossroads trying to decide whether I should take the upward-slanting route or the one that spirals down when my comm flashes. A still frame pops up in the upper left corner of my FOV. It's a broad, deep cavern seen from high above.

Every square meter of it is covered in creepers.

They're the smaller ones, the kind that took down Dugan and ripped through the floor of the main lock.

There must be thousands of them.

Tens of thousands.

"Seven! Seven, are you seeing this?"

"I see it," I say. "Eight, listen . . ."

I trail off then. Listen to what? I think back to that spider I set loose in my mother's garden all those years ago. If it had come back into the house, would I have saved it again, or would I have just crushed it and been done with it?

And what if I'd found a nest of spiders out there, hundreds of them, and realized they'd come to colonize the garden?

"Eight?"

Eight doesn't answer.

"Eight? You there?"

A final image drops into my cache. It's almost too blurred to interpret. I'd guess most people seeing this would have no idea what they were looking at.

I recognize it, though. It's the maw and feeding arms of a giant creeper, seen from no more than a couple of meters away.

That's when I realize that Eight is dead.

What now? I have no idea where he was, no idea how far away the crèche might be.

No idea if he had time to pull the trigger before they took him.

These tunnels are a blind maze. I could be kilometers from where Eight died, or it could be around the next bend.

I could try to find him.

I could pull the trigger now, and be done.

I close my eyes, start to reach for the cord, then hesitate.

There before me is the campfire, burning backward, sucking in smoke and turning ash into wood.

There before me is the caterpillar. The grin is gone, though. Its eyes are narrowed, and its mouth is a thin, hard line.

A chat window opens in the corner of my FOV.

<Mickey8>:Understa*d?

I open my eyes.

Something moves in the darkness.

Something that nearly fills the tunnel.

\<Mickey8\>: You understand?

I blink, run my tongue across my teeth, and swallow. My hand rests lightly on the trigger cord.

\<Mickey8\>: Yes, I understand.
\<Mickey8\>: You are Prime?

Okay, that I don't understand. The creeper moves closer. Both pairs of mandibles are spread wide. That has to be a threat posture, right? I take an involuntary step backward, and my hand tightens on the cord.

\<Mickey8\>: You are Prime?

I shake my head. Idiot. Even if it understood human body language, this thing probably doesn't have eyes.

\<Mickey8\>: We have destroyed your Ancillary. You are Prime?

Prime? Ancillary?
It's talking about Eight.
I could pull the trigger now.
I could, but I don't.
Instead, I take a leap of faith.

\<Mickey8\>: Yes, I am Prime.

The creeper's head settles to the tunnel floor, and the mandibles slowly close, inner first, then outer.

\<Mickey8\>:I am Prime also. We talk?

And so, we do.

IN ALL THE hundreds of worlds that make up the Union, there's only one where humans and native sentients have managed to coexist. It's a lonely little dwarf planet orbiting a gas giant, that is itself orbiting an M-class star at the far end of the spiral arm, almost twenty lights from the next-nearest colony. The mission that brought our people there was the single longest successful jump that we've managed. They named the planet Long Shot.

There's a whole other story behind that.

The natives on Long Shot are tree-dwelling cephalopods. I've seen vids of them zipping from branch to branch, changing colors on the fly to blend in with the canopy so effectively that you can really only see them in the infrared. Their population is concentrated in the central highlands of the planet's only continent. At the time of landfall they were scientifically and culturally advanced, but materially not much farther along than humans were prior to the development of agriculture. There's been a great deal of speculation over exactly why that is. The best explanation I've seen is that the entire reason humans wound up developing spears and houses and flitters and starships is that we were lousy at being regular animals.

The natives on Long Shot were not lousy at being regular animals. They had completely mastered their environment, and they hadn't needed rifles to do it. They ignored the colonists when they landed, because the beachhead was on the coast, hundreds of klicks from their mountains. The colonists ignored them because the natives were shy, localized, and nearly invisible, and for the first twenty years post-landfall, we had no idea they were there.

The histories don't say much about why this encounter turned out so differently from all the others. I've got a theory, though: by the time they finally bumped into one another, the colonists were well established enough to stop being constantly afraid.

Time. That's the key.

We just need time.

FOR THE SECOND time, for reasons that I still don't and probably never will understand, I walk alive out of the creepers' tunnels and into the low winter sun.

It's a beautiful morning by Niflheim standards. The sky is a
clear light ocher with just a hint of blue, and the sun makes the
snow between here and the dome look like a field of diamonds. I
take a deep breath in, hitch up my pack, and start walking.

The snow is knee-deep, with drifts up to my waist, and even
with the rebreather I'm not getting nearly as much oxygen out of
Niflheim's atmosphere as my muscles are demanding, so I've got
a good long while to game out how this is likely to go while I slog
the kilometer or so back to the perimeter. I think about letting
them know I'm coming. I even pop open a chat window before
realizing that, no, that might tempt Marshall to try to stop me. If
he ordered it, would Nasha or Berto be willing to drop a plasma
bomb on my head?

Nasha wouldn't. I'm confident of that. Berto, though?

I honestly have no idea what would happen to the bundle of
death on my back if he did.

Probably best for everyone if we don't find out.

I swing my route around so that I'm approaching, as near as I can make it, exactly between two pylons. I'd like to make it all the way to the dome before being challenged, but considering that the place is on high alert for creeper incursions I guess that's a lost hope. As it happens, I'm still a hundred meters out from the perimeter proper when both of the nearest pylons come to life. I keep walking as lights flash around their bases, and the burners rise from their peaks and swing around to orient on me.

"Don't," I say over the general comm channel, and hold up the trigger cord in my right hand. "Please. I don't want to pull this."

The burners don't withdraw, but they don't fire either. After what feels like hours but is probably actually more like thirty seconds, Marshall's voice speaks in my ear.

"Remove the pack, Barnes. Set it down carefully, and step away."

My hand on the cord starts shaking, and I have to stifle a giggle rising in the back of my throat.

"No," I say when I've got control of my voice. "I don't think I'll do that."

The comm cuts, this time for almost a minute. When the line opens again, I can hear the barely suppressed fury in Marshall's voice.

"Which one are you?"

"Seven," I say. "I'm Mickey7."

"Where is Eight?"

"Dead."

"Did he trigger his weapon?"

"No," I say. "He did not."

The comm cuts again. I glance over at the nearer of the two pylons. There's a dull red glow in the center of the barrel. I've never seen that before.

Which is to say, I guess, that I've never stared into the mouth of a primed burner before.

What would happen if it opened up on me? With a handheld burner I'm sure I'd have time to pull the cord before I died, even if it took me full in the face. With this thing, though?

Doesn't matter. Even if I died instantly, my arm might spasm. They can't risk it.

Can they?

I'm contemplating that question when a chat window opens.

<RedHawk>:Mickey? What the shit are you doing, man?

Oh well. At least he's not in a cockpit right now, getting ready to drop ordnance on me.

<Mickey8>:Hey there, Berto. Surprised to see me?

<RedHawk>:Seriously, Mickey. Have you gone completely insane? What are you trying to accomplish?

<Mickey8>:Send Marshall out here. We need to talk.

<RedHawk>: ...

<Mickey8>:Not joking, Berto. Send him out.

<RedHawk>:Come on, Mickey. You know that's not gonna happen.

<Mickey8>:It is, Berto.

<RedHawk>:Take off the pack, Mick. That thing you're carrying ... it's a war crime. If you pull that cord, you'll be killing every human left on this planet. You don't want to do this.

<Mickey8>:Yeah. I'm pretty sure I led with "I don't want to do this." I don't want to kill you. Well, actually I kind of do want to kill you. I don't want to kill Nasha, though, or Cat, or even that asshole Tonio from Security. I don't want to kill anybody other than maybe you. What I want is to talk to Marshall, face-to-face. Send. Him. Out.

The window snaps closed, and I'm left to contemplate the burners on the pylons again.

They leave me standing there for almost an hour, staring up into that dull red glow while the cold seeps through the layers of my thermals, down into my skin and muscles, and finally straight through to my bones. Here is a hard, true fact: if you're left standing still for long enough in subzero weather, you will eventually be miserably, unbearably, bone-rattlingly cold, no matter how many layers of high-tech heat-retaining clothing you happen to be wearing. After forty minutes or so I find myself wishing that they'd just go ahead and open up on me with the burners so that at least I can die warm.

They don't, though. Instead, just when I've almost decided to pull the cord and be done with it, the secondary lock on the dome cycles open two hundred meters distant, and Marshall comes stomping out.

I think it's Marshall, anyway. It's a little difficult to tell through the rebreather and goggles and half dozen layers of cold-weather gear. The height is about right, though, and he's followed through the lock by two goons in full combat armor, so by the time that's all done with, I'm pretty confident it's him. I open a comm channel.

"Seriously? What's the escort for, Marshall? You've already got two cannons trained on me. How much more firepower do you think you need?"

"The security officers," he replies, his voice a low growl, "are here because I strongly suspect that this may be some sort of ambush."

I almost laugh at that. "An ambush? By who?"

"We are at war," Marshall says. "And for reasons that I honestly cannot fathom, you seem to have taken the enemy's side."

I don't have anything to say to that, so I stand silent and shivering, and watch him struggle toward me through the snow. He stops just at the perimeter, maybe ten meters away. The two goons stop a half pace behind him.

"Well?" Marshall says. "Here I am, Barnes. Do what you came here to do."

I wonder what he expects now. For me to wave my arms, I suppose, and summon an army of creepers up out of the snow to eat him. For just a moment I actually consider shouting, *Get him*, just to see what he'd do, but the goons both have accelerators at the ready, and they're probably nervous. This isn't the time for fun.

"I didn't do it," I say. "I didn't pull the trigger."

"I can see that," Marshall says. "What about your . . . friend?"

"You mean Eight?"

"Yes. Eight. Did he trigger his device?"

"No," I say. "I already told you that he didn't. He was killed before he could."

"I see," Marshall says. "What happened to his device?"

"The creepers have it."

The silence following that one stretches on for what feels like an eternity.

"Do they know what they have?" Marshall finally asks. There's a tremor in his voice that wasn't there before.

"Yes," I say. "They do."

"How do you know that?" Marshall asks.

"Because I told them what it was, and how it operates."

Marshall turns to the goon on his left. "Kill him."

"Sir?"

It's Cat. I should have recognized her armor. Marshall raises one trembling hand to point at me.

"This man has betrayed our colony, Corporal Chen. He has betrayed the Union. He has betrayed humanity. I have no doubt at this point that our time left on this planet will be measured in hours, if not minutes, but before that clock runs out I want to see him dead. Kill him."

"That's not a good idea," the goon on Marshall's other side says. It's Lucas, I think, but his voice is hard to make out over the comm. "He's carrying a bubble bomb, sir."

"Listen," I say. "I had to tell them what they had. Otherwise, they might have tried to take it apart, tried to see what makes it tick. If they'd done that—"

"If they'd done that," Marshall says, "this problem would have taken care of itself."

"Unless they decided to do it underneath the dome," Cat says. "That's what I would have done if I were them."

"It doesn't matter what you would have done," Marshall says. "It doesn't matter what justifications Barnes has dreamed up for what he's already done. This man has conspired with the enemy in a time of war. There is no greater crime."

"What about genocide?" I say. "That's a pretty great crime. It wasn't conspiring with the enemy that led us to abandon old Earth, you know. Also, not for nothing, we're not at war."

Marshall rounds back on me. "Those things out there have killed five of my people, you monster! Hell, they've killed *you* twice now. We've killed them as well. If we're not at war, then what are we?"

I shake my head. "You're thinking like a human. The creepers don't see it that way. They don't seem to have much of a concept of individual life. As far as I can tell, they're a communal intelligence. They don't care at all about the creepers we've killed, and they don't have an inkling of why we'd care about the people they've taken. The idea that dissecting a few ancillaries would be considered an act of aggression is beyond them. As far as they're concerned, all we've done so far is exchange a bit of information."

"Ancillaries?" Cat says.

"Yeah," I say. "That's my best translation for what they call the little ones that we've seen around the dome. They're just parts of the whole, not intelligent things themselves. They've been assuming that individual humans are the same."

"Great," Cat says. "Did you at least correct them on that?"

"I tried. Their grasp of the language is surprisingly good considering that everything they know, they've learned from snooping on my comms, but where the concepts aren't there, there's not much you can do to translate. Anyway, they say they're sorry."

Cat starts to say something more, but Marshall cuts her off.

"Enough! Be silent, Chen, or by God you'll go down the corpse hole with him."

"I'm not going down the corpse hole," I say.

"Oh, you are. Unless we're all blown to hell first, you are definitely going down the hole, and I do not care in the least if you're alive or dead when it happens. You have to take that pack off sometime, Barnes, and the minute you do, I'll put a round in you myself."

"Not to criticize," Lucas says, "but you're not giving him a lot of incentive not to kill us all right now, sir."

Marshall turns to glare at him, then Chen, then back at me.

"You can't kill me," I say. "Much though you might want to, you can't. I'm your only liaison to the creepers, and they've got an antimatter weapon now, just like we do."

"Thanks to you," he says. "Thanks to you, Barnes. You've killed us all, you bastard."

I shake my head. "Sending a doomsday weapon down into their tunnels wasn't my idea, and it wasn't my fault that they took Eight before he could pull the trigger. That's on you, Marshall."

"But you could have ended it," he says. "If you'd just done your goddamned job, this would all be over. You're an Expendable, you coward, and you were afraid to die."

I sigh, and let my eyes fall closed. When I open them again, Cat and Lucas have shouldered their weapons.

"Maybe," I say. "Maybe I didn't want to die . . . or maybe I just didn't want to have a genocide on my conscience when I did. I get that you think I should have just pulled the cord, and killed the creepers, and died—but I didn't, and now we've got to move on from there. There's another intelligent species on this planet, and you've just handed them an antimatter weapon. You're in desperate need of diplomacy, and I'm your only diplomat. Do you really think killing me is in anybody's best interests at this point?"

Marshall stares me down for a solid thirty seconds. His hands are shaking and I can see his jaw working under his rebreather, but he doesn't say a word. In the end, he turns on his heel and stalks back toward the lock. Cat and Lucas stand and watch him go.

"So?" I say when the outer door cycles shut behind him. "Are we good?"

Cat glances over at Lucas. He turns to look at the nearest pylon. As we watch, the burner goes dark and sinks back onto its bearings.

"Yeah," Cat says. "I think so. For the moment, anyway."

She closes the distance between us and offers me her hand. I stow the trigger cord, take it, and pull her into a hug.

"I'm sorry," she says, and I can hear the tears in her voice.

"I know," I say. "It's okay, Cat. You did what you had to do."

We stand there for another ten seconds, until she finally says, "Hugging in armor is weird."

She's not wrong.

I let her go, and the three of us walk back to the dome together.

I'M BACK IN my rack, stretched out on the bed with my eyes closed and my hands folded behind my head, just thinking about drifting off, when Eight's death finally hits me. It makes no sense for so many reasons—I mean, even setting aside the fact that he pretty much had to go if I was going to stay, and also the fact that he was kind of annoying most of the time, and that I only actually knew him for a few days, he's not really gone, is he? After all, I'm him, and he was me. It's like mourning your reflection when you've broken a mirror.

Doesn't matter. Maybe it's for him, or maybe it's for me, or maybe it's just a release of everything that's been building up inside me ever since I fell down that fucking hole, but in the span of five seconds I go from totally fine to full-on ugly crying.

That goes on for a while.

I'm just winding down when someone knocks at my door.

"Come," I say, then sit up, swing my feet to the floor, and wipe my face mostly clean with the front of my shirt. When I look up, Nasha's closing the door behind her.

"Hey," she says softly. "Welcome back."

"Thanks." I shift to make room, and she sits down on the bed beside me. "Sorry it's just me this time."

She laughs, then slides an arm around my shoulder and rests the side of her head against mine. "Was it bad, what happened to Eight?"

I shrug. "I don't know. We were separated. He'd found a . . . nest, I guess? Thousands of creepers crawling over one another in a huge domed cavern. He was sending me stills of it when his signal cut." I can feel her shudder against me. "It must have been quick, anyway. He was set on pulling the trigger. Whatever happened to him, it was sudden enough that he didn't get the chance."

I don't really know that, of course. He was me, after all. Maybe he had a change of heart at the last minute. Maybe he could have pulled the trigger, but chose not to.

Nasha sniffles, then laughs.

"Sorry," she says. "I have no idea what to feel right now."

I slide my arm around her waist. She sighs, leans into me, and pushes me down onto the bed.

"You know," she says as she settles her head against my chest, "Marshall actually tried to order me to do a bombing run on your friends out there."

"Huh," I say, my eyes already drifting shut. "What did you say?"

She laughs again, softly, and slides one leg across mine. "I said that if what you told us is true, they're buried under a hundred or more meters of bedrock, and we don't have anything in our arsenal at this point that's powerful enough to so much as knock the dust off of their chandeliers. The most we could hope to do would be to annoy them, and that seems like a bad idea right now."

"Good call. How'd he take it?"

She slides her hand up my chest, cups my cheek, and pulls my head up far enough to kiss me. "About how you'd expect."

She settles in again, then reaches up to stroke my cheek. "Is it true?"

I kiss her hand, then move it back down to my chest. "Is what true?"

"What you told us," she says. "About the creepers. Are they really gonna leave us be?"

I shrug. "I think so? The truth is, though, that I don't know for sure how much either one of us understood what the other was saying. They said they'd leave us alone as long as we stayed clear of their tunnels and didn't try to build anything in the foot-hills south of the dome. Do they actually know what 'the dome' means, though? Are they totally clear on the fact that leaving us alone implies not grabbing the occasional human and tearing him to shreds? Who the hell knows?"

"Wow," she says. "You're a hell of a negotiator, huh?"

"Sorry," I say. "I did my best, you know?"

She rises up on one elbow, kisses my cheek, and then pulls my arm back around her and nuzzles her head into the hollow be-tween my shoulder and neck. "I know you did, babe." She sighs, and pulls me closer. "I know you did."

It's no more than a minute or two more before she's sleeping. I'm drifting as well. It's been a long few days. I close my eyes, and soon enough I slide into the dream of the caterpillar. We're back on Midgard, sitting across the backward-burning campfire from one another, watching the smoke spiral down out of a clear black sky.

"Is this an ending," he asks, "or a beginning?"

I look up from the fire. "You can speak now?"

"I could always speak. You couldn't understand."

I shrug. That's fair.

"I think it's both," I say. "I hope it's both."

That seems to satisfy him. We sit together then in companion-able silence until, bit by bit, he fades away.

026

NASHA'S GONE WHEN I wake. She's left a message on my tablet, though.

Gotta fly today. See you when I'm back?

That makes me smile. I get out of bed, give myself a quick dry-scrub, and pull on my last set of semi-clean clothes.

I can't quite pin it down, but something is different today.

I feel a weird sense of . . . lightness? I don't know. I just . . .

And then it hits me. For the first time in I have no idea how long, *I'm not afraid.*

I'm savoring that feeling, wallowing in it, letting it soak straight into my bones, when my ocular pings.

<Command1>:You are required to report to the Commander's office immediately.

<Command1>:Failure to do so by 09:00 will be construed as desertion.

Oh well. So much for that.

I take my time responding to Marshall's summons. I've got

a pretty good idea what he's planning to say to me, and I don't want to hear it.

It's 08:59 when I open the door to Marshall's office. He's leaned back behind his desk, hands folded across his belly, with what could almost be a subtle half smile on his face.

Huh. That is not what I was expecting.

"Barnes," he says. "Have a seat."

I step into the office, close the door behind me, and pull a chair up to the desk.

"Good morning, sir. You asked to see me?"

"Yes," he says. "I did. Mostly, I wanted to apologize to you."

That's *really* not what I was expecting.

"It seems," he continues, "that I misjudged the situation yesterday. When I learned that you'd left our device with those creatures, when I learned that you'd told them what it was, well . . ."

"As I explained," I say, "I didn't leave the device with them. They seized it from Eight when they killed him. I had to explain what it was and how it operated, or they might have triggered it accidentally."

He nods. "You did mention that. I naturally assumed that they would immediately turn our weapon back on us. However, the fact that we're sitting here having this conversation tells me that I was wrong. I was wrong, and you were right. So, again—I apologize. I should not have reacted the way I did yesterday."

"You mean when you tried to get Cat and Lucas to kill me?"

His right eye twitches, but beyond that he maintains his composure. "Yes, Barnes. That was wrong. I'm sorry."

"Huh. Well. Apology accepted, I guess?"

"Excellent," he says. "You're a bigger man than most."

He leans forward, and reaches across the desk to offer me his hand. After a moment's hesitation, I shake it.

"So," I say when he releases me and leans back again. "Um . . . will that be all, sir?"

"Well," he says, and the smile returns, slightly bigger this time. "Not quite. Now that things are hopefully on their way back to normal, we have a job for you."

Right. Here we go. "A job, sir?"

"Yes," he says. "Assuming that our friends will keep to their tunnels and away from our dome in the future—and I hope we can assume that—it's time for us all to get back to the business of making sure this colony survives, don't you think?"

I lean back in my own chair and fold my arms across my chest. "Yes, sir. I suppose it is."

"Good. Good. Well, as I'm sure you can guess, producing those two devices yesterday put a dangerous dent in our remaining store of antimatter. We don't have any prospect of being able to produce new fuel stores anytime in the foreseeable future, and I'm sure I don't need to tell you what happens to all of us if our power plant shuts down."

"No," I say. "I'm sure you don't."

He leans forward now and plants both elbows on the desk, looking for all the world like a flitter salesman trying to close a deal.

"Half the fuel we pulled is lost, of course. No help for that. It is vital, however, that the antimatter contained in the device that you brought back with you goes back into the core."

Oh, for shit's sake.

"You pulled it out," I say. "Just do whatever you did then, only backward."

He tries for a sorrowful look now, but it's not working. "Unfortunately, that's not possible. We extracted that fuel by using the normal drive feed mechanism. As I'm sure you know, that only runs in one direction. There is no mechanism for feeding individual fuel elements back into the core. I'm afraid it's going to have to be done manually, from the inside."

I close my eyes, take a deep breath in, and let it out slowly.

What's the neutron flux in an active antimatter core? I don't think Jemma ever covered that one, but I'm guessing it's a lot.

"Don't worry," he says. "I won't ask you to upload before or after. You won't need to remember any of this."

"I won't have to upload?"

He shakes his head. "Absolutely not."

"I haven't uploaded since I came out of the tank, you know. If I do this, it'll be like this part of me never existed."

"Nonsense," he says. "This part of you, as you say, will have saved the colony. We'll remember, even if you don't." He looks down at his hands, then back up with what might even be sincere emotion. "I know I don't say this often enough, but the truth is, you've saved this colony more than once already, and I'm sure you will again in the future. That's a debt that can't be repaid. On behalf of all of us—thank you, Mickey. Your courage is an inspiration."

Mickey. For the first time in nine fucking years, he called me Mickey.

My courage is an inspiration.

Fuck you, Marshall.

I slide my chair back and get to my feet.

"No."

The sincerity drops from his face like a mask, replaced almost instantly by pure rage.

"What?"

"No," I say. "I won't do it. You obviously had plans for the colony to survive without that fuel when you sent me down into the tunnels. Use those. Or burn a drone getting your war-crime bomb back into the core. Or do it yourself. I'm not doing it."

He surges to his feet now, his face darkening and his eyes narrowing to slits.

"You will do it," he hisses. "You will, or as God is my witness I will wipe your pattern and your recordings from the servers, and I will shove the last instantiation of you down the corpse hole myself."

Now that the decision is made, I can feel a weight that I didn't realize was there lifting from my shoulders. It almost feels like flying.

"You can wipe the servers, Marshall. In fact, please do, because I am hereby resigning as this colony's Expendable. Find a replacement. I honestly don't care. You won't kill me, though, because I'm your only liaison to the creepers, and you were stupid enough to hand them an antimatter bomb yesterday. Have your people lay a hand on me, and I'll tell the creepers that the truce is off."

His mouth opens, closes, then opens again.

I can't help it. I burst out laughing.

"You wouldn't fucking dare," he finally manages when I'm halfway out the door.

"I've died seven goddamn times," I say over my shoulder. "That's six times more than anyone should. Don't tell me what I wouldn't dare."

I don't bother to close the door behind me.

"Hey, there, buddy. How's it going?"

I look up from my cricket and yam scramble. Berto sets his tray down on the table across from mine and drops onto the bench.

"Oh," I say. "It's you."

"Yeah," he says. "I heard you resigned."

I shrug. "Seems like it."

"Wild," he says. "I didn't know you could do that."

"You can't," I say. "Not unless you're holding an antimatter bomb over Marshall's head, anyway."

He takes a bite, chews, and swallows. I'm just turning back to my own food when he says, "Back on a solid diet, huh?"

"Yeah," I say. "I'm not sharing a ration anymore, am I?"

"Oh," he says. "Right."

"Yeah."

We eat in silence for a solid minute, long enough to be uncomfortable if I cared about that kind of stuff right now.

"I'm glad you made it back," he says finally.

I look up. "Thanks, I guess. Didn't feel up to inventing some story about what happened to me for Nine, huh?"

That gets a wince out of him, anyway. "Ouch. I said I was sorry about that."

"Yeah," I say. "You did."

We sit through another thirty seconds of silence. I'm almost done eating by now, but Berto's barely touched his food.

"So," he says. "Are we, uh . . . good?"

I close my eyes, take a deep breath in, and let it out. When I open them again, he's watching me expectantly. I lean across the table toward him. He leans forward in response.

I pop him right in the eye, hard enough to split my knuckle and snap his head back.

"Yeah," I say. "We're good."

I stand, pick up my tray, and go. When I glance back as the door to the corridor slides open, he's staring at me, mouth slightly open, hands flat on the table in front of him. The eye is already purpling up nicely.

I know it's a cliché, but I don't care. This is the first day of the rest of my life.

So APPARENTLY THERE'S such a thing as springtime on Nifl-heim. Who knew?

About a year post-landfall, the temperature starts rising and the snow begins to melt. We get our first look at exposed soil a few weeks later. A month after that, the ground is covered in lichen.

Nobody seems to have a clear explanation for why this is happening. Niflheim's orbit is nearly circular, and its axial tilt is negligible. We shouldn't have seasons of any kind here, theoretically. The best guess that anyone can come up with about what's happening is that our sun is actually a marginally variable star, and its cycle is on the upswing.

That's the sort of thing you'd think the mission planners back on Midgard would have been aware of, isn't it? I mean, they observed this place for almost thirty years before we boosted out. After a little digging, I find out that they did observe a periodic swing in observed stellar output here. It was pretty well documented. They didn't ascribe it to the star, though, because nobody had a decent theory as to how that would work from a stellar physics standpoint. Instead, they decided that it must have had something to do with dust clouds in the interstellar medium, and then they filed it away. That's why they thought we'd be warm and happy here. They thought the high marks for stellar output were the real deal, and the low points were due to interference.

Oops.

At first everyone is pretty happy about the change in the weather, until some guy in the Physics Section thinks to wonder whether we're going to swing from one extreme to the other and wind up roasting in our own juices.

Spooky thought, but we don't. After a few months things level out somewhere between brisk and balmy, and eventually the folks in Agriculture actually manage to get an experimental plot going outside the dome.

It's right around that time, when our fellow colonists are finally starting to spend a bit of time outside and they're talking about decanting the first few embryos and everyone other than me and Marshall seems to have mostly forgotten about the creepers, that I ask Nasha if she'd like to go for a walk.

We still have to wear rebreathers. The partial pressure of oxygen has been rising, slowly but perceptibly, since green things started growing, but the change won't be enough to keep one of us alive unaided for a long while yet—if it ever is, of course. We have no idea how long this season will last. It could be years. It could be over tomorrow.

In the meantime, though, it's a nice day for a hike.

"Where are we going?" Nasha asks after Lucas has waved us through the perimeter.

"Away from the dome. Isn't that enough?"

She takes my hand, and we walk.

Back on Midgard, there was an enormous desert that straddled the equator and stretched nearly the width of the only continent.

Broad swaths of land there could go years without seeing any significant rain. Every once in a long while, though, when weather conditions were just right, a massive storm would roll over and dump a year's worth of water over those bone-dry plains and arroyos in a day or two. Whenever that happened, we got a reminder that life had been waiting there, poised to spring out at the first opportunity. Plants practically leapt out of the mud, and animals crawled up out of hibernation to eat and drink and hunt and mate.

Niflheim's biosphere seems to be a bit like that. The snow has only been gone for a couple of months, but already the lichen has given way to something that could be grass, and there are even a few woody-looking shrubs poking up here and there. There are animals too—mostly little crawly things that bear a striking resemblance to the creepers, but a klick or so out from the dome I spot what looks like an eight-legged reptile sunning itself on an exposed shelf of rock.

When I point it out to Nasha, she scowls and puts a hand to the burner she's brought along, because of course she did.

"Come on," I say. "It's cute."

She shoots me a sideways glance, then shakes her head and lets her hand fall to her side.

We keep walking.

After another five minutes or so, I have to stop to get my bearings. It's been a long time now, and everything looks so different without the snow. Nasha takes a half step back, folds her arms across her chest, and tilts her head to one side.

"This isn't just a walk-around, is it?"

I smile behind my rebreather. "Not exactly. I needed to check on something."

I've got my landmark now. We start up a hillside, then turn down into a gully that takes us out of sight of the dome.

"You sure about this?" Nasha asks. I glance back. Her hand is back on the burner. "This looks like creeper country."

"Yeah," I say. "We're actually pretty close to an entrance to their tunnel system."

"Okay," she says. "Why?"

"I told you," I say. "I have to check on something."

I miss the spot at first. The boulder I'd taken as my marker must have been held in place by the ice, or maybe it was pushed down the slope by runoff. In any case, it's twenty meters or more down the gully from where it was supposed to be. I finally recognize it, though, and once I've done that it's not too difficult to trace back to the little shelf where it was resting when I came out of the tunnels. Under that shelf is a jumble of smaller rocks. I drop to my knees and start pulling them away.

"Mickey?" Nasha says. "Do you want to tell me what we're doing here?"

I would, but I don't have to, because by now I've pulled enough of the scree out of the way to expose the hollow space under the rock shelf.

"Holy shit," Nasha says.

I turn back to look at her, to gauge her reaction. She's surprised, but not horrified or murderous. I take that as a good sign. Carefully, I reach into the dark space and pull Eight's pack out into the light.

"You sneaky little shit," she says.

I laugh. "You didn't think I'd actually leave this with the creepers, did you?"

She crouches down beside me, reaches out, and runs a hand across the top of the pack. "How?"

"How what? How did I manage to get this atrocity back from the creepers after they'd murdered Eight?"

Nasha turns to look at me. I can tell from her eyes that she's not smiling under the rebreather. "Yeah, Mickey."

I shrug. "I asked for it."

She shakes her head, then turns her attention back to the bomb. "Is it loaded?"

"Well, there's enough antimatter in here to sterilize a medium-sized city, if that's what you mean."

She pulls her hand back.

"Don't worry," I say. "As long as the bubbles are intact, the antimatter is basically in a different universe. It can't touch us."

"And what if some of them aren't intact?"

I laugh. "Trust me. You'd know."

"Why, Mickey?"

"Why, what? Why did I leave a doomsday weapon buried out here like pirate's treasure?"

"Yeah," she says. "That."

I rock back on my heels and turn to look at her. "Well, here's the thing. If I'd actually left it with the creepers like I told Marshall, they might have eventually gotten it into their heads to use it. I honestly couldn't have given a shit about most of the people in that dome at that point, but . . ."

She grins. "But what, Mickey?"

"You know," I say. "I'd rather let Marshall shove me down the corpse hole than risk having anything happen to you."

"Okay," she says. "I get that. So why didn't you bring it back?"

"Oh, that's easy. If I'd turned both bombs back over to Marshall, he definitely would have killed me on the spot, and then he would have sent Nine down into the tunnels to finish his genocide. The only reason I'm still alive, and the only reason the creepers are still here, is that he thinks I'm the only thing keeping the creepers from popping this thing off underneath the dome."

"I guess you're probably right about that," she says. "The part I don't get, though, is why the creepers let you walk out with both bombs. Weren't they worried about deterrence or whatever?"

I laugh again, a little harder. "Seriously? You think I actually told them what we were carrying? You think I told them we came into their home with the intent of committing genocide? Holy crow, Nasha. I'm no genius, but I'm not *that* dumb."

She seems taken aback by that. Apparently she thought I actually was that dumb.

"So what did you tell them?"

"I mean, the language thing was a major barrier, but I tried to tell them we were emissaries. They never actually asked about the packs. They don't really look like doomsday weapons, do they?"

"No," Nasha says. "I guess not."

I shove the pack back into the hollow, and then carefully push the rocks back into place until it's invisible again. When I'm done, I get to my feet and take a half dozen steps back to examine my work.

"What do you think?" I ask Nasha. "Will it stay hidden there?"

She shrugs. "Maybe for now. Probably not forever. Do you have a long-term plan, or are you just going to wait around until somebody stumbles across this place and accidentally kills us all?"

I sigh. "My plan was to wait until Marshall dies, then come back here and get it, and tell whoever the new commander is that the creepers decided to return the bomb as a gesture of goodwill."

"Seriously?"

"Yeah, seriously. If you've got a better plan, I'd love to hear it."

She stares back at me for a long moment, then shakes her head. "I've got nothing. How long do you expect this to go on, though? Is Marshall sick?"

"Not that I know of."

She takes my hand. "Do you have a backup plan, just in case he doesn't die?"

"I do not."

She cups my cheek in her free hand, then lifts her rebreather and leans in to kiss me. "You really aren't a genius," she says, then lets my hand fall and turns to start back up the gully. "It's a good thing you're cute."

I turn to look back at the bomb's hiding place. It just looks like a jumble of rocks, no different from all the other jumbles of rocks that cover ninety percent of this planet.

Is it good enough?

Marshall seems pretty healthy.

I guess it'll have to be.

With a final backward glance, I put our would-be war crime behind me.

I follow Nasha out of the shadows, up the gully, and into the sun.

Acknowledgments

The list of people who contributed to this book is a long one. I'm probably going to forget some of them. If you're one of those, I hope you will forgive me. As you are probably well aware, I'm not nearly as smart as I look.

First, the obvious: my deepest gratitude to Paul Lucas and the good folks at Janklow & Nesbit, without whose guidance and encouragement I would almost certainly have given up on this business long ago, and also to Michael Rowley of Rebellion Publishing and Michael Homler of St. Martin's Press, both of whom were willing to take a chance on an odd little book written by an extremely obscure author. Slightly less obviously, I would also like to give sincere and heartfelt thanks to Navah Wolfe, who read this story when it was a modestly depressing novella and encouraged me to turn it into a much less depressing novel. If you read this, Navah, I hope you see your fingerprints on the final product, and I do hope that you approve.

My sincere thanks also go out to (in no particular order):

- Kira and Claire, for their tough but fair criticism of the earliest drafts of this story.
- Heather, for buying me endless chais on my own credit card.
- Anthony Taboni, for being the future president of my nascent fan club.
- Therese, Craig, Kim, Aaron, and Gary, for reading through multiple versions of this manuscript without ever telling me to just pack it in already.
- Karen Fish, for teaching me what it means to be a writer.
- John, for being my go-to sounding board on all things literary.
- Mickey, for not getting mad after I put him into a book and then murdered him multiple times.
- Jack, for keeping my ego in check when it was needed most.
- Jen, for finally reading one of my manuscripts prepublication.
- Max and Freya, for never letting me forget what's really important in life.

As I said, this is a partial list. This book would not be what it is without any of these folks, and probably a whole mess of others besides. Thanks, friends. Now on to the next one, right?

21982320173002